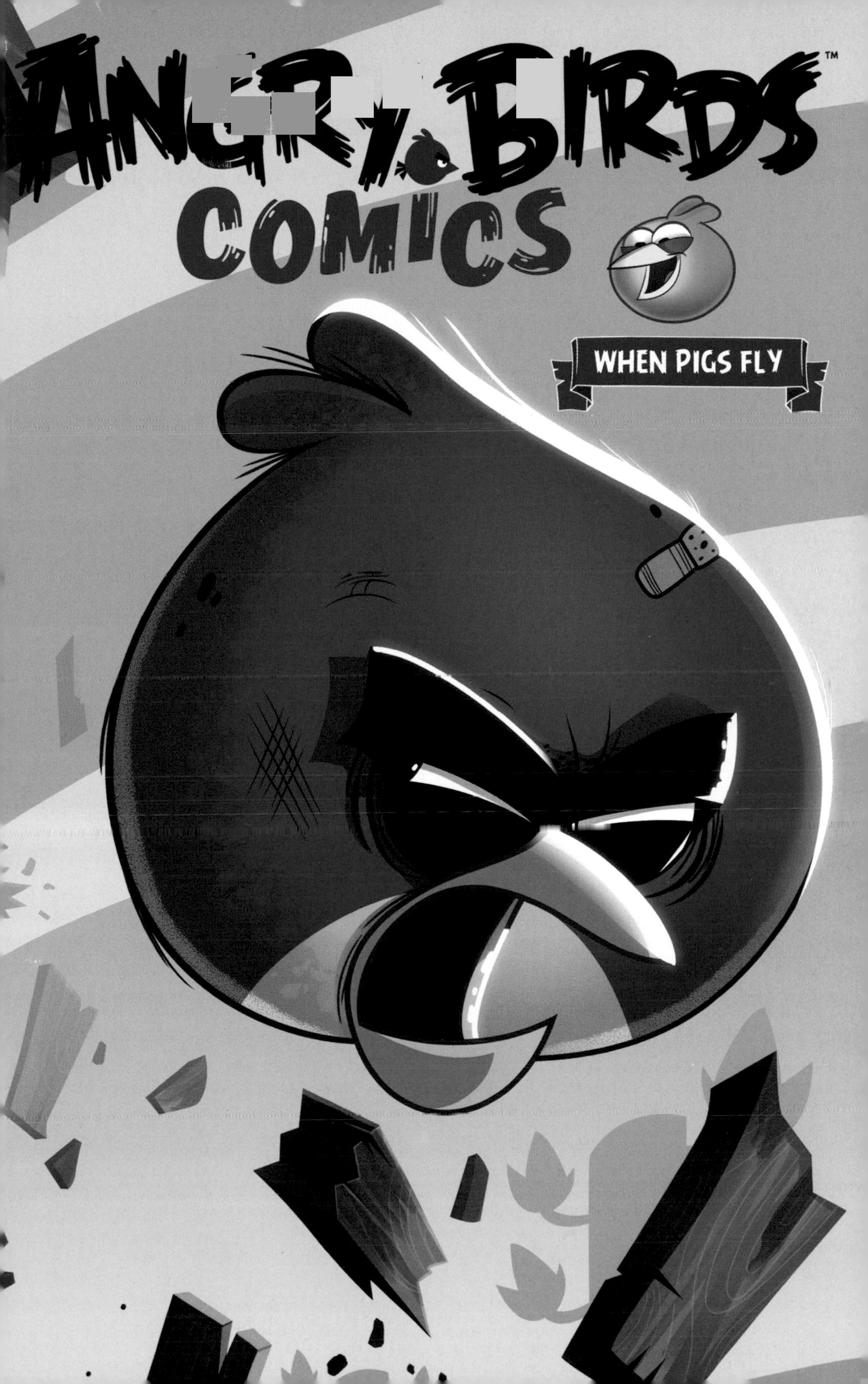
ANGRY BIRDS™
COMICS
WHEN PIGS FLY

Cover Artwork by: Paco Rodriquez
Cover Colors by: Nicole Pasquetto

Original Series Edits by: David Hedgecock
Collection Edits by: Justin Eisinger & Alonzo Simon
Collection Production by: Chris Mowry

ROVIO BOOKS

Laura Nevanlinna, Publishing Director
Jukka Heiskanen, Editor-in-Chief, Comics
Juha Mäkinen, Editor, Comics
Jan Schulte-Tigges, Art Director, Comics
Henri Sarimo, Graphic Designer
Nathan Cosby, Freelance Editor

Thanks to Jukka Heiskanen, Juha Mäkinen, and the Rovio team for their hard work and invaluable assistance.

ISBN: 978-1-63140-248-7

18 17 16 15 1 2 3 4

IDW®
www.IDWPUBLISHING.com
IDW founded by Ted Adams, Alex Garner, Kris Oprisko, and Robbie Robbins

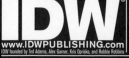

Ted Adams, CEO & Publisher
Greg Goldstein, President & COO
Robbie Robbins, EVP/Sr. Graphic Artist
Chris Ryall, Chief Creative Officer/Editor-in-Chief
Matthew Ruzicka, CPA, Chief Financial Officer
Alan Payne, VP of Sales
Dirk Wood, VP of Marketing
Lorelei Bunjes, VP of Digital Services
Jeff Webber, VP of Digital Publishing & Business Development

Facebook: facebook.com/idwpublishing
Twitter: @idwpublishing
YouTube: youtube.com/idwpublishing
Instagram: instagram.com/idwpublishing
deviantART: idwpublishing.deviantart.com
Pinterest: pinterest.com/idwpublishing/idw-staff-faves

Originally published in ANGRY BIRDS COMICS issues #5–8.

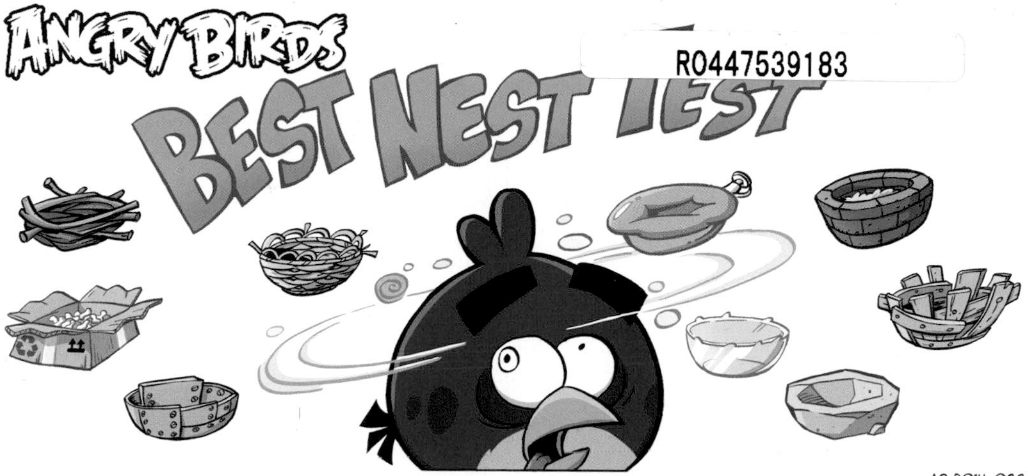
ANGRY BIRDS
BEST NEST TEST

AB 2014-066

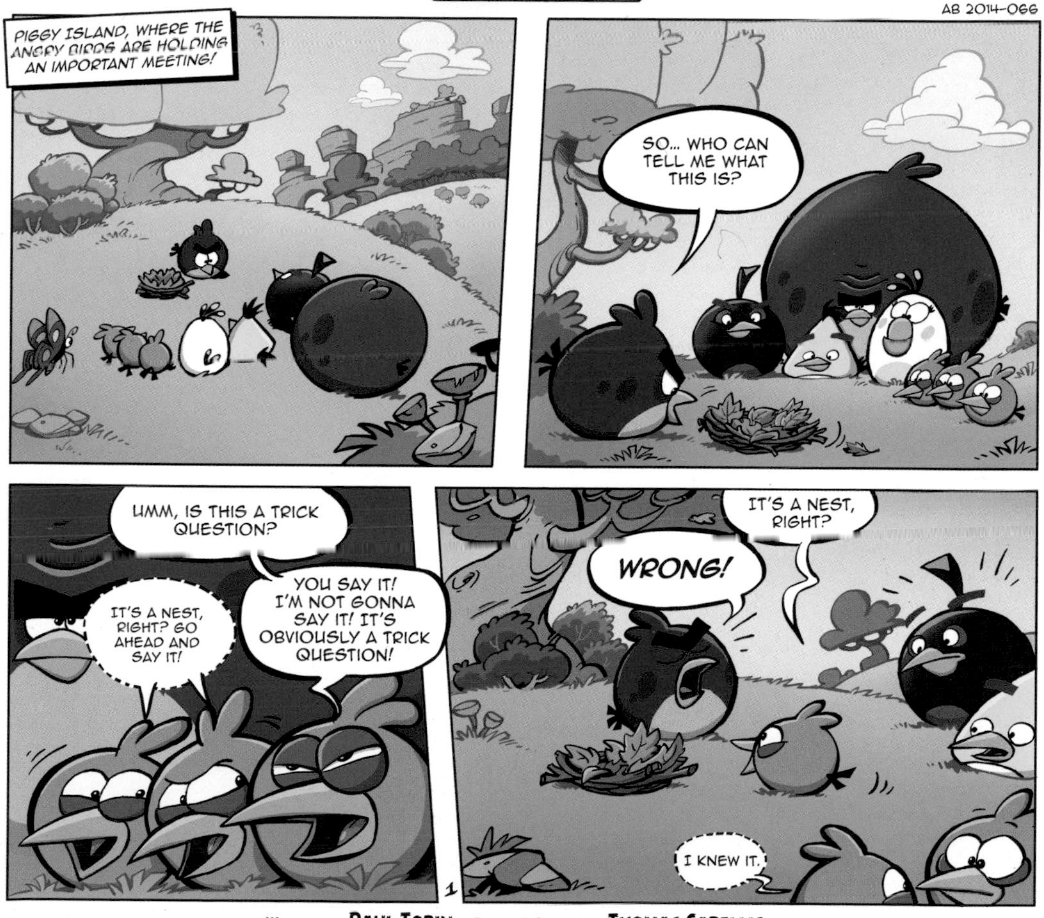
PIGGY ISLAND, WHERE THE ANGRY BIRDS ARE HOLDING AN IMPORTANT MEETING!
SO... WHO CAN TELL ME WHAT THIS IS?
UMM, IS THIS A TRICK QUESTION?
IT'S A NEST, RIGHT? GO AHEAD AND SAY IT!
YOU SAY IT! I'M NOT GONNA SAY IT! IT'S OBVIOUSLY A TRICK QUESTION!
IT'S A NEST, RIGHT?
WRONG!
I KNEW IT.
1

WRITTEN BY: PAUL TOBIN • ART AND COLORS BY: THOMAS CABELLIC

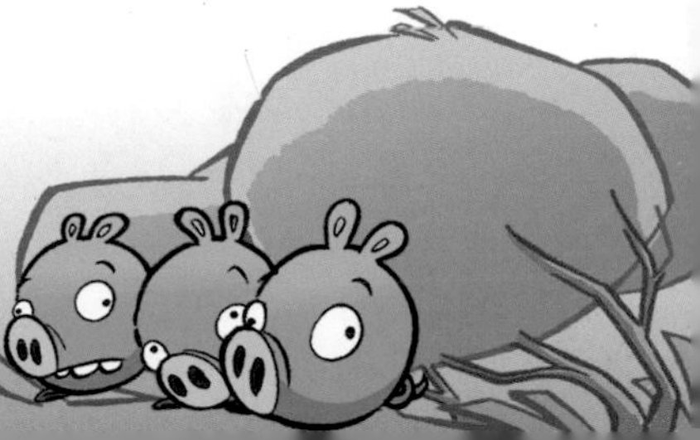

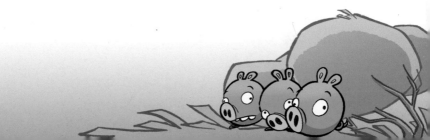

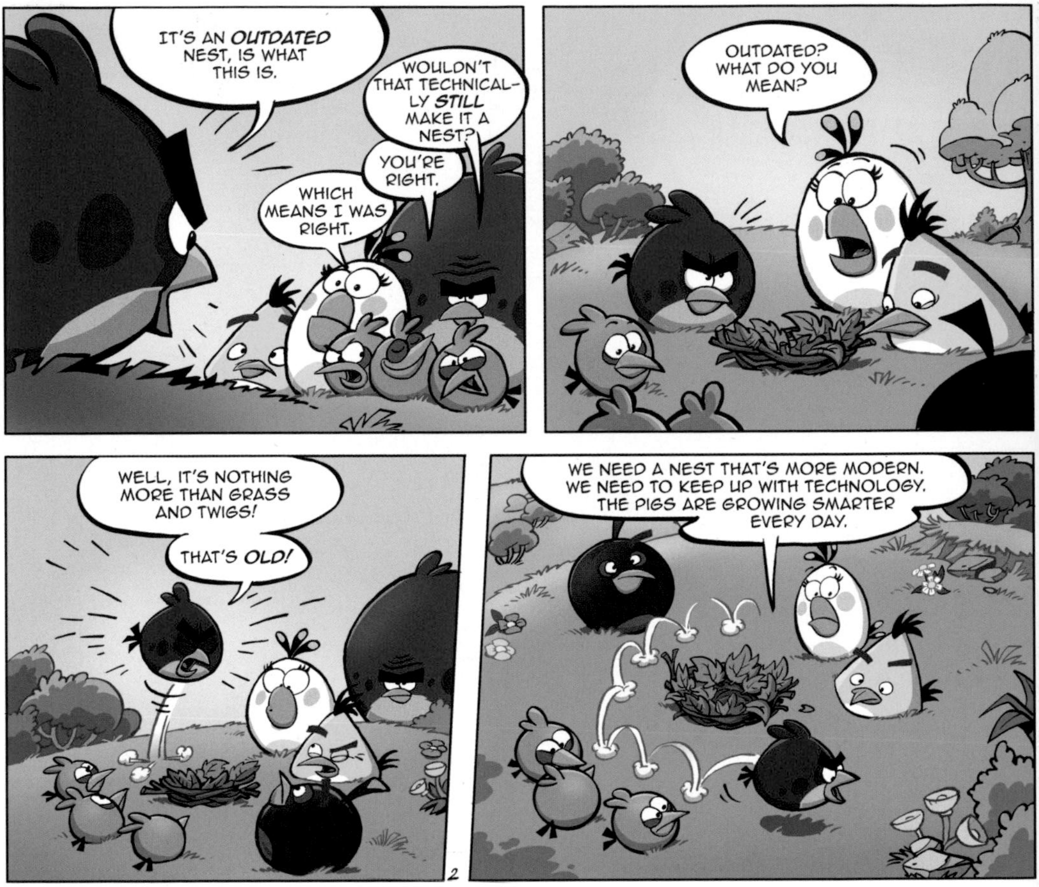

IT'S AN OUTDATED NEST, IS WHAT THIS IS.
WOULDN'T THAT TECHNICAL-LY STILL MAKE IT A NEST?
YOU'RE RIGHT.
WHICH MEANS I WAS RIGHT.
OUTDATED? WHAT DO YOU MEAN?
WELL, IT'S NOTHING MORE THAN GRASS AND TWIGS!
THAT'S OLD!
WE NEED A NEST THAT'S MORE MODERN. WE NEED TO KEEP UP WITH TECHNOLOGY. THE PIGS ARE GROWING SMARTER EVERY DAY.
2

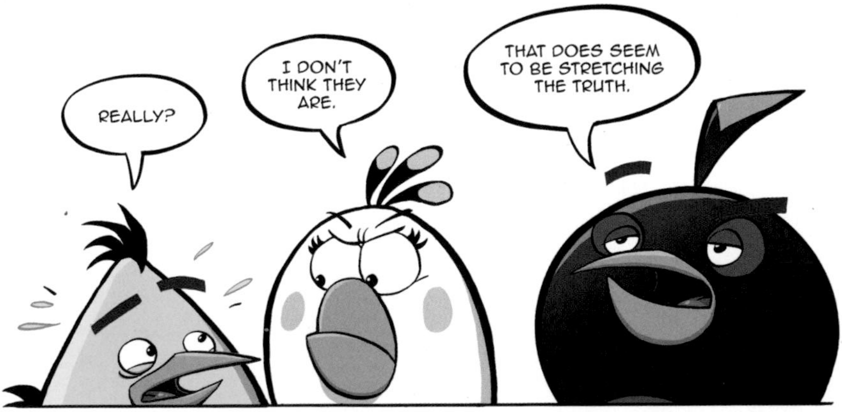

REALLY?
I DON'T THINK THEY ARE.
THAT DOES SEEM TO BE STRETCHING THE TRUTH.

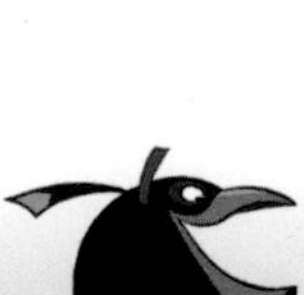

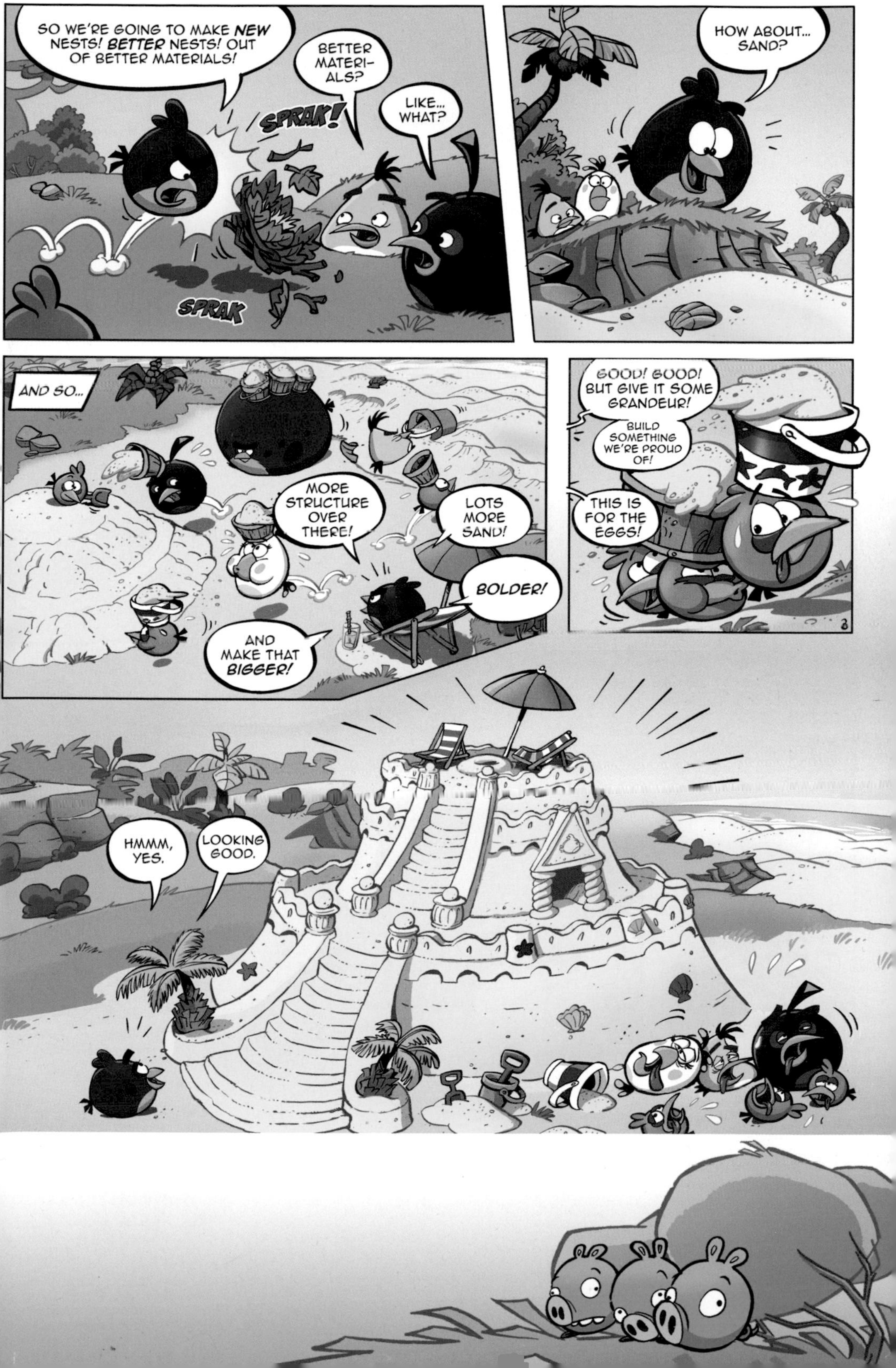
SO WE'RE GOING TO MAKE NEW NESTS! BETTER NESTS! OUT OF BETTER MATERIALS!
SPRAK!
SPRAK
BETTER MATERI-ALS?
LIKE... WHAT?
HOW ABOUT... SAND?
AND SO...
MORE STRUCTURE OVER THERE!
LOTS MORE SAND!
BOLDER!
AND MAKE THAT BIGGER!
GOOD! GOOD! BUT GIVE IT SOME GRANDEUR!
BUILD SOMETHING WE'RE PROUD OF!
THIS IS FOR THE EGGS!
HMMM, YES.
LOOKING GOOD.

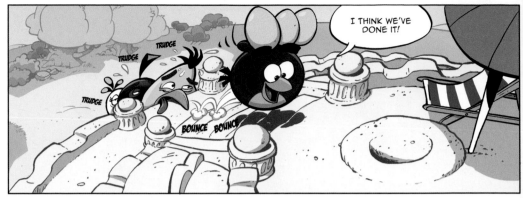

TRUDGE
TRUDGE
TRUDGE
BOUNCE BOUNCE
I THINK WE'VE DONE IT!
THERE! DOESN'T THIS FEEL BETTER?
AND WE'RE HIGH ENOUGH UP TO KEEP A LOOK OUT FOR THE PIGS!
SO THIS NEST IS *MUCH* BETTER THAN THAT OLD...
PLIP
IS IT STARTING TO RAIN?
PLIP
PLOP
PLOP
PLIP
PLIP
PLOP
PLIP
PLOP
PLIP
PLIP
PLOP
PLIP
PLIP
PLIP
4

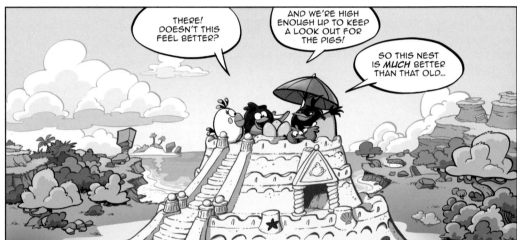

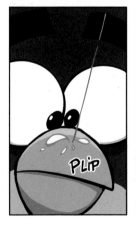

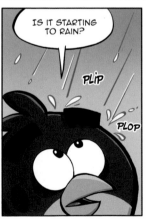

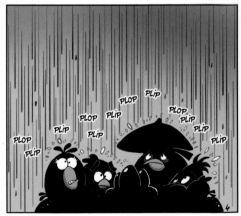

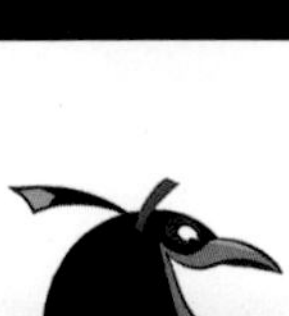

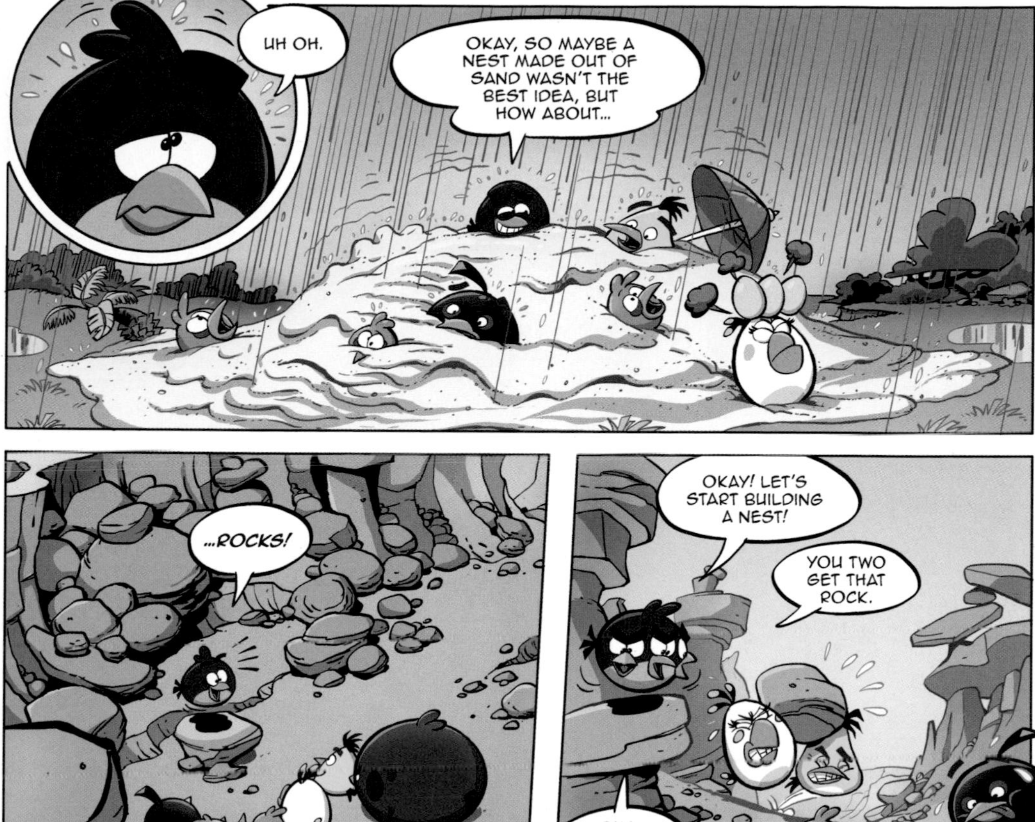
UH OH.
OKAY, SO MAYBE A NEST MADE OUT OF SAND WASN'T THE BEST IDEA, BUT HOW ABOUT...
...ROCKS!
OKAY! LET'S START BUILDING A NEST!
YOU TWO GET THAT ROCK.
JAY, JAKE, JIM... YOU START GATHERING THOSE ROCKS.
AND I'LL GET *THIS* ONE!

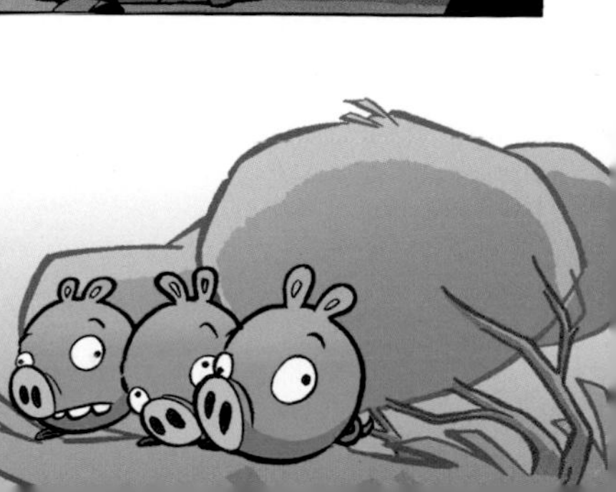

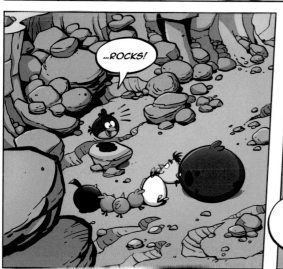

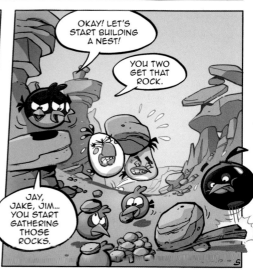

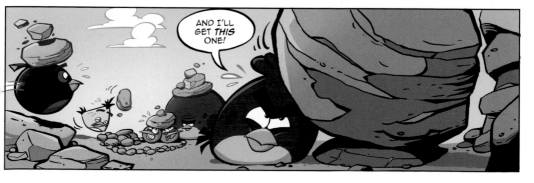

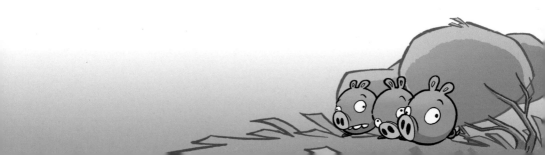

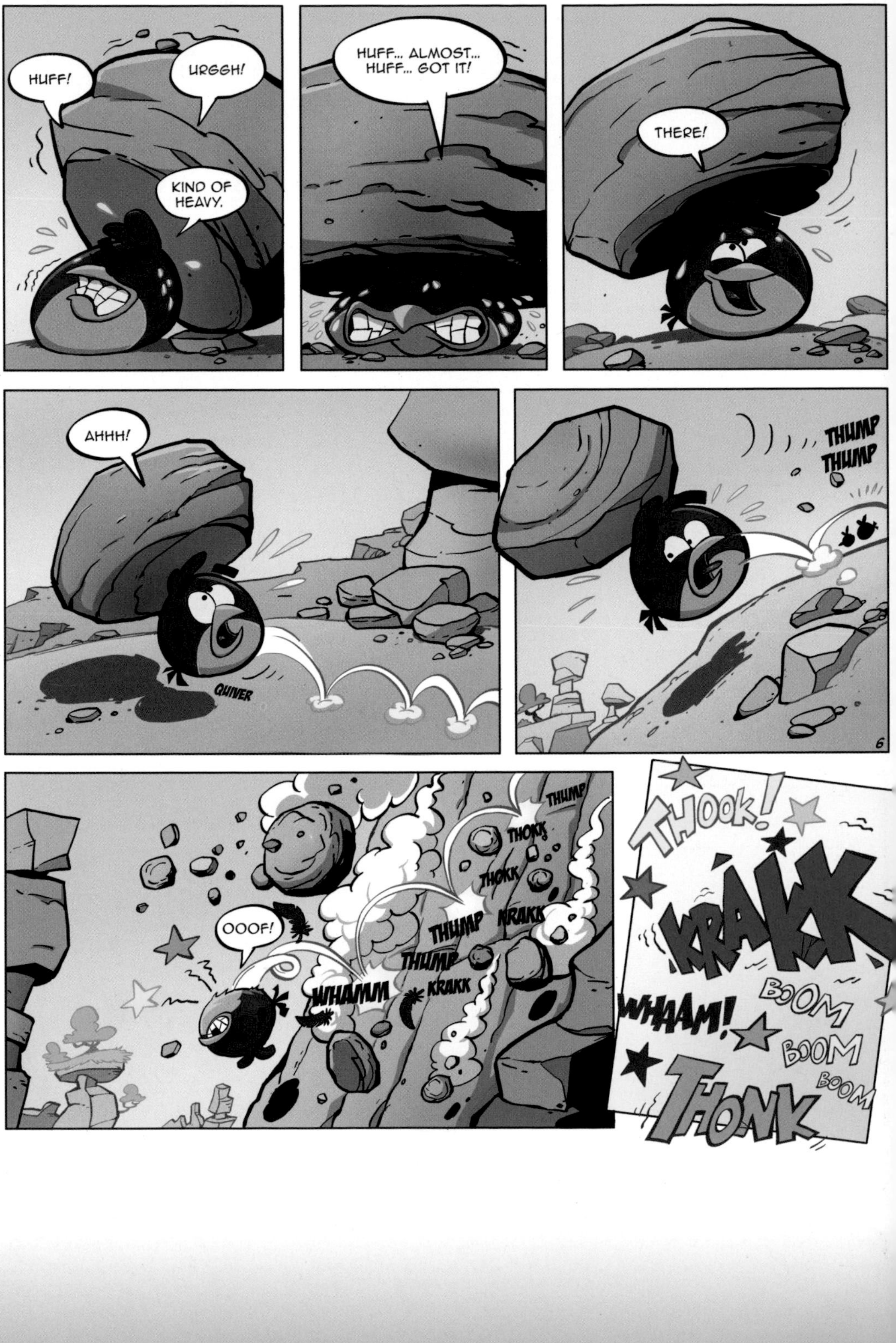
HUFF!
URGGH!
KIND OF HEAVY.
HUFF... ALMOST... HUFF... GOT IT!
THERE!
AHHH!
QUIVER
THUMP
THUMP
OOOF!
WHAMM
THUMP
KRAKK
THUMP
THOKK
THOKK
THUMP
KRAKK
THOOK!
KRAKK
WHAAM!
BOOM
BOOM
BOOM
THONK

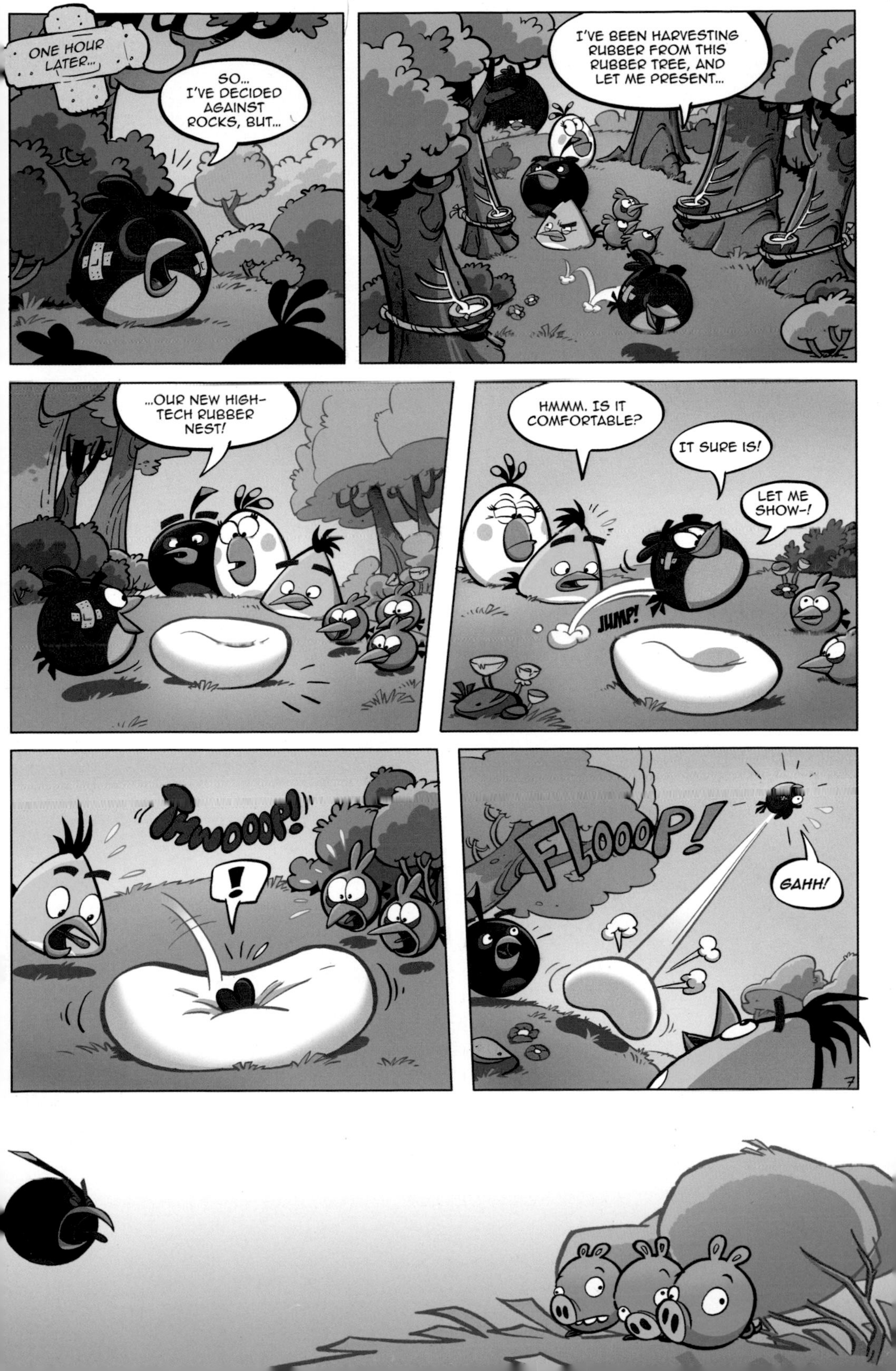
ONE HOUR LATER...
SO... I'VE DECIDED AGAINST ROCKS, BUT...
I'VE BEEN HARVESTING RUBBER FROM THIS RUBBER TREE, AND LET ME PRESENT...
...OUR NEW HIGH-TECH RUBBER NEST!
HMMM. IS IT COMFORTABLE?
IT SURE IS!
LET ME SHOW-!
JUMP!
THWOOOP!
!
FLOOOP!
GAHH!
7

WHOOOOOOOSH

AHHHH!

THUMP THUMP

WHEW! THAT WASN'T SO BAD, I...

OOOPS.

CRUMBLE

THUMP!

ACKK!

THOOK

THUMP THOOK

KRAKK

THUMP THUMP

WHAMM!!

BOOM

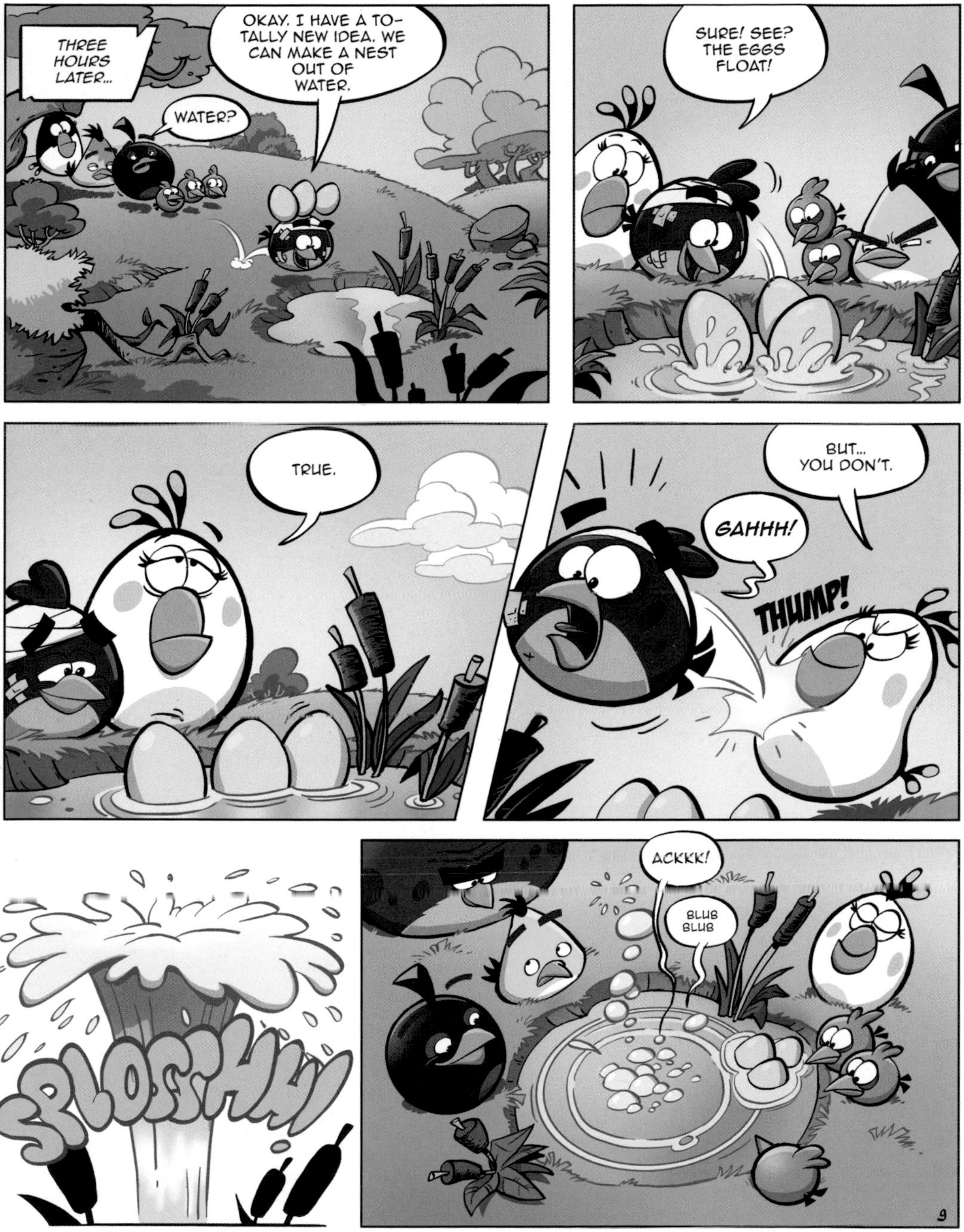
THREE HOURS LATER...
OKAY. I HAVE A TOTALLY NEW IDEA. WE CAN MAKE A NEST OUT OF WATER.
WATER?
SURE! SEE? THE EGGS FLOAT!
TRUE.
BUT... YOU DON'T.
GAHHH!
THUMP!
SPLOOSHHH!
ACKKK!
BLUB BLUB

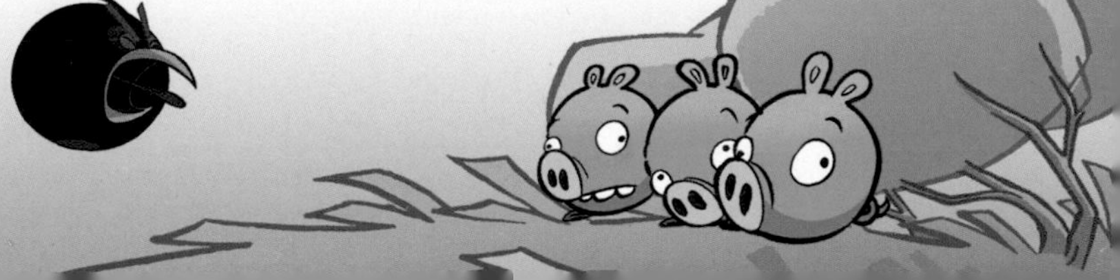

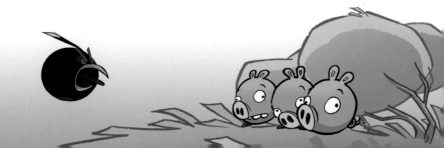

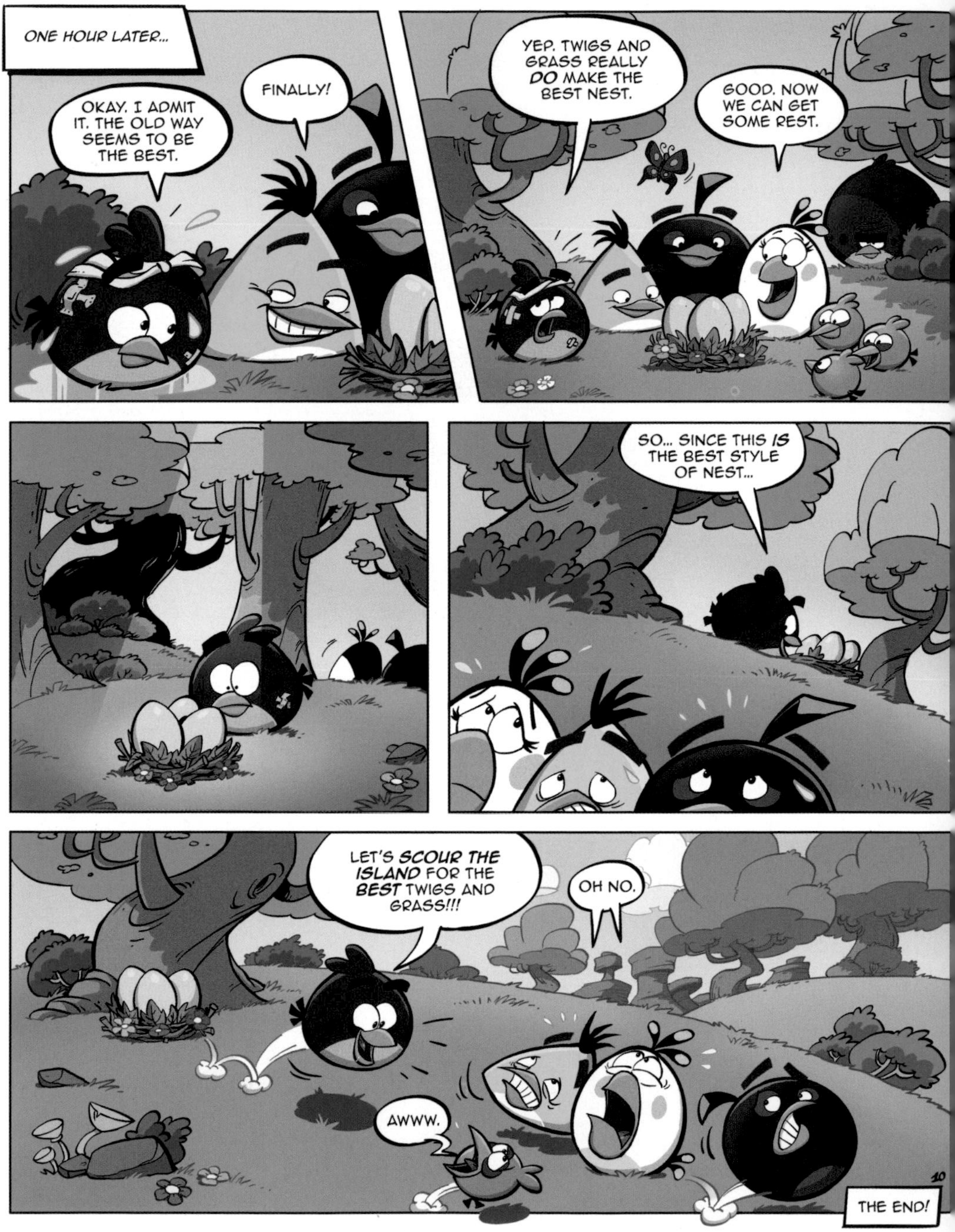
ONE HOUR LATER...
OKAY. I ADMIT IT. THE OLD WAY SEEMS TO BE THE BEST.
FINALLY!
YEP. TWIGS AND GRASS REALLY DO MAKE THE BEST NEST.
GOOD. NOW WE CAN GET SOME REST.
SO... SINCE THIS IS THE BEST STYLE OF NEST...
LET'S SCOUR THE ISLAND FOR THE BEST TWIGS AND GRASS!!!
OH NO.
AWWW.
THE END!

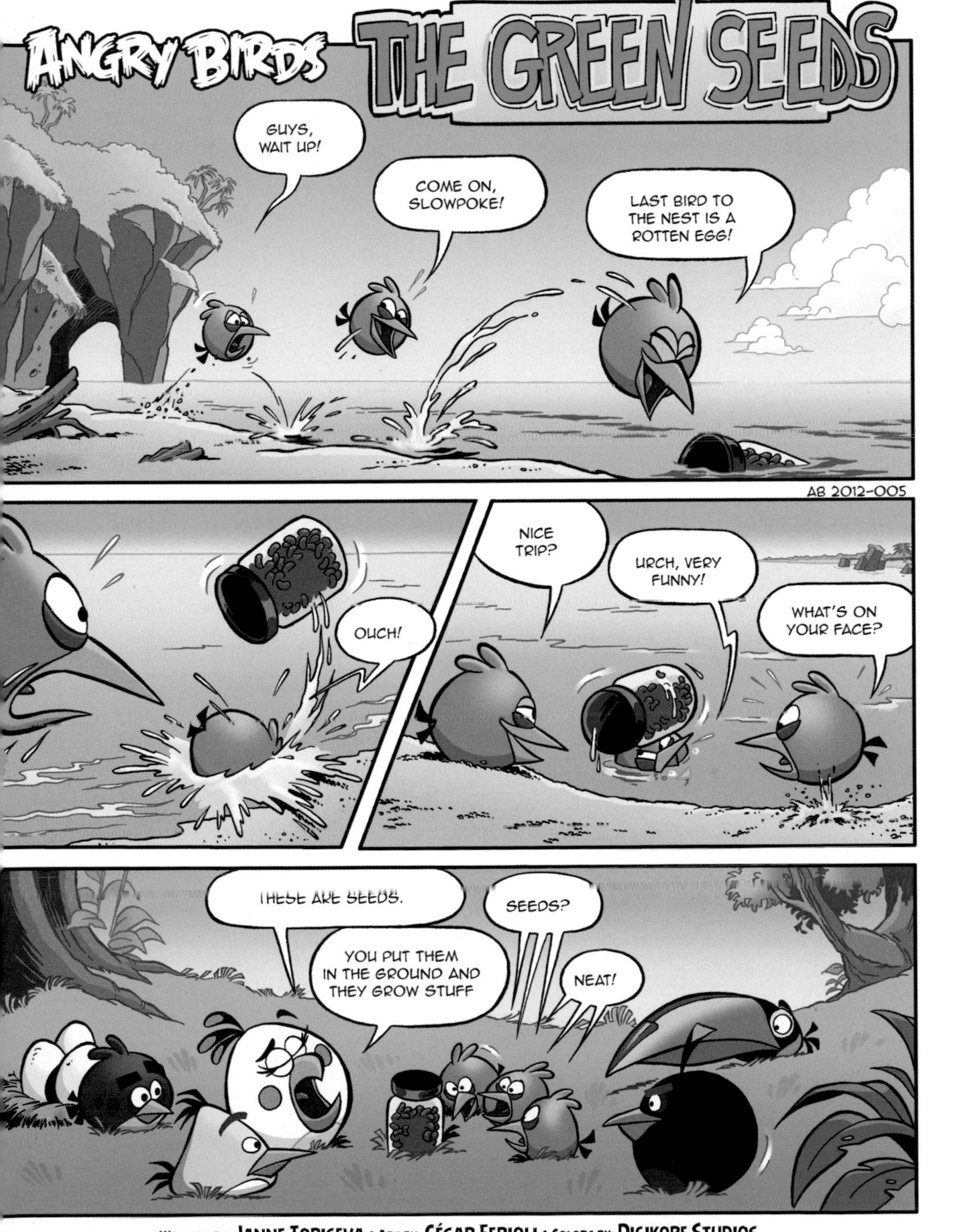
ANGRY BIRDS
THE GREEN SEEDS
GUYS, WAIT UP!
COME ON, SLOWPOKE!
LAST BIRD TO THE NEST IS A ROTTEN EGG!
AB 2012-005
OUCH!
NICE TRIP?
URCH, VERY FUNNY!
WHAT'S ON YOUR FACE?
THESE ARE SEEDS.
SEEDS?
YOU PUT THEM IN THE GROUND AND THEY GROW STUFF
NEAT!

WRITTEN BY: JANNE TORISEVA • ART BY: CÉSAR FERIOLI • COLORS BY: DIGIKORE STUDIOS

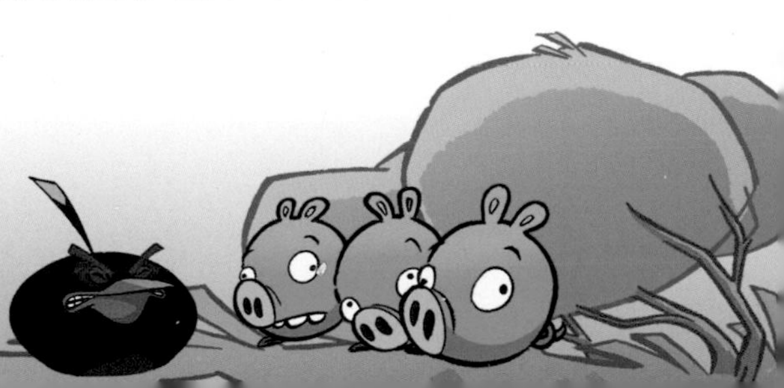

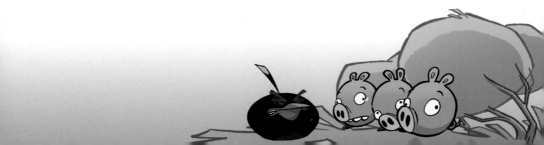

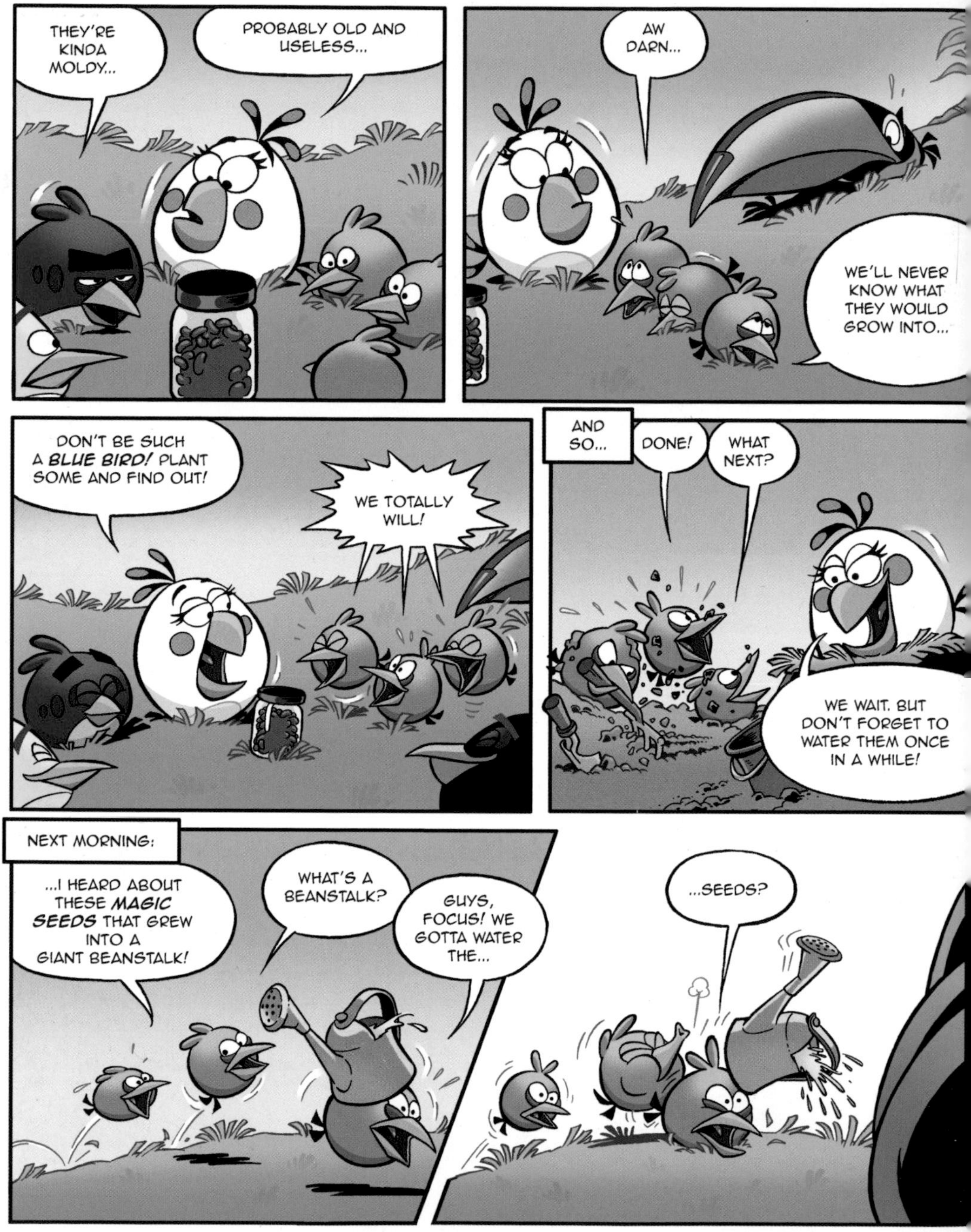
THEY'RE KINDA MOLDY...
PROBABLY OLD AND USELESS...
AW DARN...
WE'LL NEVER KNOW WHAT THEY WOULD GROW INTO...
DON'T BE SUCH A BLUE BIRD! PLANT SOME AND FIND OUT!
WE TOTALLY WILL!
AND SO...
DONE!
WHAT NEXT?
WE WAIT. BUT DON'T FORGET TO WATER THEM ONCE IN A WHILE!
NEXT MORNING:
...I HEARD ABOUT THESE MAGIC SEEDS THAT GREW INTO A GIANT BEANSTALK!
WHAT'S A BEANSTALK?
GUYS, FOCUS! WE GOTTA WATER THE...
...SEEDS?

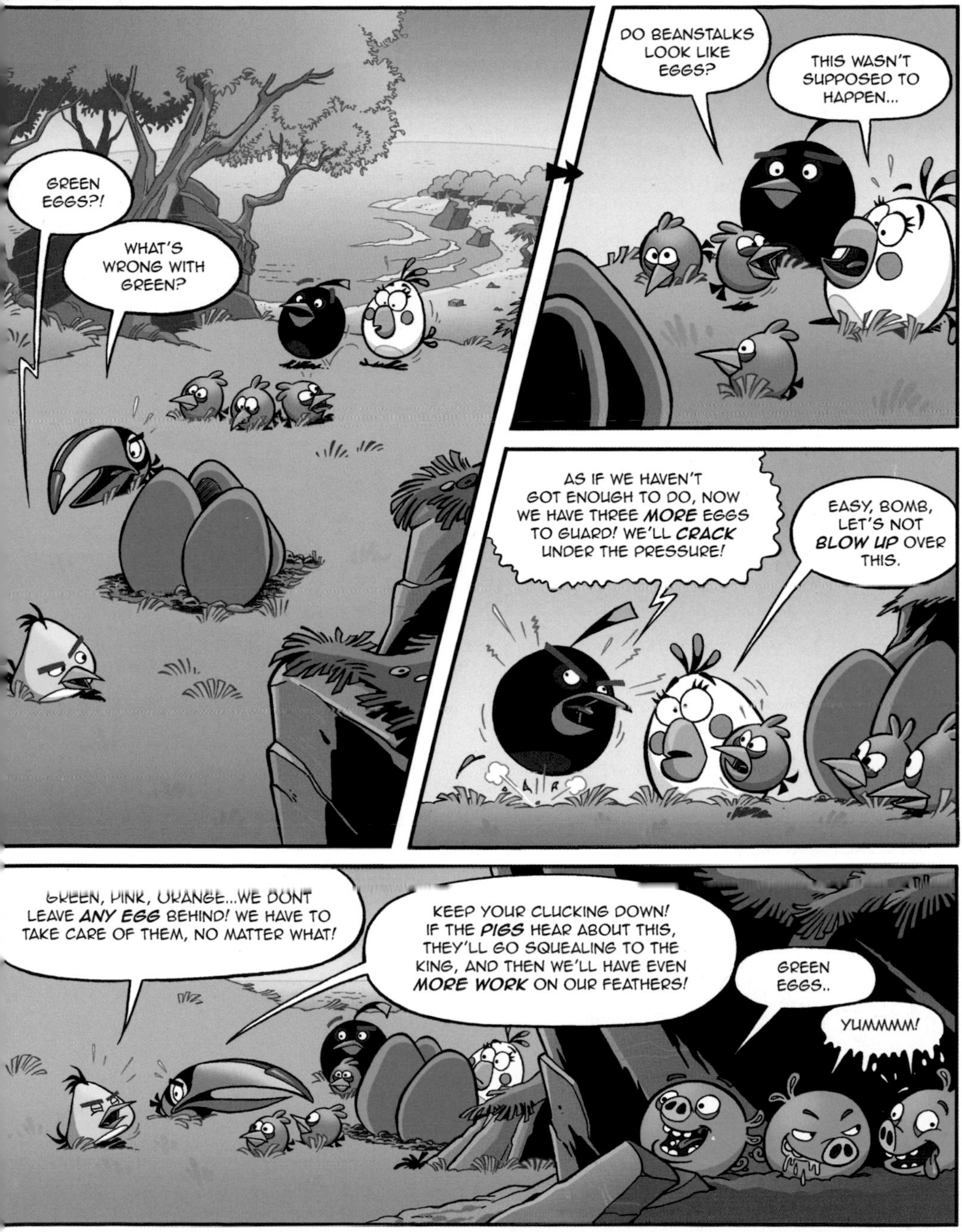
GREEN EGGS?!
WHAT'S WRONG WITH GREEN?
DO BEANSTALKS LOOK LIKE EGGS?
THIS WASN'T SUPPOSED TO HAPPEN...
AS IF WE HAVEN'T GOT ENOUGH TO DO, NOW WE HAVE THREE MORE EGGS TO GUARD! WE'LL CRACK UNDER THE PRESSURE!
EASY, BOMB, LET'S NOT BLOW UP OVER THIS.
GREEN, PINK, ORANGE...WE DONT LEAVE ANY EGG BEHIND! WE HAVE TO TAKE CARE OF THEM, NO MATTER WHAT!
KEEP YOUR CLUCKING DOWN! IF THE PIGS HEAR ABOUT THIS, THEY'LL GO SQUEALING TO THE KING, AND THEN WE'LL HAVE EVEN MORE WORK ON OUR FEATHERS!
GREEN EGGS..
YUMMMM!

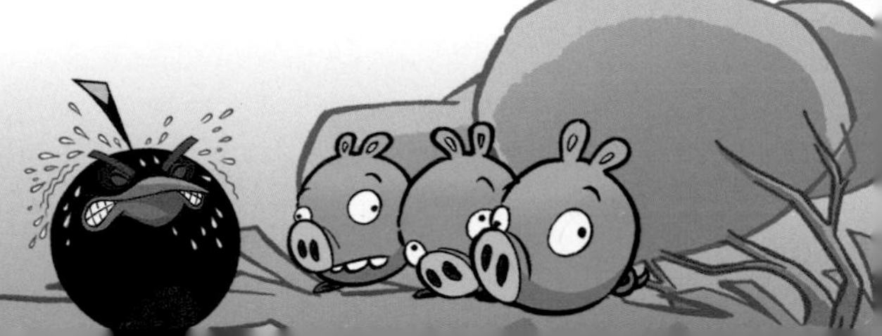

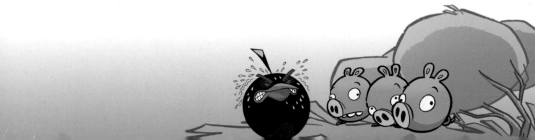

(SNORT) MMMM, WHAT'S ON THE MENU TODAY, CHEF?
AW SNOT! GRASS AGAIN...
I'M SORRY, SIRE. I WEEDED OUT THE WORST BITS...
YOUR ROYAL PIGNESS! YOU HAVE TO HEAR THIS!
THE BIRDS ARE ALL IN A FLAP OVER SOME GREEN EGGS!
YOU ARE DISTURBING THE KING'S GRASS DINNER!
WAIT...MORE EGGS? WHERE DID THEY COME FROM?
A LITTLE BIRD TOLD US ABOUT SOME SEEDS, YOUR MAJESTY!
THE SEEDS GROW INTO EGGS, YOUR HIGHNESS!
WE GOT A PIG'S-EYE-VIEW OF THE WHOLE THING, YOUR HOGINESS!

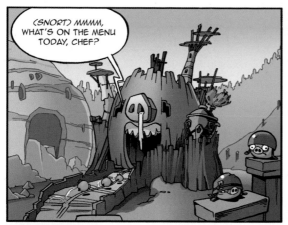

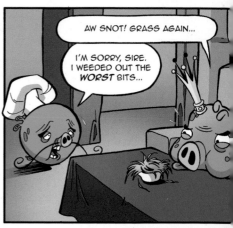

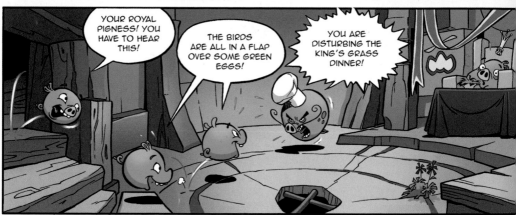

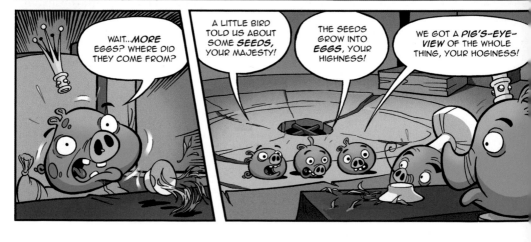

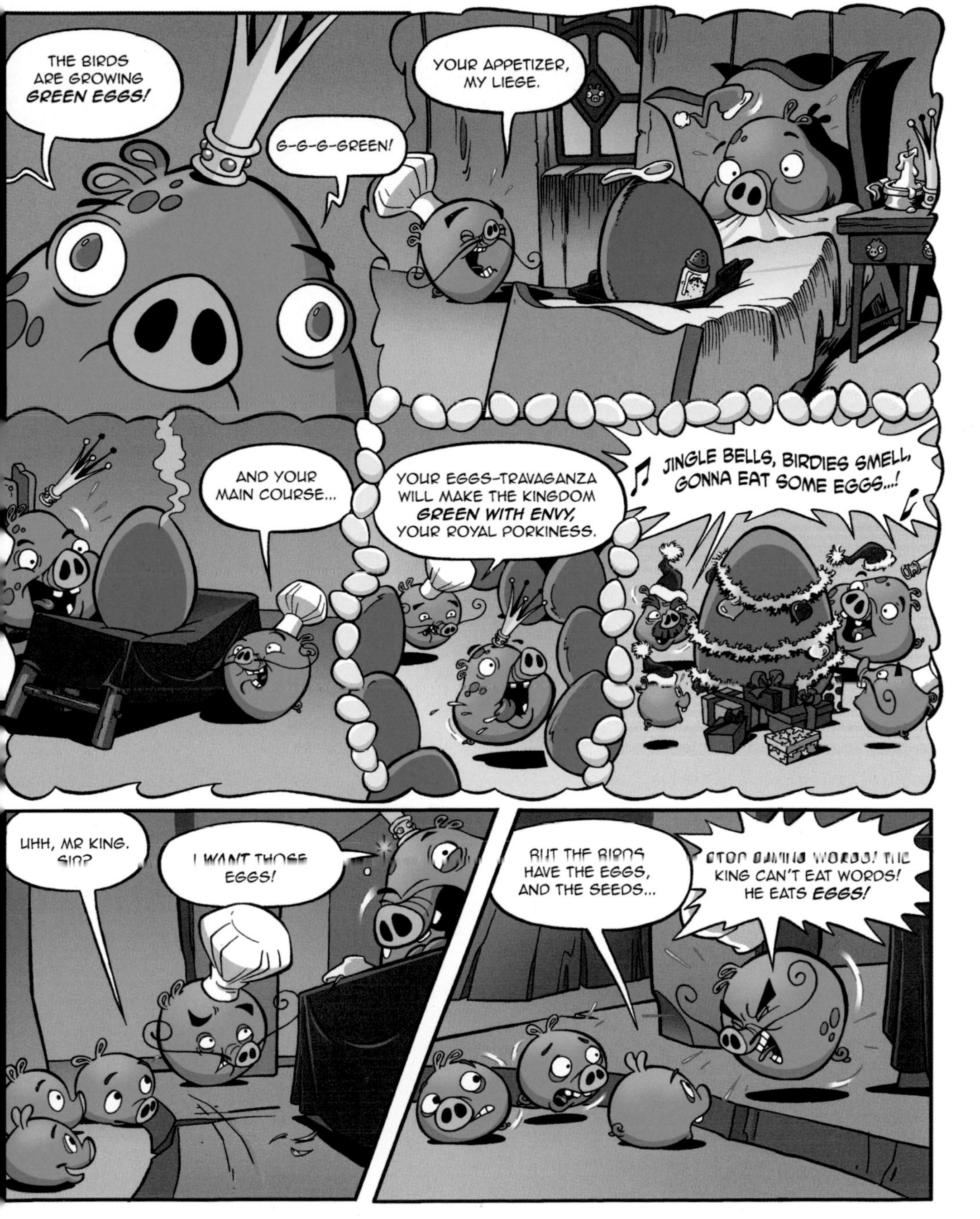
THE BIRDS ARE GROWING GREEN EGGS!
G-G-G-GREEN!
YOUR APPETIZER, MY LIEGE.
AND YOUR MAIN COURSE...
YOUR EGGS-TRAVAGANZA WILL MAKE THE KINGDOM GREEN WITH ENVY, YOUR ROYAL PORKINESS.
JINGLE BELLS, BIRDIES SMELL, GONNA EAT SOME EGGS...!
UHH, MR KING. SIR?
I WANT THOSE EGGS!
BUT THE BIRDS HAVE THE EGGS, AND THE SEEDS...
KING CAN'T EAT WORDS! HE EATS EGGS!

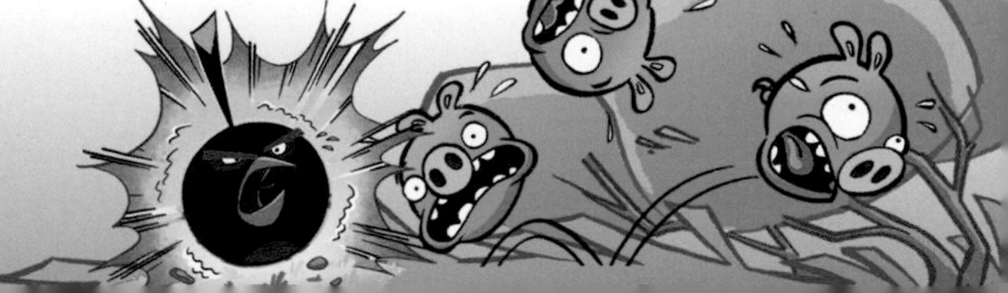

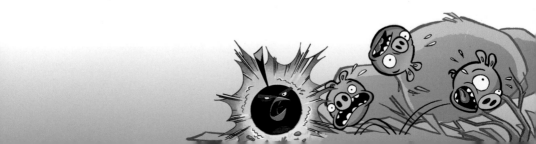

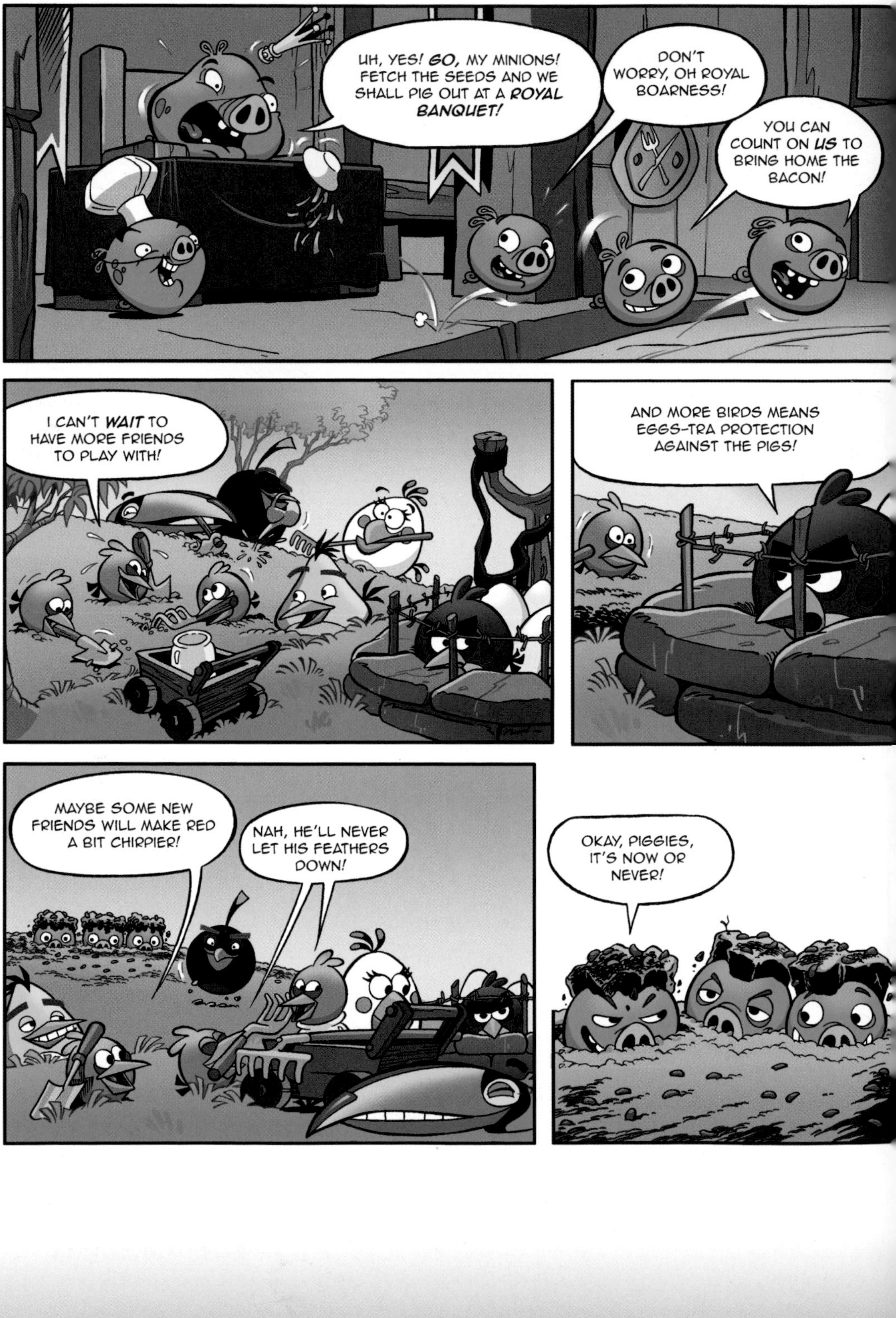
UH, YES! GO, MY MINIONS! FETCH THE SEEDS AND WE SHALL PIG OUT AT A ROYAL BANQUET!
DON'T WORRY, OH ROYAL BOARNESS!
YOU CAN COUNT ON US TO BRING HOME THE BACON!
I CAN'T WAIT TO HAVE MORE FRIENDS TO PLAY WITH!
AND MORE BIRDS MEANS EGGS-TRA PROTECTION AGAINST THE PIGS!
MAYBE SOME NEW FRIENDS WILL MAKE RED A BIT CHIRPIER!
NAH, HE'LL NEVER LET HIS FEATHERS DOWN!
OKAY, PIGGIES, IT'S NOW OR NEVER!

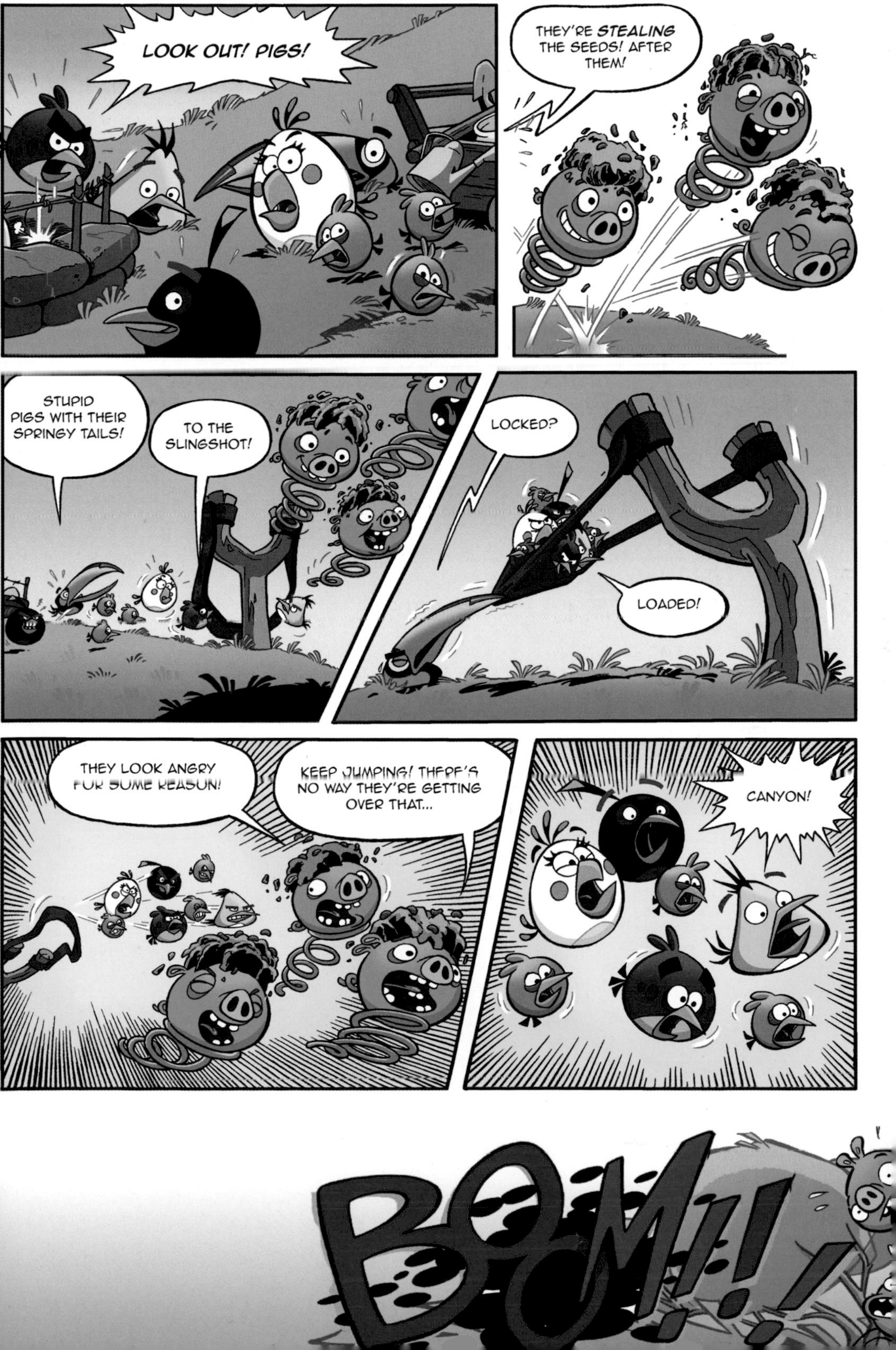
LOOK OUT! PIGS!
THEY'RE STEALING THE SEEDS! AFTER THEM!
STUPID PIGS WITH THEIR SPRINGY TAILS!
TO THE SLINGSHOT!
LOCKED?
LOADED!
THEY LOOK ANGRY FOR SOME REASON!
KEEP JUMPING! THERE'S NO WAY THEY'RE GETTING OVER THAT...
CANYON!
BOOM!!!

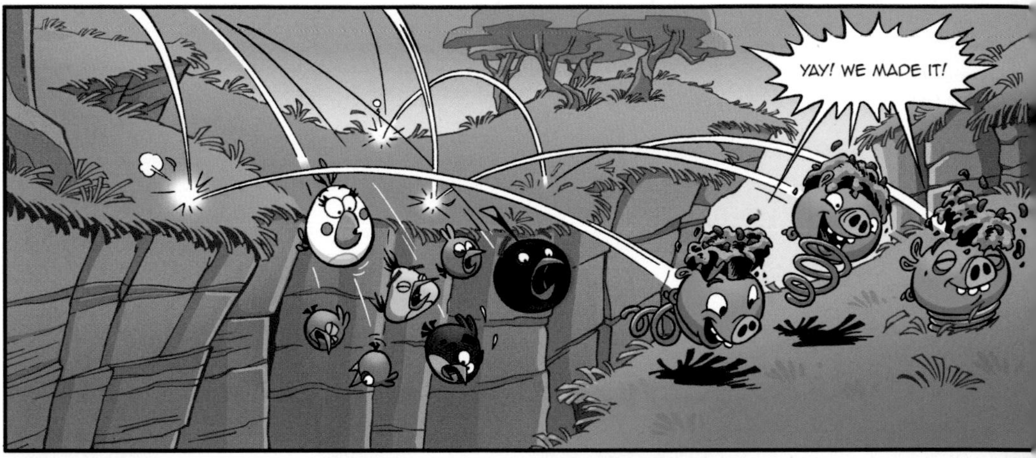
YAY! WE MADE IT!

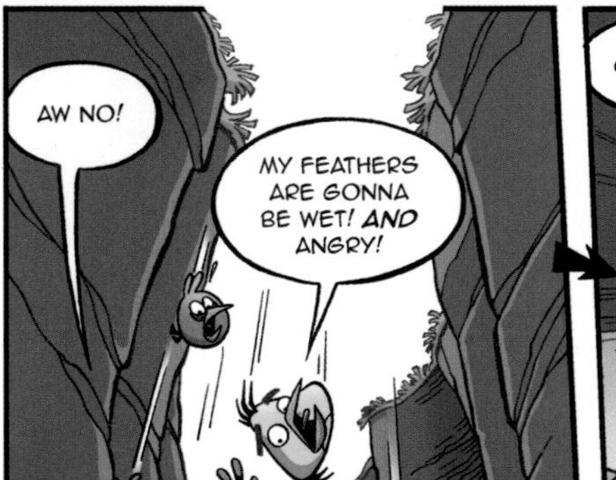
AW NO!
MY FEATHERS ARE GONNA BE WET! AND ANGRY!

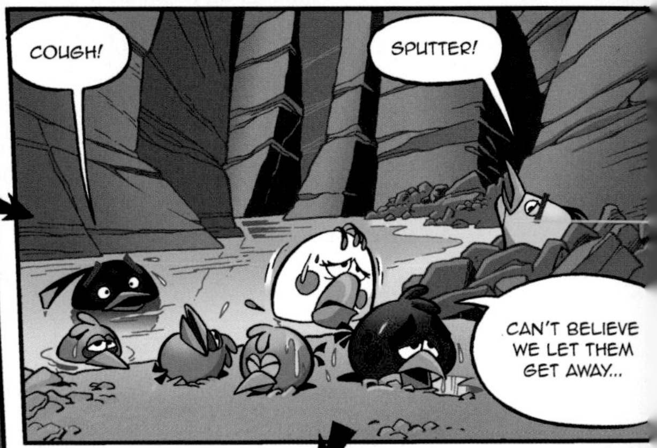
COUGH!
SPUTTER!
CAN'T BELIEVE WE LET THEM GET AWAY...

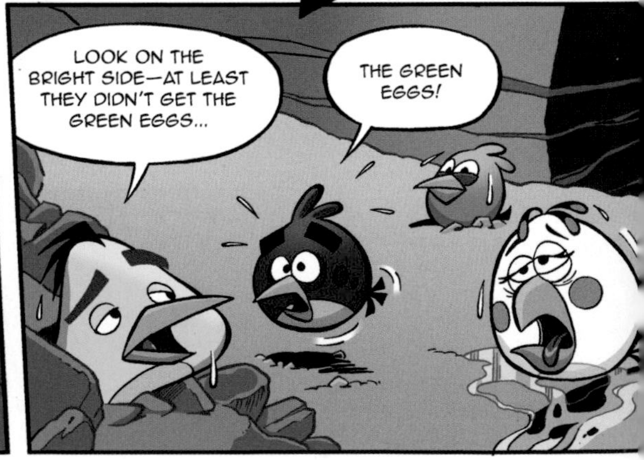
LOOK ON THE BRIGHT SIDE—AT LEAST THEY DIDN'T GET THE GREEN EGGS...
THE GREEN EGGS!

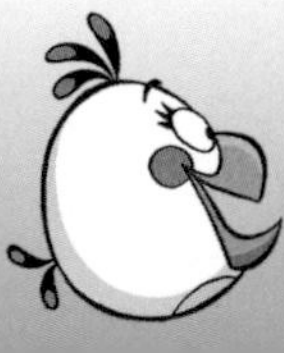

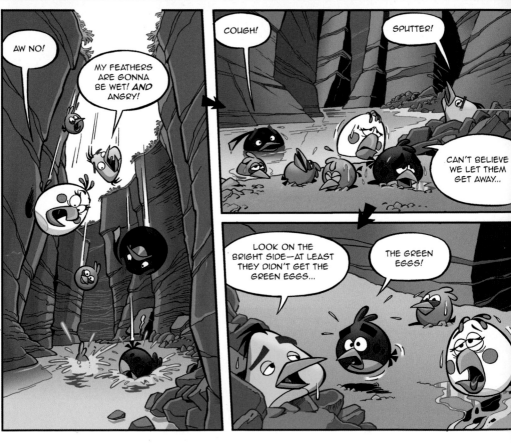

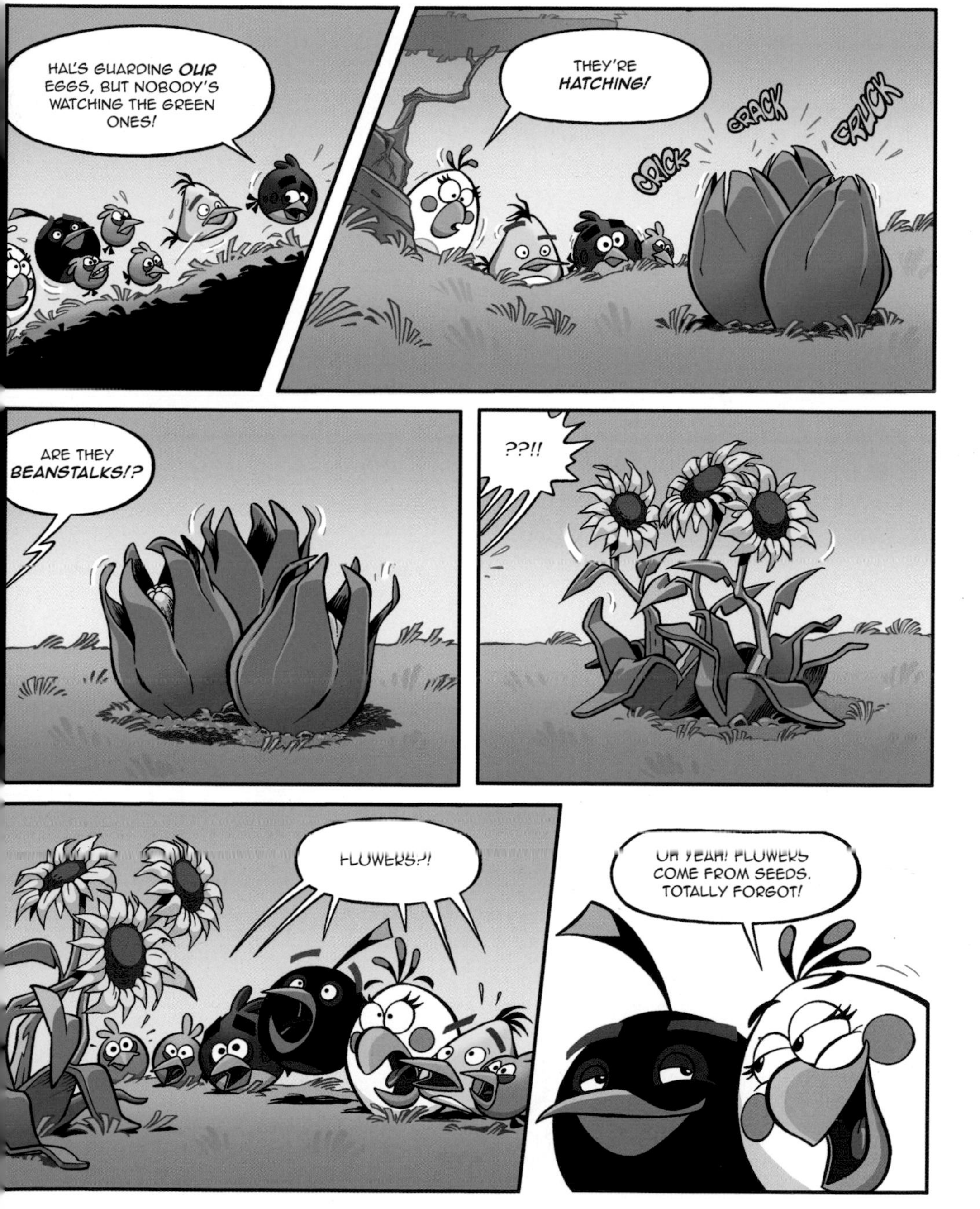
HAL'S GUARDING OUR EGGS, BUT NOBODY'S WATCHING THE GREEN ONES!
THEY'RE HATCHING!
CRICK
CRACK
CRUCK
ARE THEY BEANSTALKS!?
??!!
FLOWERS?!
OH YEAH! FLOWERS COME FROM SEEDS. TOTALLY FORGOT!

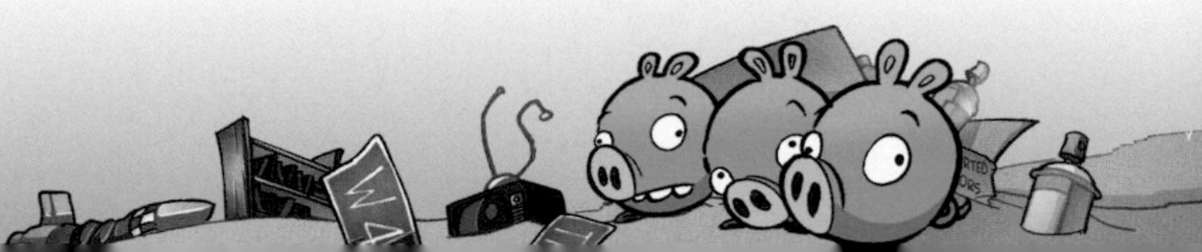

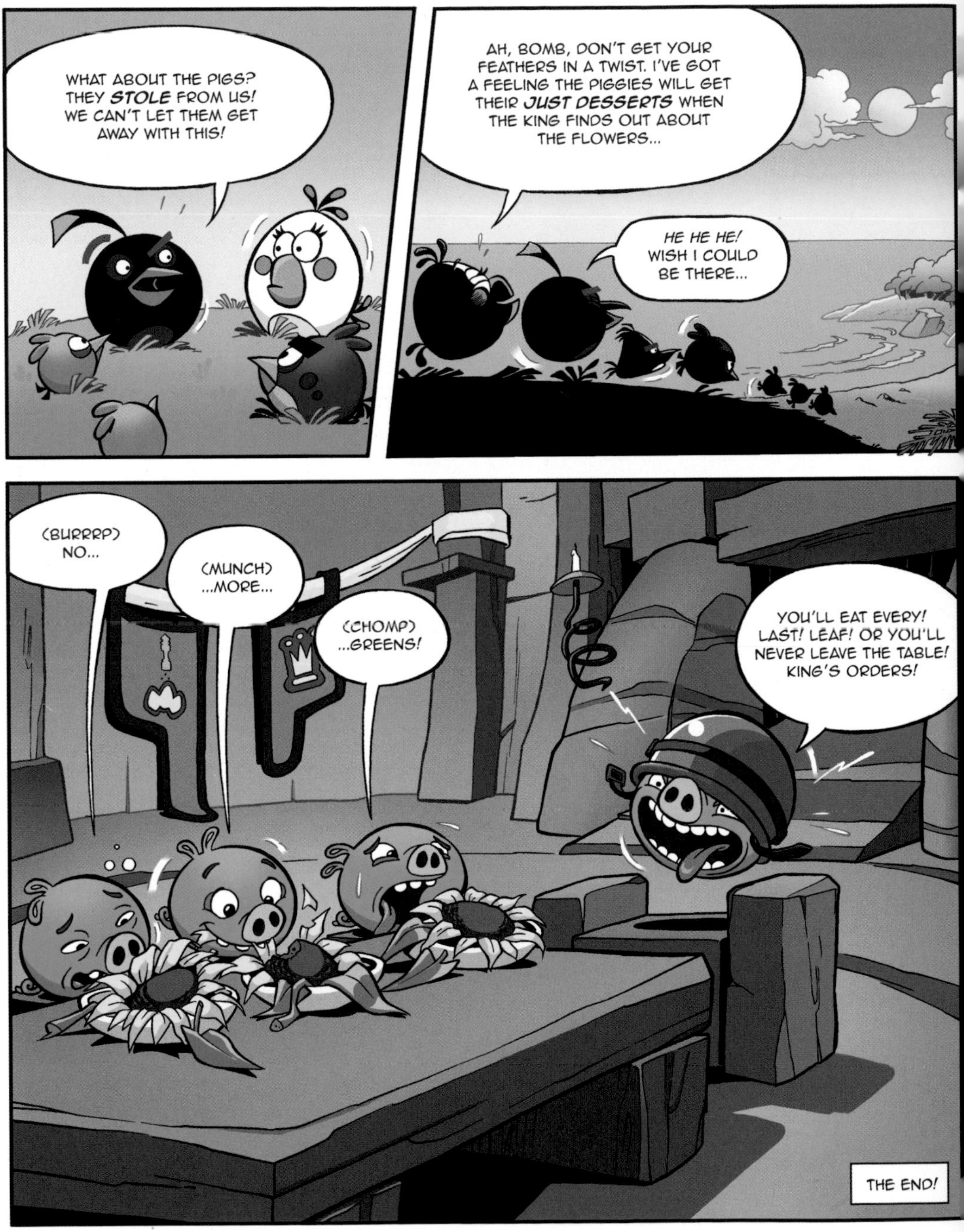
WHAT ABOUT THE PIGS? THEY **STOLE** FROM US! WE CAN'T LET THEM GET AWAY WITH THIS!
AH, BOMB, DON'T GET YOUR FEATHERS IN A TWIST. I'VE GOT A FEELING THE PIGGIES WILL GET THEIR ***JUST DESSERTS*** WHEN THE KING FINDS OUT ABOUT THE FLOWERS...
HE HE HE! WISH I COULD BE THERE...
(BURRRP) NO...
(MUNCH) ...MORE...
(CHOMP) ...GREENS!
YOU'LL EAT EVERY! LAST! LEAF! OR YOU'LL NEVER LEAVE THE TABLE! KING'S ORDERS!
THE END!

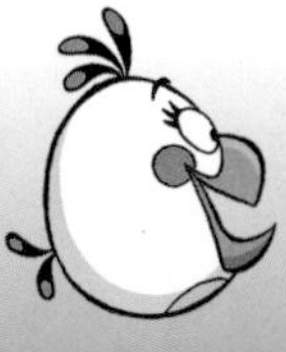

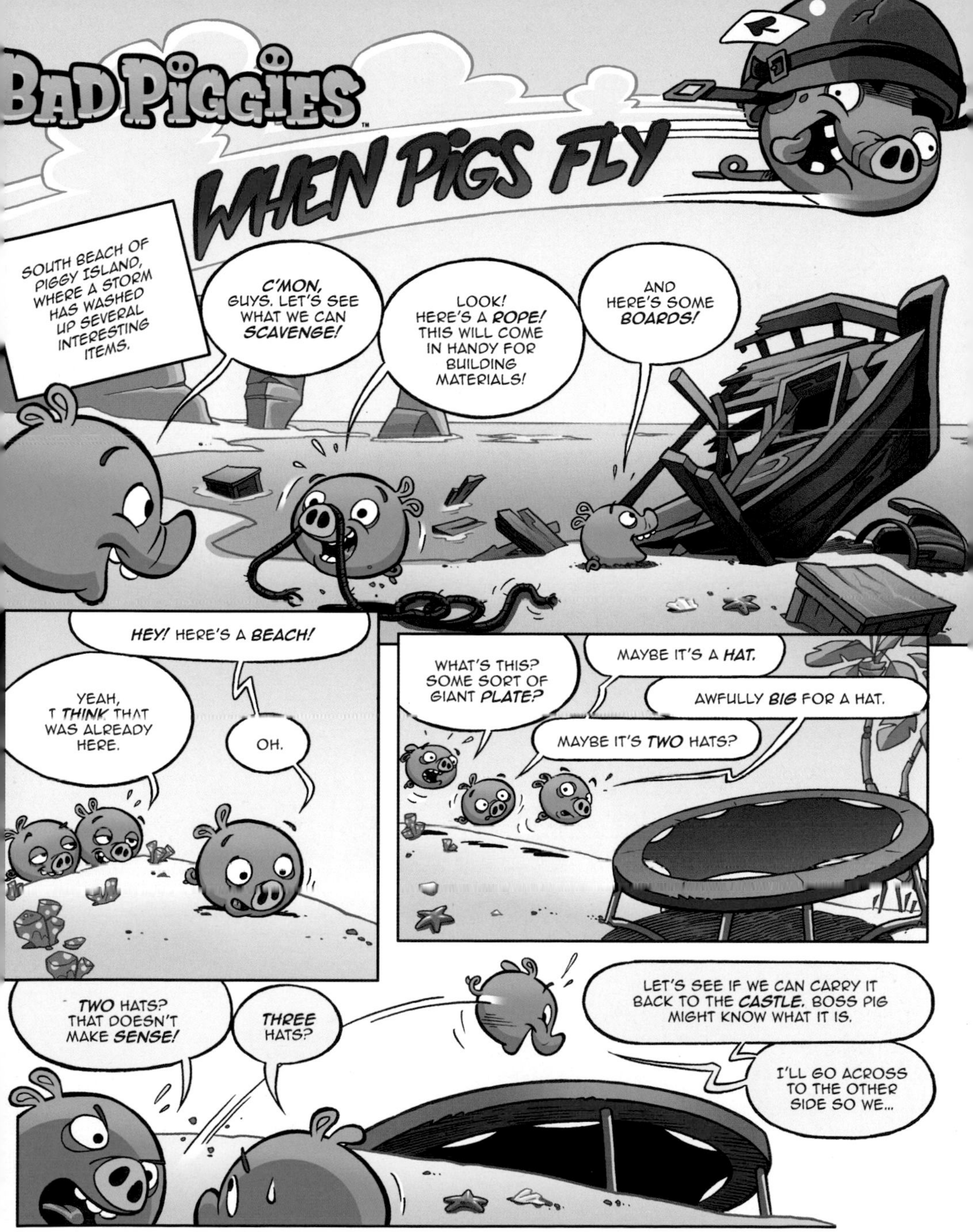
BAD PIGGIES™
WHEN PIGS FLY
SOUTH BEACH OF PIGGY ISLAND, WHERE A STORM HAS WASHED UP SEVERAL INTERESTING ITEMS.
C'MON, GUYS. LET'S SEE WHAT WE CAN SCAVENGE!
LOOK! HERE'S A ROPE! THIS WILL COME IN HANDY FOR BUILDING MATERIALS!
AND HERE'S SOME BOARDS!
HEY! HERE'S A BEACH!
YEAH, I THINK THAT WAS ALREADY HERE.
OH.
WHAT'S THIS? SOME SORT OF GIANT PLATE?
MAYBE IT'S A HAT.
AWFULLY BIG FOR A HAT.
MAYBE IT'S TWO HATS?
TWO HATS? THAT DOESN'T MAKE SENSE!
THREE HATS?
LET'S SEE IF WE CAN CARRY IT BACK TO THE CASTLE. BOSS PIG MIGHT KNOW WHAT IT IS.
I'LL GO ACROSS TO THE OTHER SIDE SO WE...

WRITTEN BY: PAUL TOBIN • ART BY: CÉSAR FERIOLI • COLORS BY: DIGIKORE STUDIOS • LETTERS BY: PISARA OY

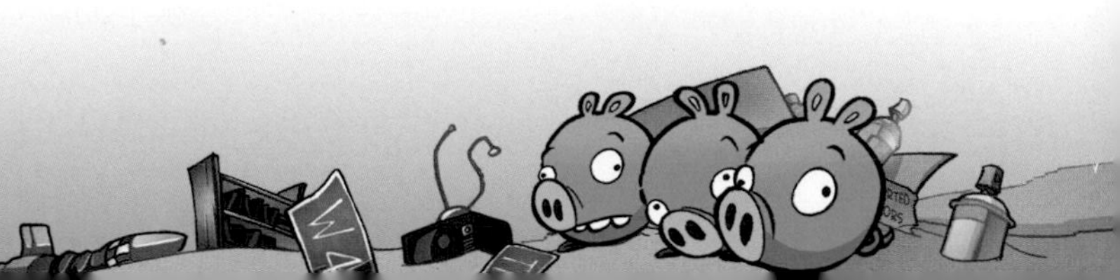

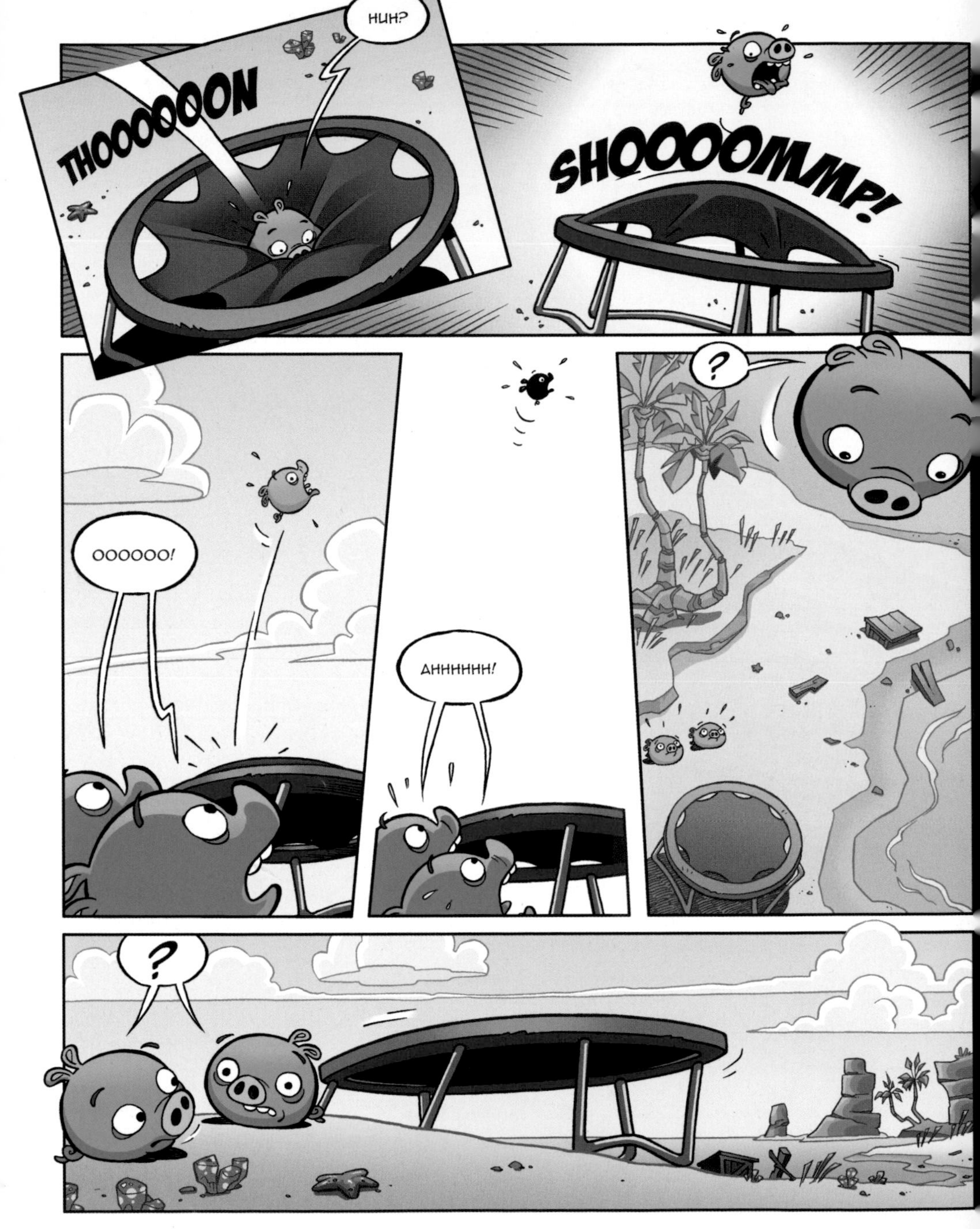
HUH?
THOOOOOON
SHOOOOMMP!
OOOOOO!
AHHHHHH!
?
?

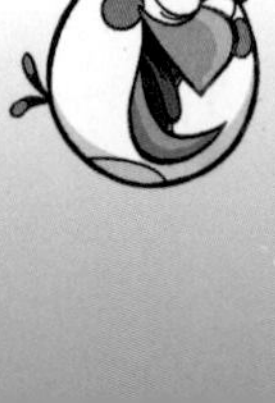

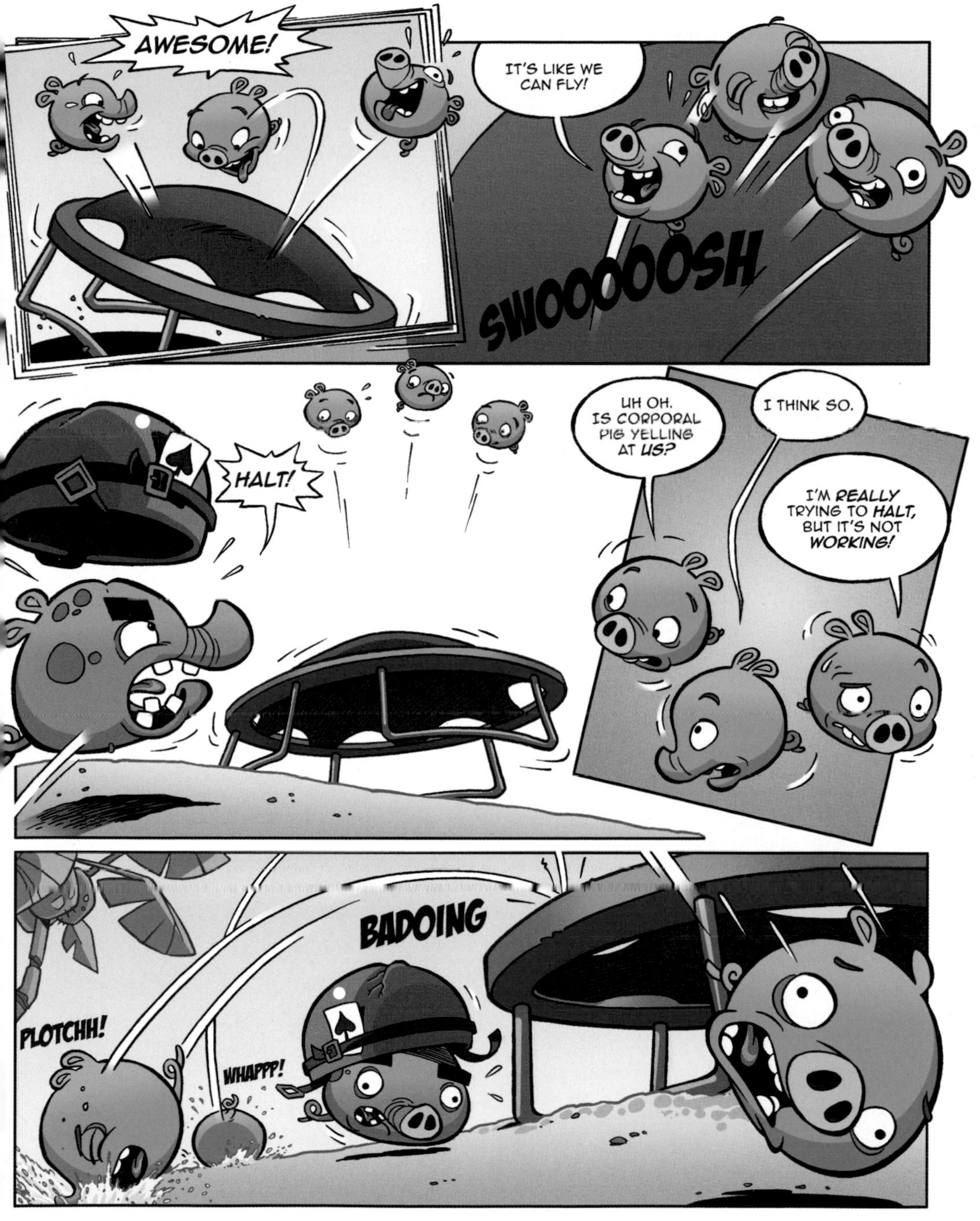

AWESOME!
IT'S LIKE WE CAN FLY!
SWOOOOOOSH
HALT!
UH OH. IS CORPORAL PIG YELLING AT US?
I THINK SO.
I'M REALLY TRYING TO HALT, BUT IT'S NOT WORKING!
BADOING
PLOTCHH!
WHAPPP!

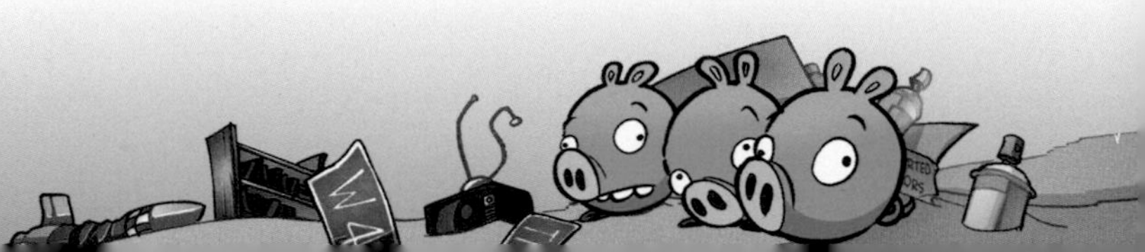

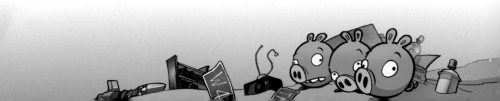

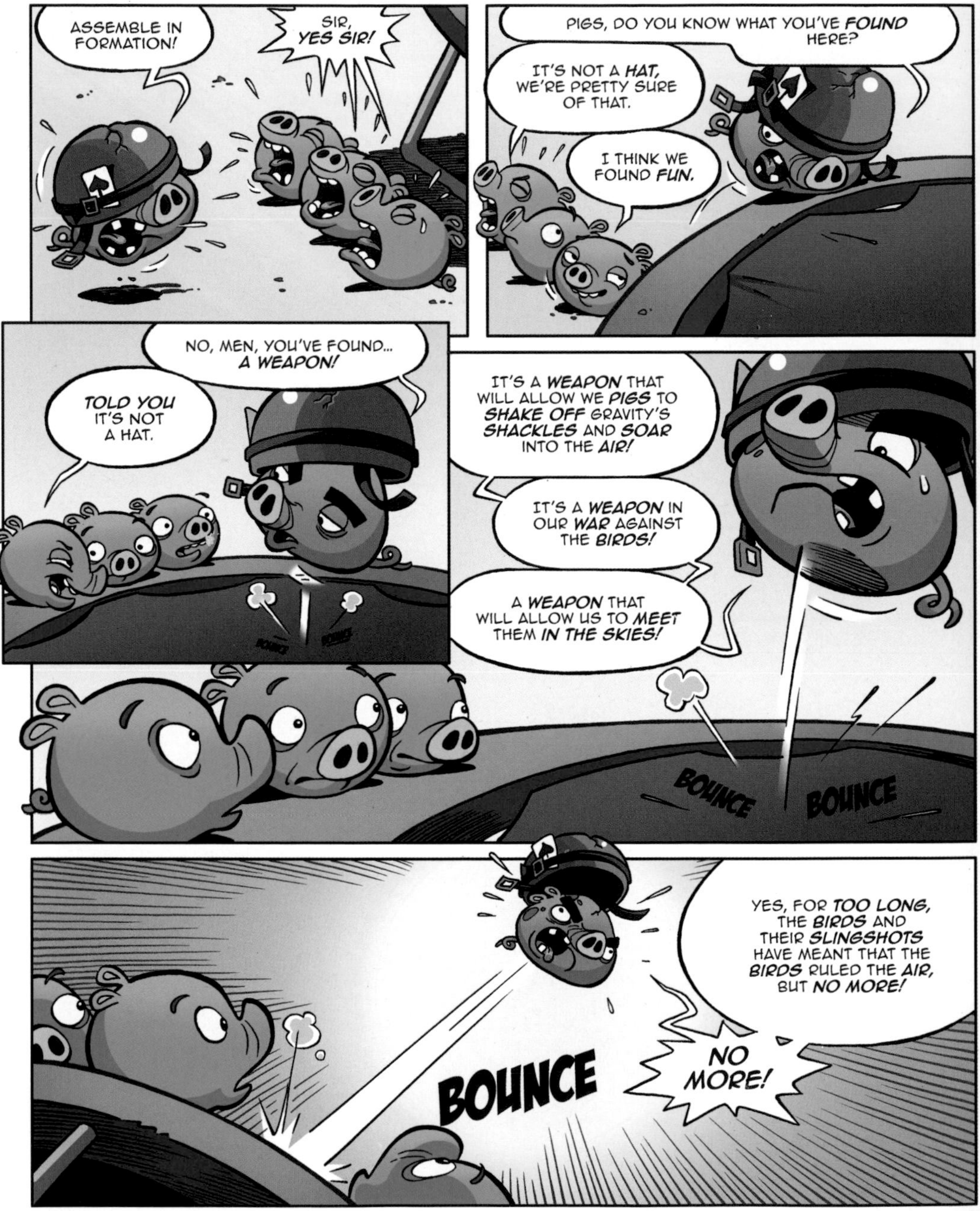
ASSEMBLE IN FORMATION!
SIR, YES SIR!
PIGS, DO YOU KNOW WHAT YOU'VE FOUND HERE?
IT'S NOT A HAT, WE'RE PRETTY SURE OF THAT.
I THINK WE FOUND FUN.
NO, MEN, YOU'VE FOUND... A WEAPON!
TOLD YOU IT'S NOT A HAT.
BOUNCE
BOUNCE
IT'S A WEAPON THAT WILL ALLOW WE PIGS TO SHAKE OFF GRAVITY'S SHACKLES AND SOAR INTO THE AIR!
IT'S A WEAPON IN OUR WAR AGAINST THE BIRDS!
A WEAPON THAT WILL ALLOW US TO MEET THEM IN THE SKIES!
BOUNCE
BOUNCE
YES, FOR TOO LONG, THE BIRDS AND THEIR SLINGSHOTS HAVE MEANT THAT THE BIRDS RULED THE AIR, BUT NO MORE!
NO MORE!
BOUNCE

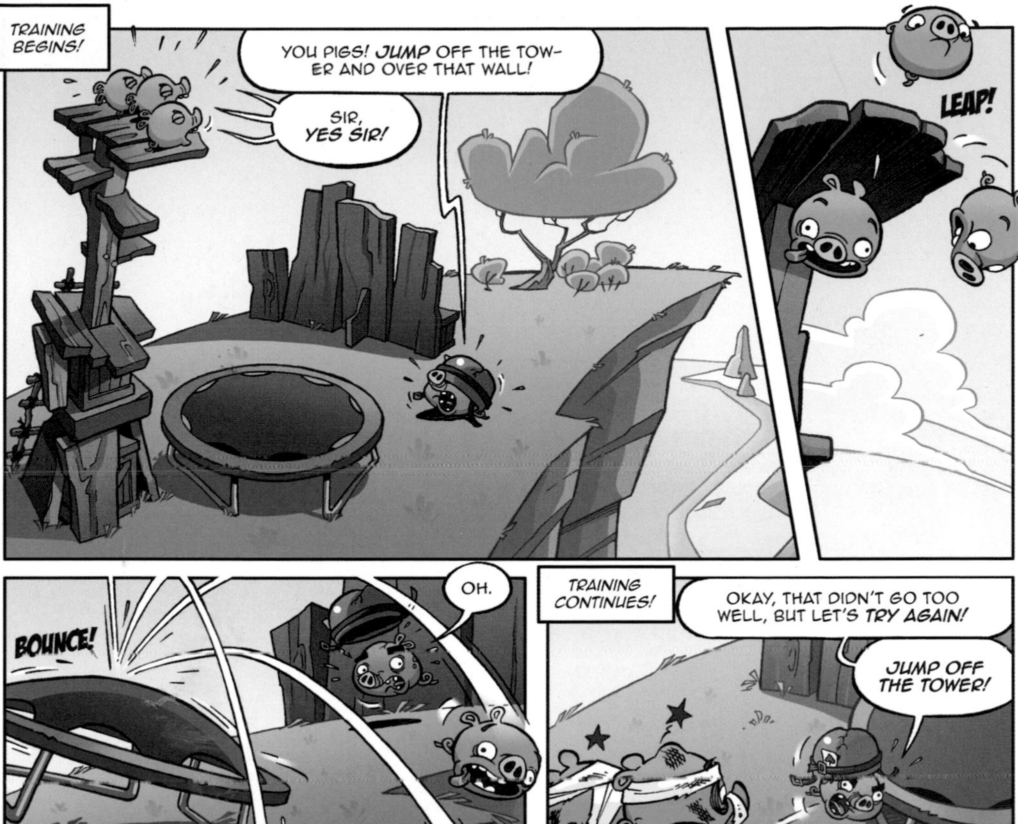
TRAINING BEGINS!
YOU PIGS! JUMP OFF THE TOWER AND OVER THAT WALL!
SIR, YES SIR!
LEAP!
BOUNCE!
OH.
TRAINING CONTINUES!
OKAY, THAT DIDN'T GO TOO WELL, BUT LET'S TRY AGAIN!
JUMP OFF THE TOWER!
SIR, YES SIR!
!
THUD!
THUD!

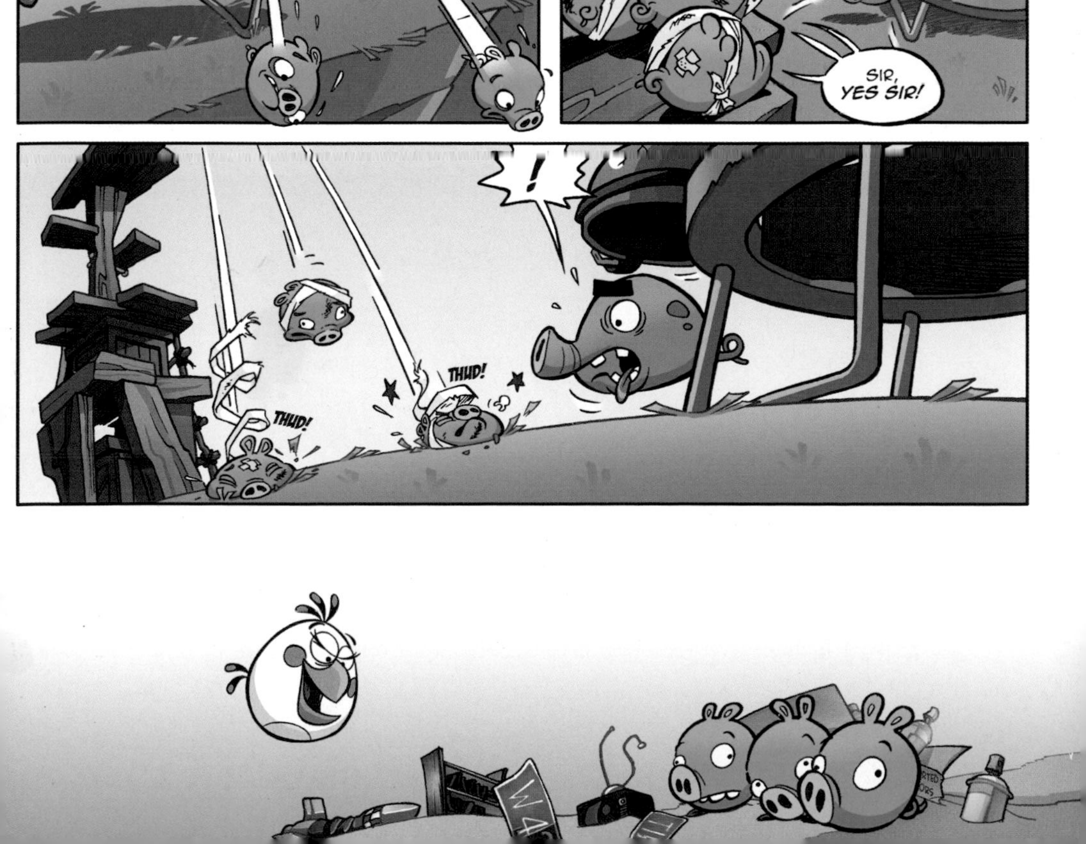

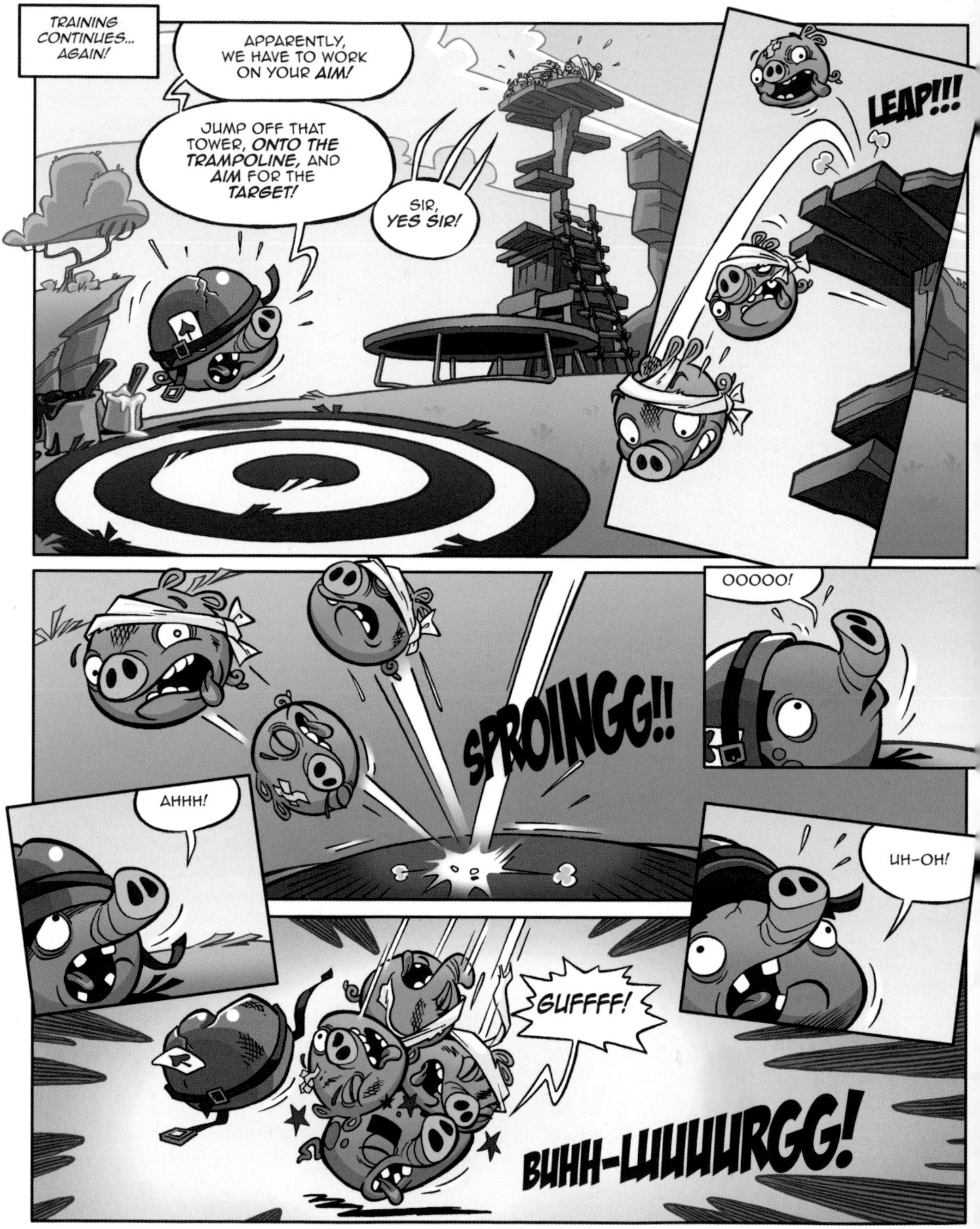
TRAINING CONTINUES... AGAIN!
APPARENTLY, WE HAVE TO WORK ON YOUR AIM!
JUMP OFF THAT TOWER, ONTO THE TRAMPOLINE, AND AIM FOR THE TARGET!
SIR, YES SIR!
LEAP!!!
SPROINGG!!
OOOOO!
AHHH!
UH-OH!
GUFFFF!
BUHH-WUUURGG!

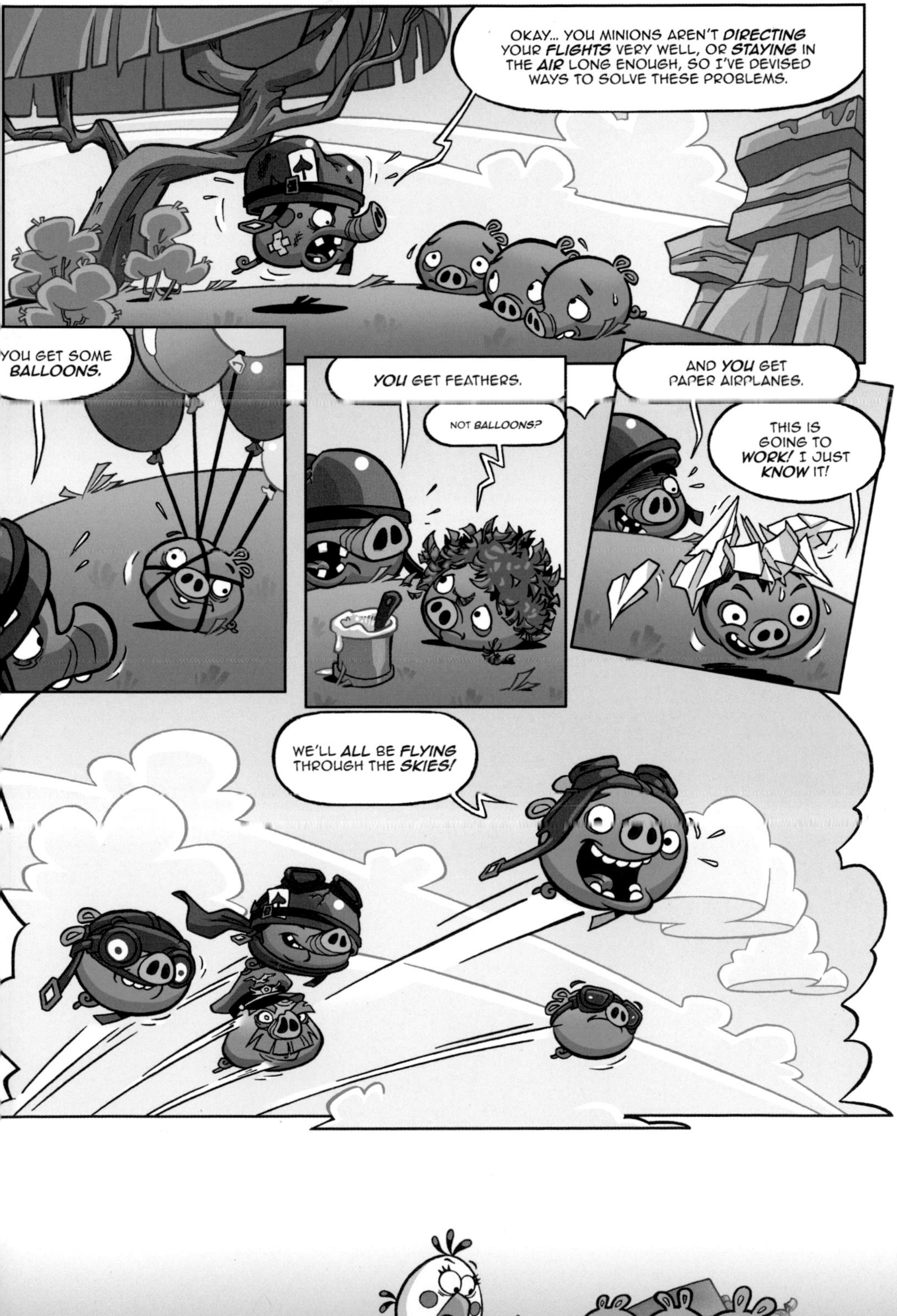
OKAY... YOU MINIONS AREN'T DIRECTING YOUR FLIGHTS VERY WELL, OR STAYING IN THE AIR LONG ENOUGH, SO I'VE DEVISED WAYS TO SOLVE THESE PROBLEMS.
YOU GET SOME BALLOONS.
YOU GET FEATHERS.
NOT BALLOONS?
AND YOU GET PAPER AIRPLANES.
THIS IS GOING TO WORK! I JUST KNOW IT!
WE'LL ALL BE FLYING THROUGH THE SKIES!

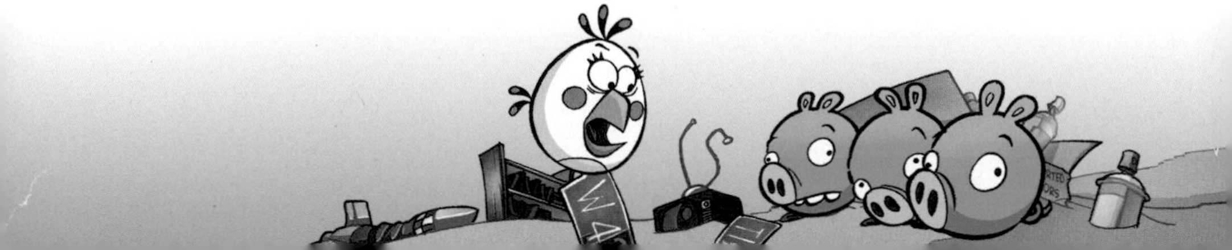

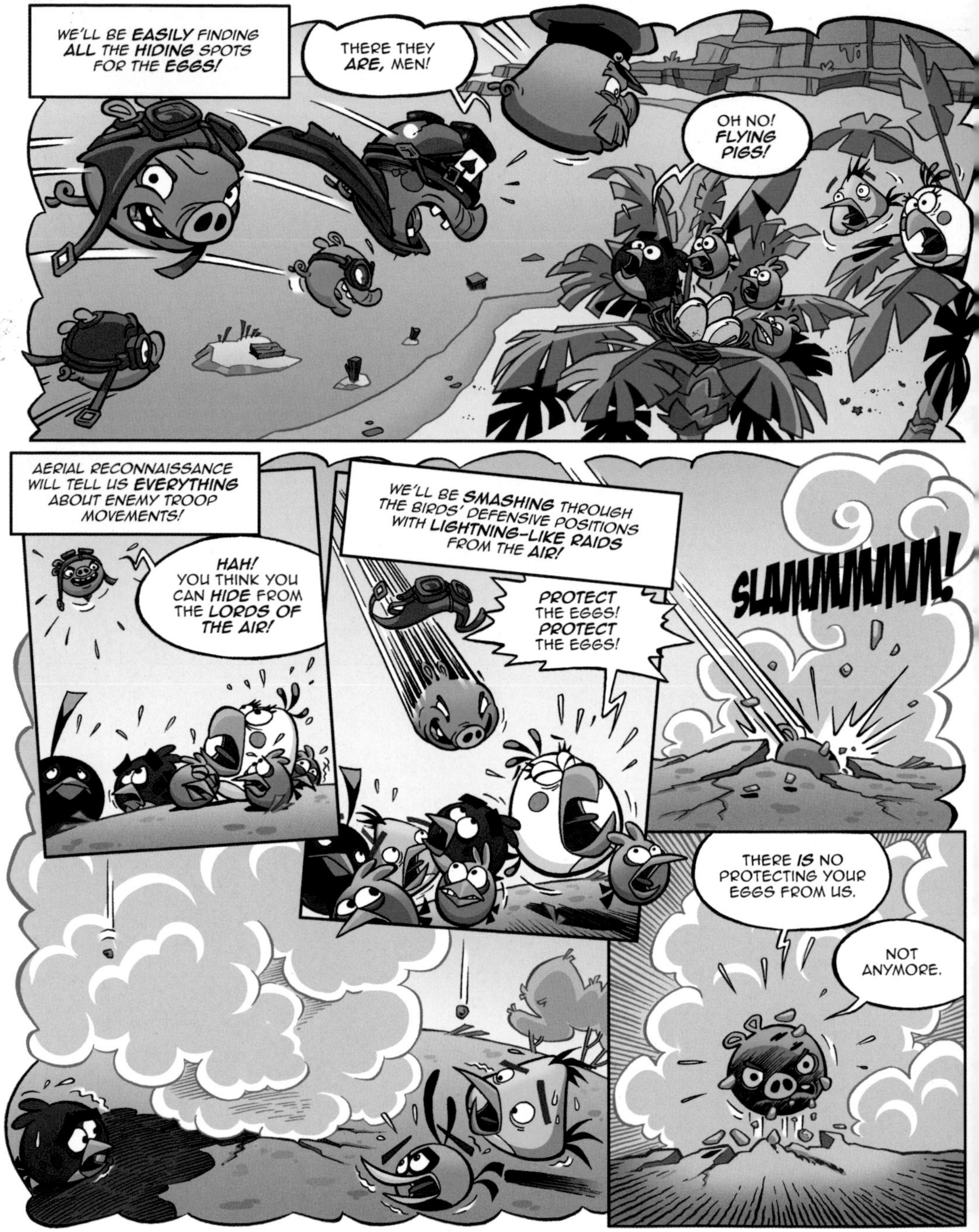
WE'LL BE EASILY FINDING ALL THE HIDING SPOTS FOR THE EGGS!
THERE THEY ARE, MEN!
OH NO! FLYING PIGS!
AERIAL RECONNAISSANCE WILL TELL US EVERYTHING ABOUT ENEMY TROOP MOVEMENTS!
HAH! YOU THINK YOU CAN HIDE FROM THE LORDS OF THE AIR!
WE'LL BE SMASHING THROUGH THE BIRDS' DEFENSIVE POSITIONS WITH LIGHTNING-LIKE RAIDS FROM THE AIR!
PROTECT THE EGGS! PROTECT THE EGGS!
SLAMMMMMM!
THERE IS NO PROTECTING YOUR EGGS FROM US.
NOT ANYMORE.

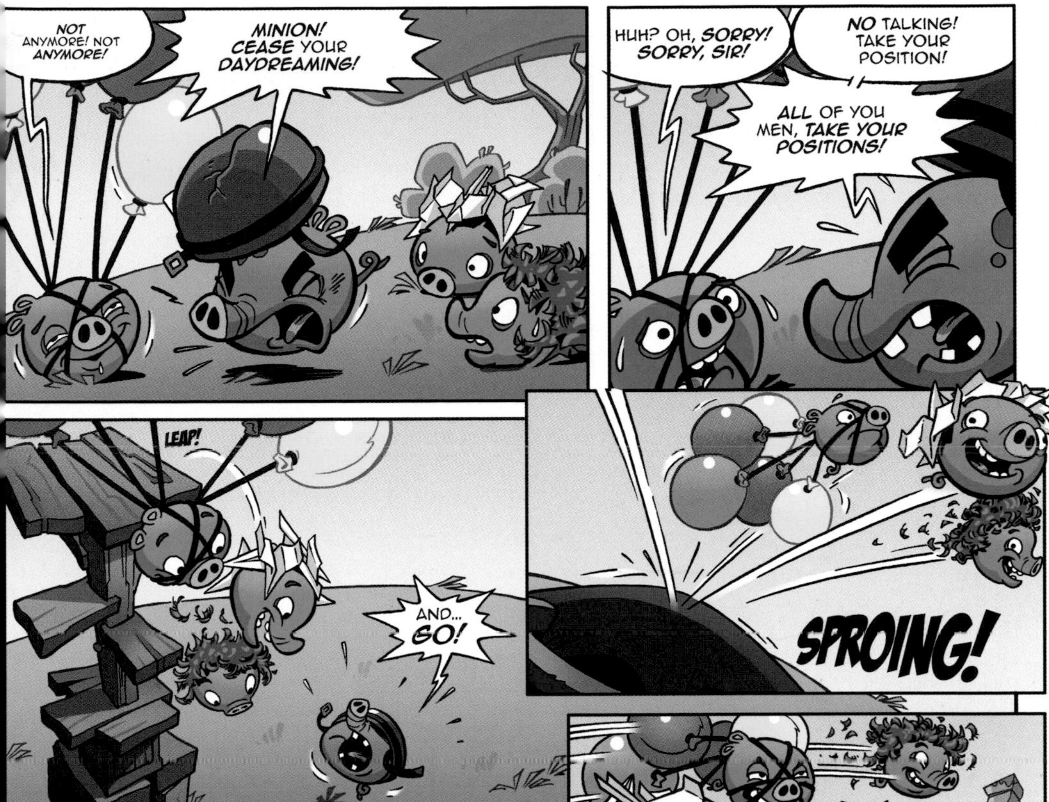
NOT ANYMORE! NOT ANYMORE!
MINION! CEASE YOUR DAYDREAMING!
HUH? OH, SORRY! SORRY, SIR!
NO TALKING! TAKE YOUR POSITION!
ALL OF YOU MEN, TAKE YOUR POSITIONS!
LEAP!
AND... GO!
SPROING!
GRRR!
UH-OH.

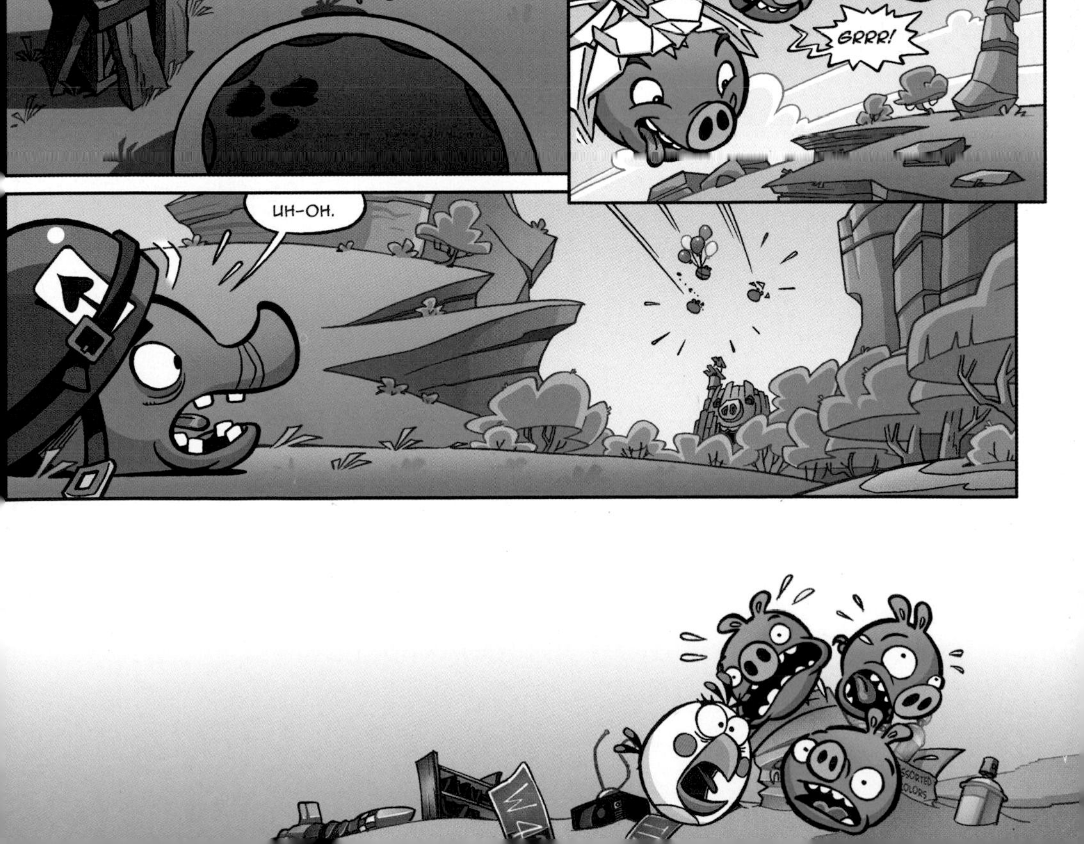

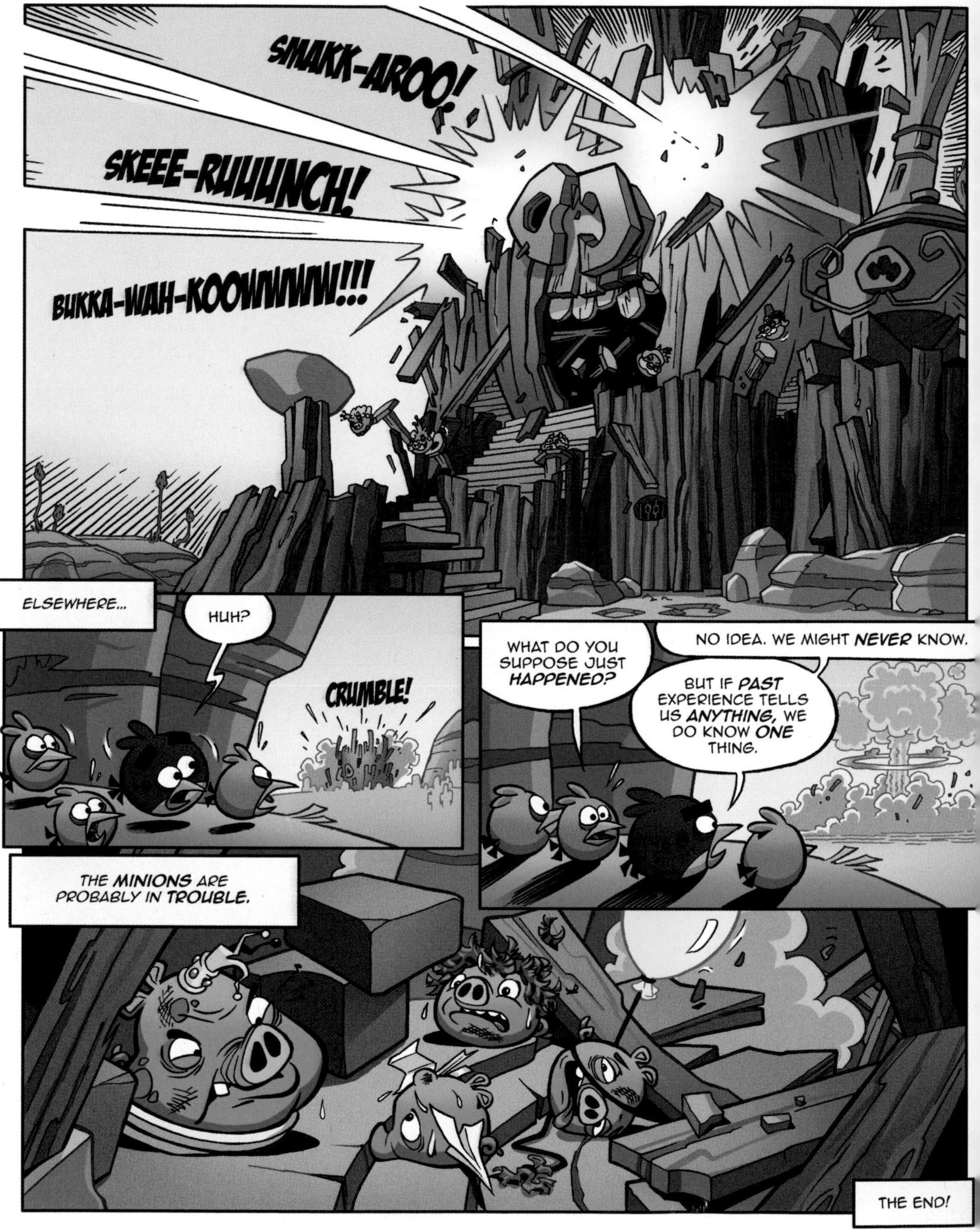
SMAKK-AROO!
SKEEE-RUUUNCH!
BUKKA-WAH-KOOWWWW!!!
ELSEWHERE...
HUH?
CRUMBLE!
WHAT DO YOU SUPPOSE JUST HAPPENED?
NO IDEA. WE MIGHT NEVER KNOW.
BUT IF PAST EXPERIENCE TELLS US ANYTHING, WE DO KNOW ONE THING.
THE MINIONS ARE PROBABLY IN TROUBLE.
THE END!

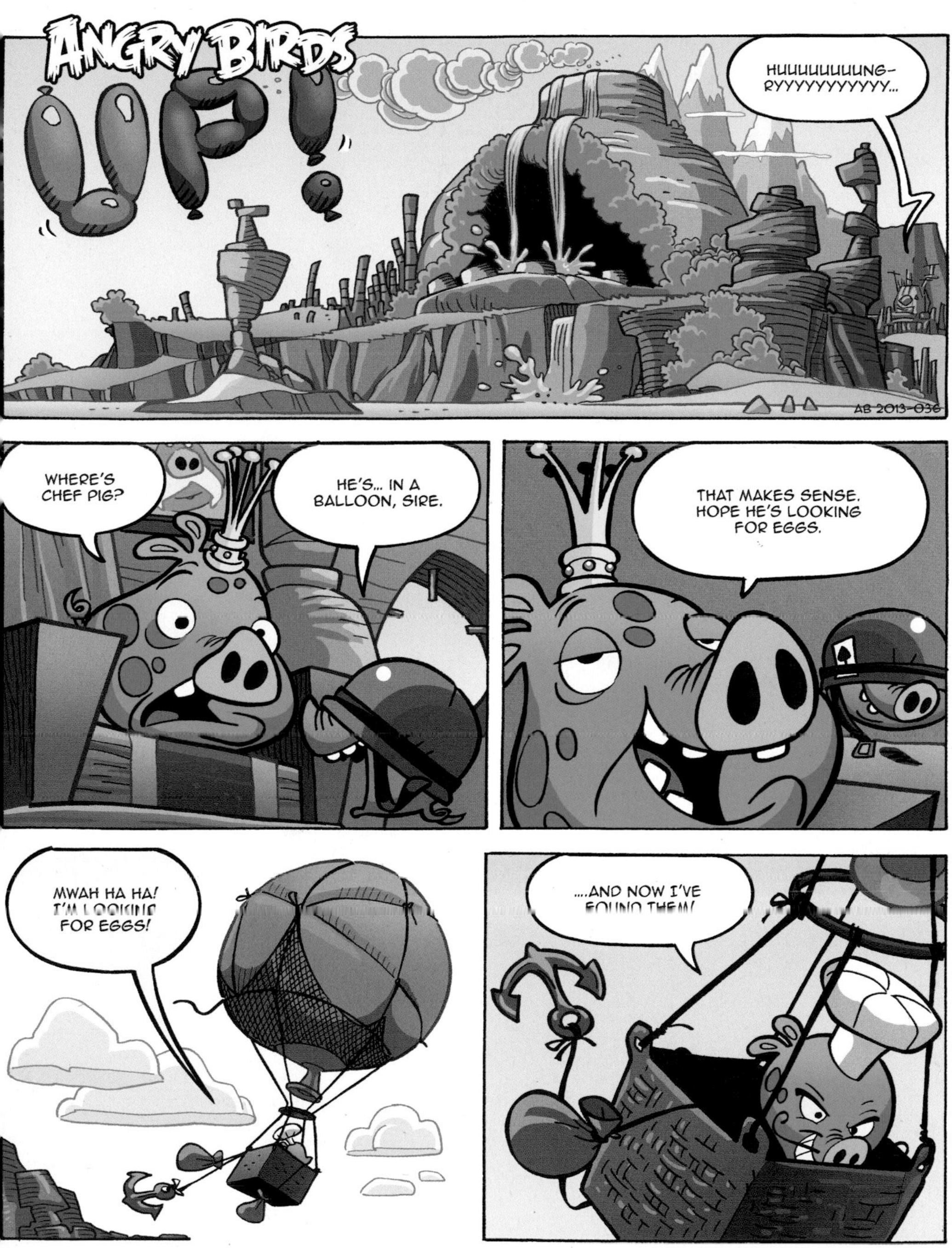
ANGRY BIRDS
UP!
HUUUUUUUUUNG-RYYYYYYYYYYY...
AB 2013-036
WHERE'S CHEF PIG?
HE'S... IN A BALLOON, SIRE.
THAT MAKES SENSE. HOPE HE'S LOOKING FOR EGGS.
MWAH HA HA! I'M LOOKING FOR EGGS!
....AND NOW I'VE FOUND THEM!

WRITTEN BY: FRANÇOIS CORTEGGIANI • ART BY: GIORGIO CAVAZZANO • COLORS BY: DIGIKORE STUDIOS • LETTERS BY: PISARA OY

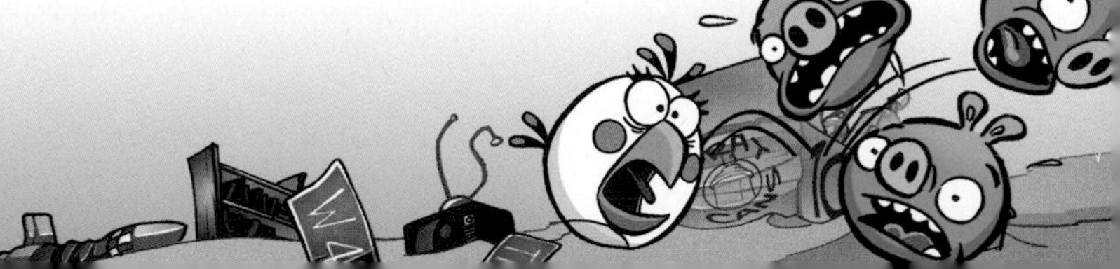

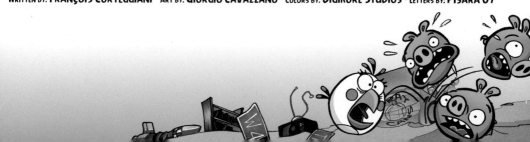

WHAT A PEACEFUL AND BEAUTIFUL DAY.

SO RARE, PEACEFUL *AND* BEAUTIFUL AT THE SAME TIME.

NOT A CLOUD IN THE SKY!

?

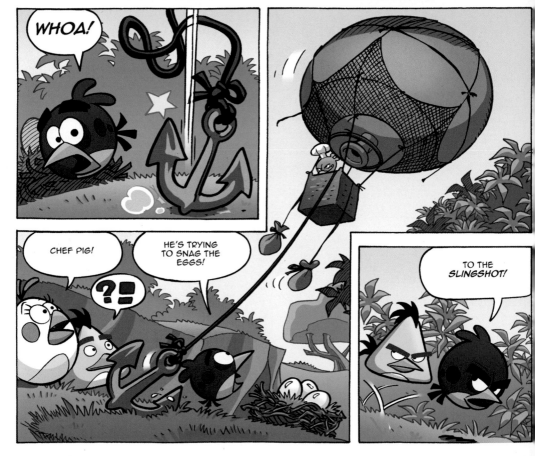

WHOA!

CHEF PIG!

HE'S TRYING TO SNAG THE EGGS!

?!

TO THE *SLINGSHOT!*

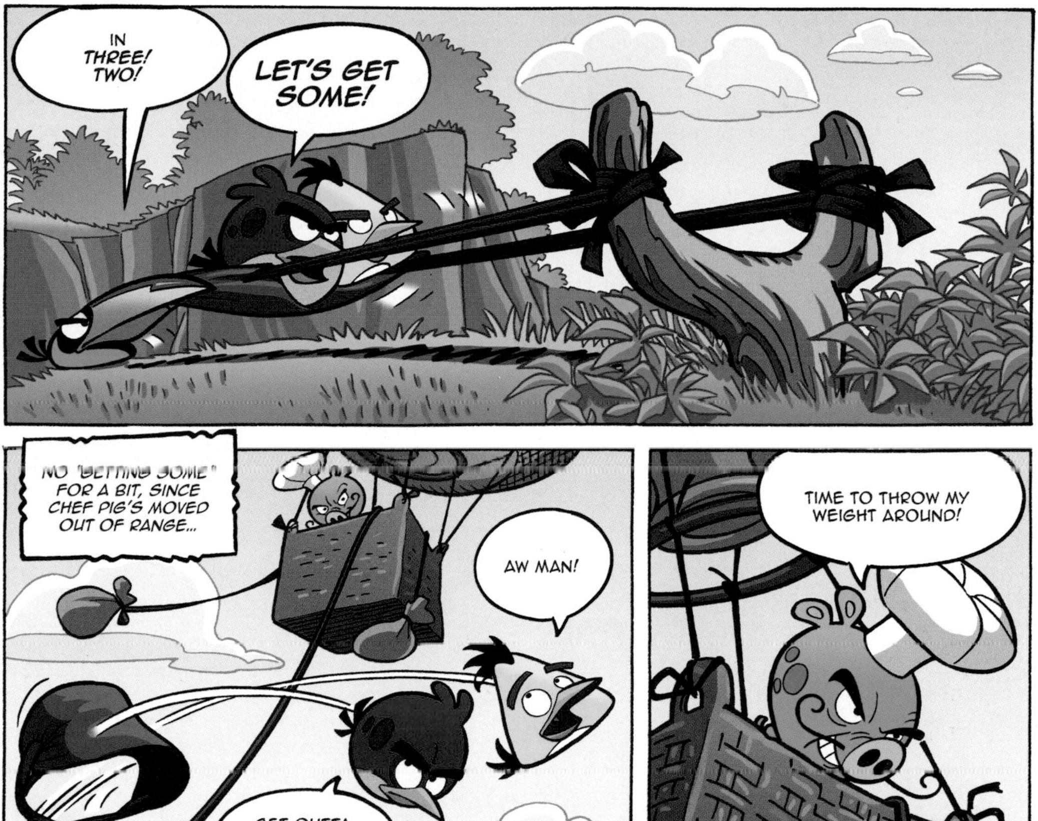
IN THREE! TWO!
LET'S GET SOME!
NO "GETTING SOME" FOR A BIT, SINCE CHEF PIG'S MOVED OUT OF RANGE...
AW MAN!
GET OUTTA HERE, PIGGY!
TIME TO THROW MY WEIGHT AROUND!
HRM?
BWAH HA HA HA!!!
MISSED AGAIN!

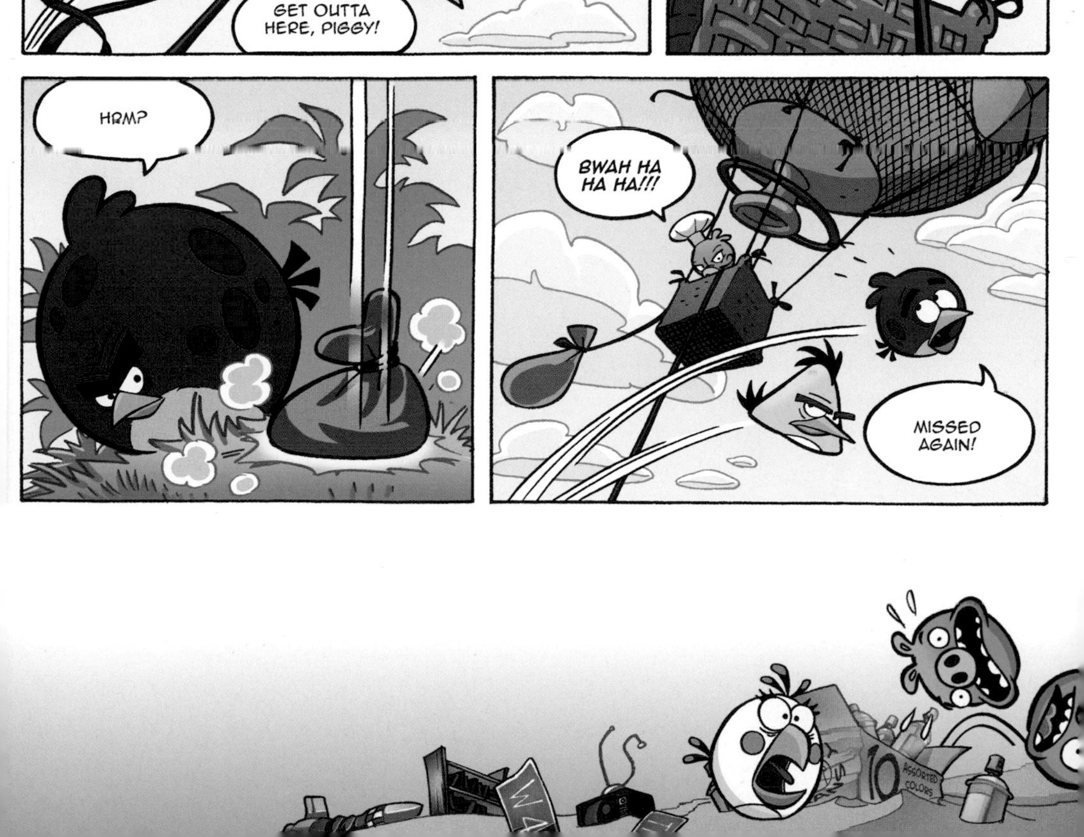
10
ASSORTED COLORS

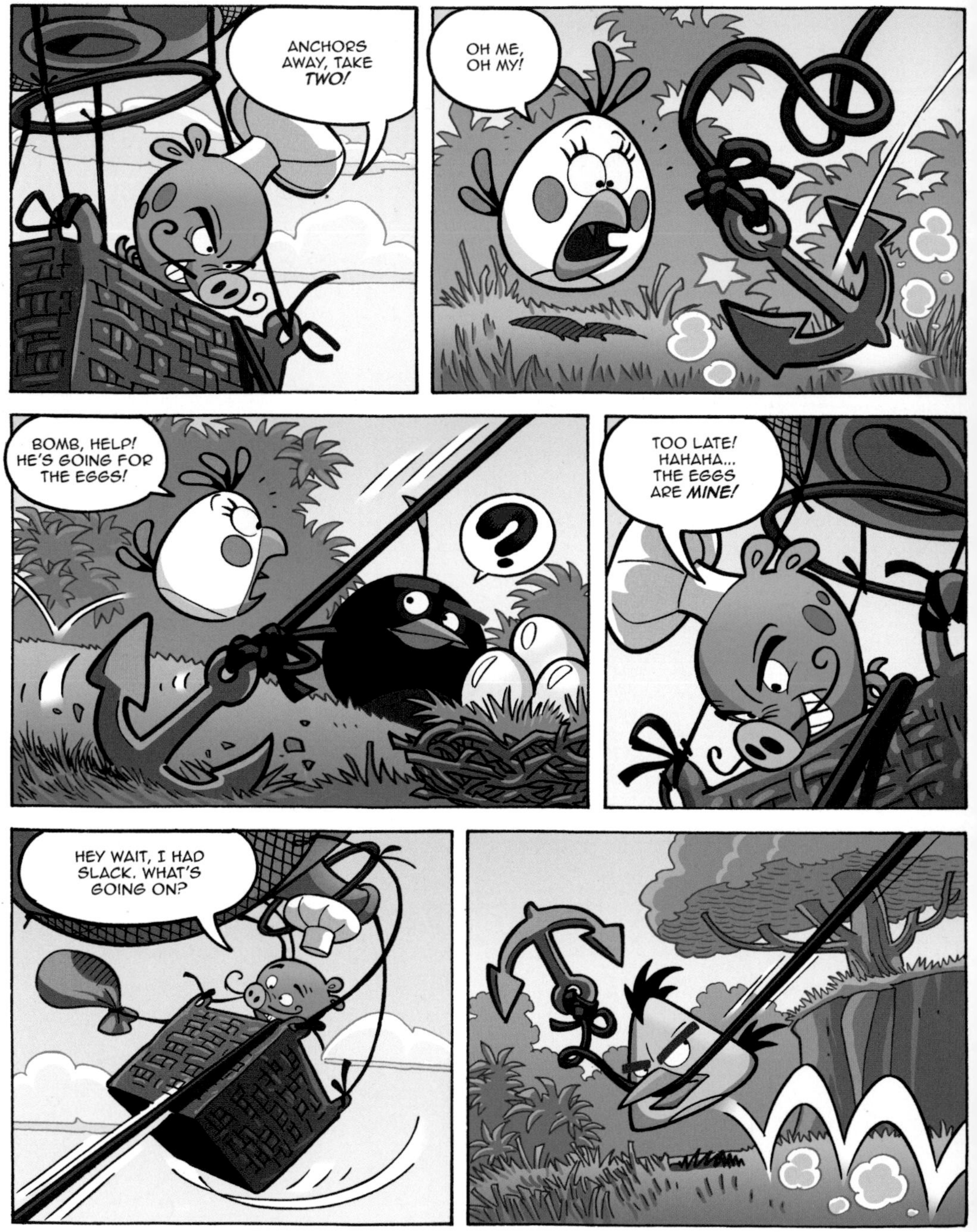
ANCHORS AWAY, TAKE *TWO!*
OH ME, OH MY!
BOMB, HELP! HE'S GOING FOR THE EGGS!
?
TOO LATE! HAHAHA... THE EGGS ARE *MINE!*
HEY WAIT, I HAD SLACK. WHAT'S GOING ON?

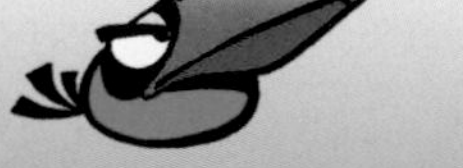

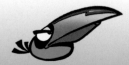

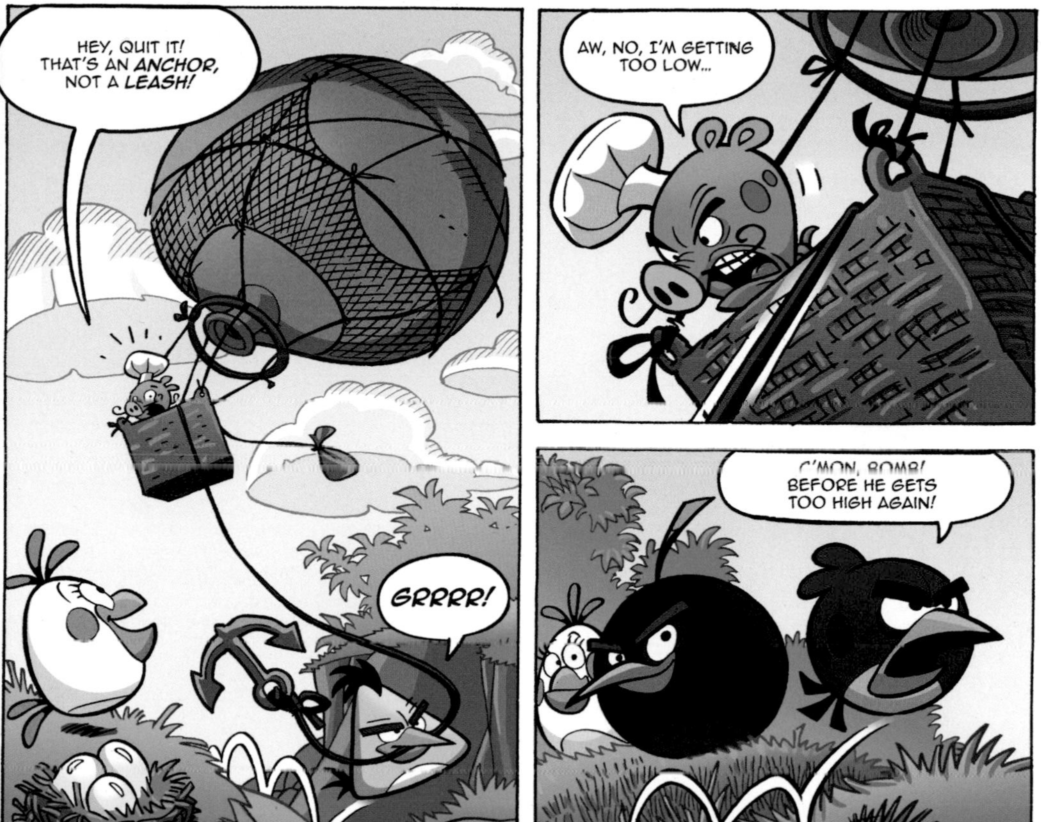
HEY, QUIT IT! THAT'S AN ANCHOR, NOT A LEASH!
GRRRR!
AW, NO, I'M GETTING TOO LOW...
C'MON, BOMB! BEFORE HE GETS TOO HIGH AGAIN!
YEE-HAW!
GET SOME RELOADED!

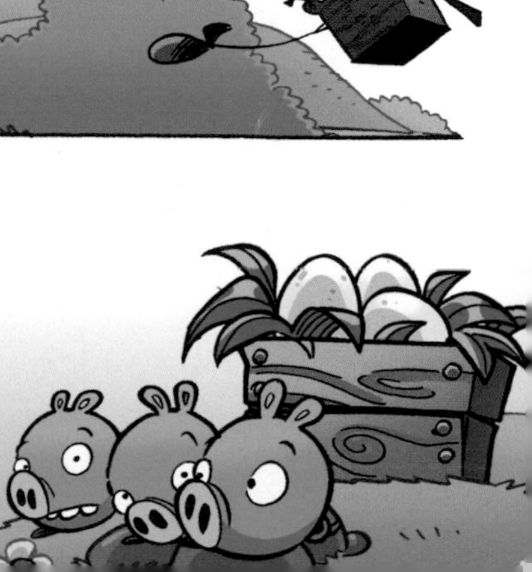

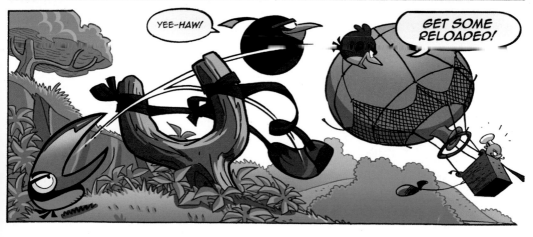

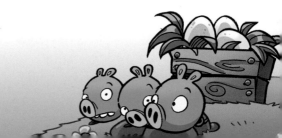

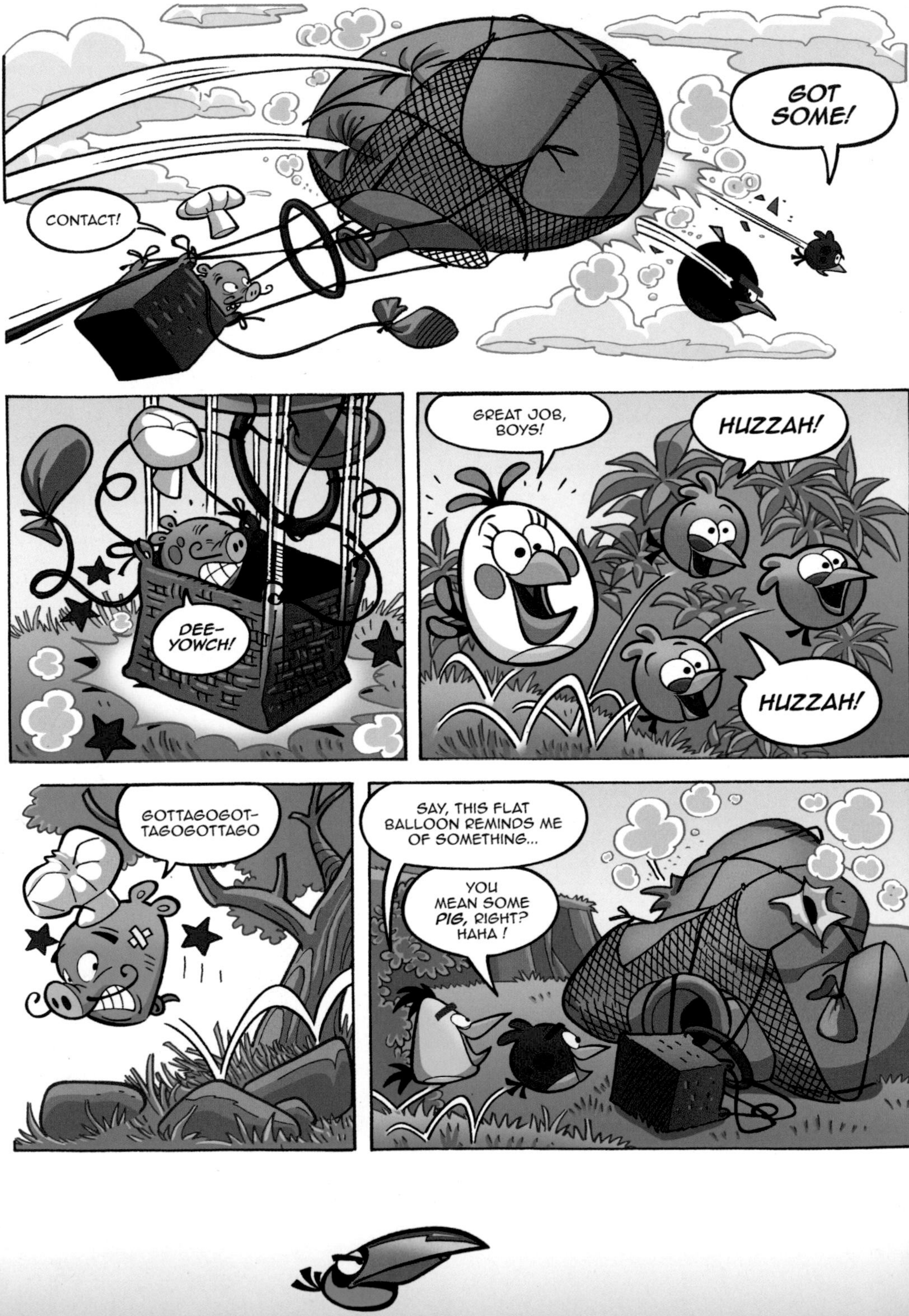
GOT SOME!
CONTACT!
DEE-YOWCH!
GREAT JOB, BOYS!
HUZZAH!
HUZZAH!
GOTTAGOGOT-TAGOGOTTAGO
SAY, THIS FLAT BALLOON REMINDS ME OF SOMETHING...
YOU MEAN SOME PIG, RIGHT? HAHA !

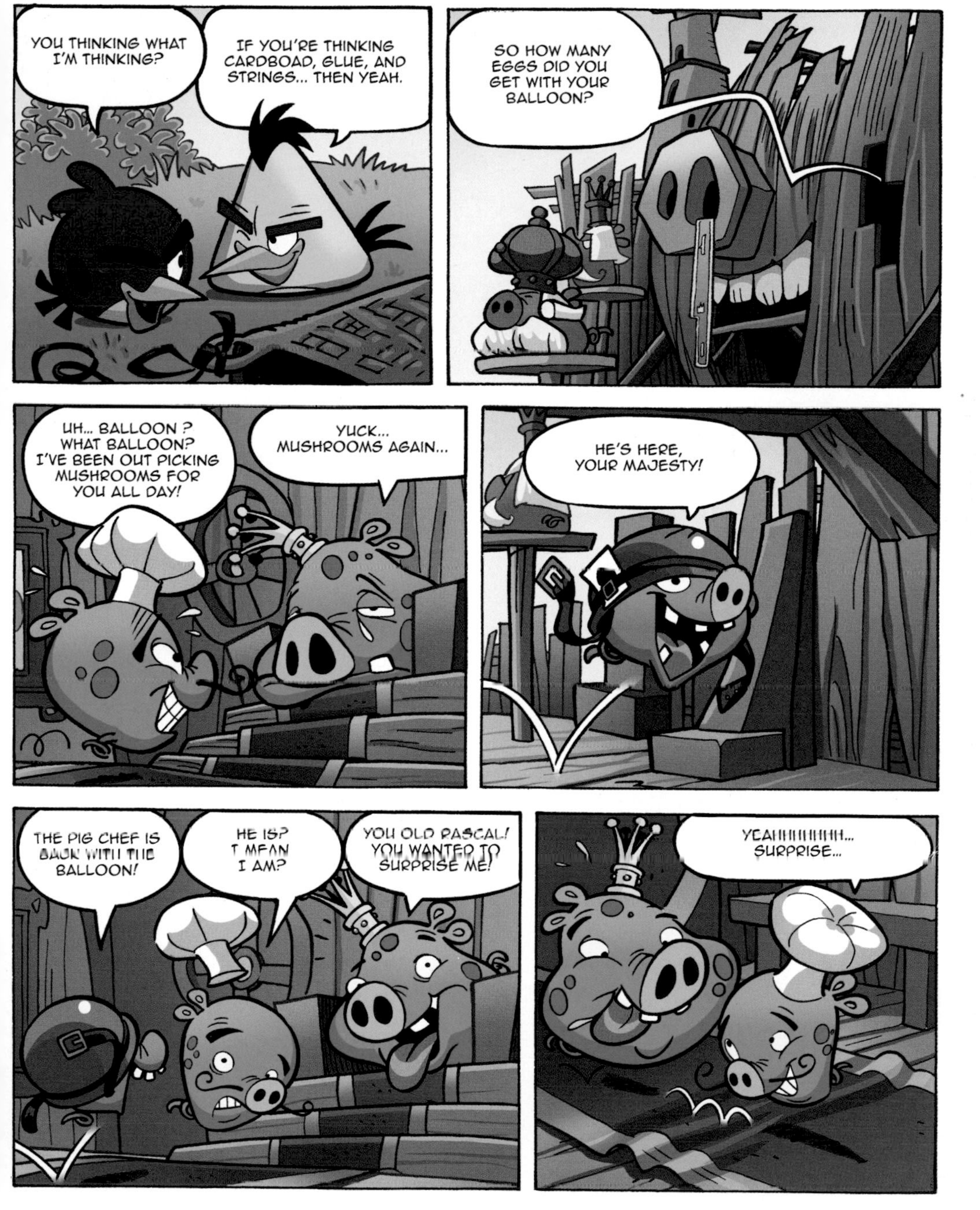
YOU THINKING WHAT I'M THINKING?
IF YOU'RE THINKING CARDBOAD, GLUE, AND STRINGS... THEN YEAH.
SO HOW MANY EGGS DID YOU GET WITH YOUR BALLOON?
UH... BALLOON ? WHAT BALLOON? I'VE BEEN OUT PICKING MUSHROOMS FOR YOU ALL DAY!
YUCK... MUSHROOMS AGAIN...
HE'S HERE, YOUR MAJESTY!
THE PIG CHEF IS BACK WITH THE BALLOON!
HE IS? I MEAN I AM?
YOU OLD RASCAL! YOU WANTED TO SURPRISE ME!
YEAHHHHHHH... SURPRISE...

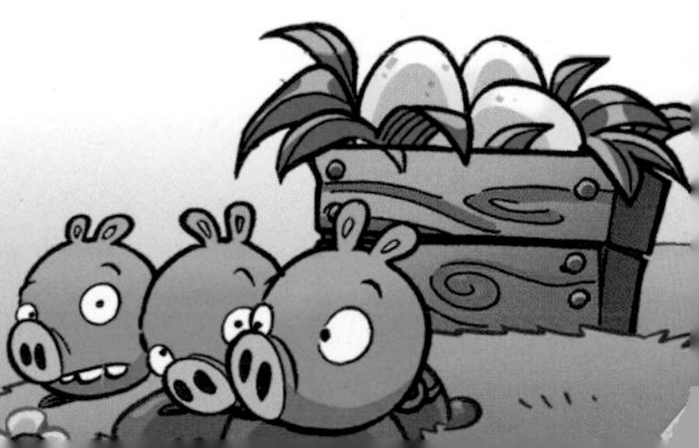

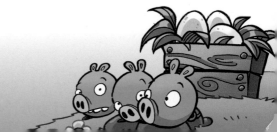

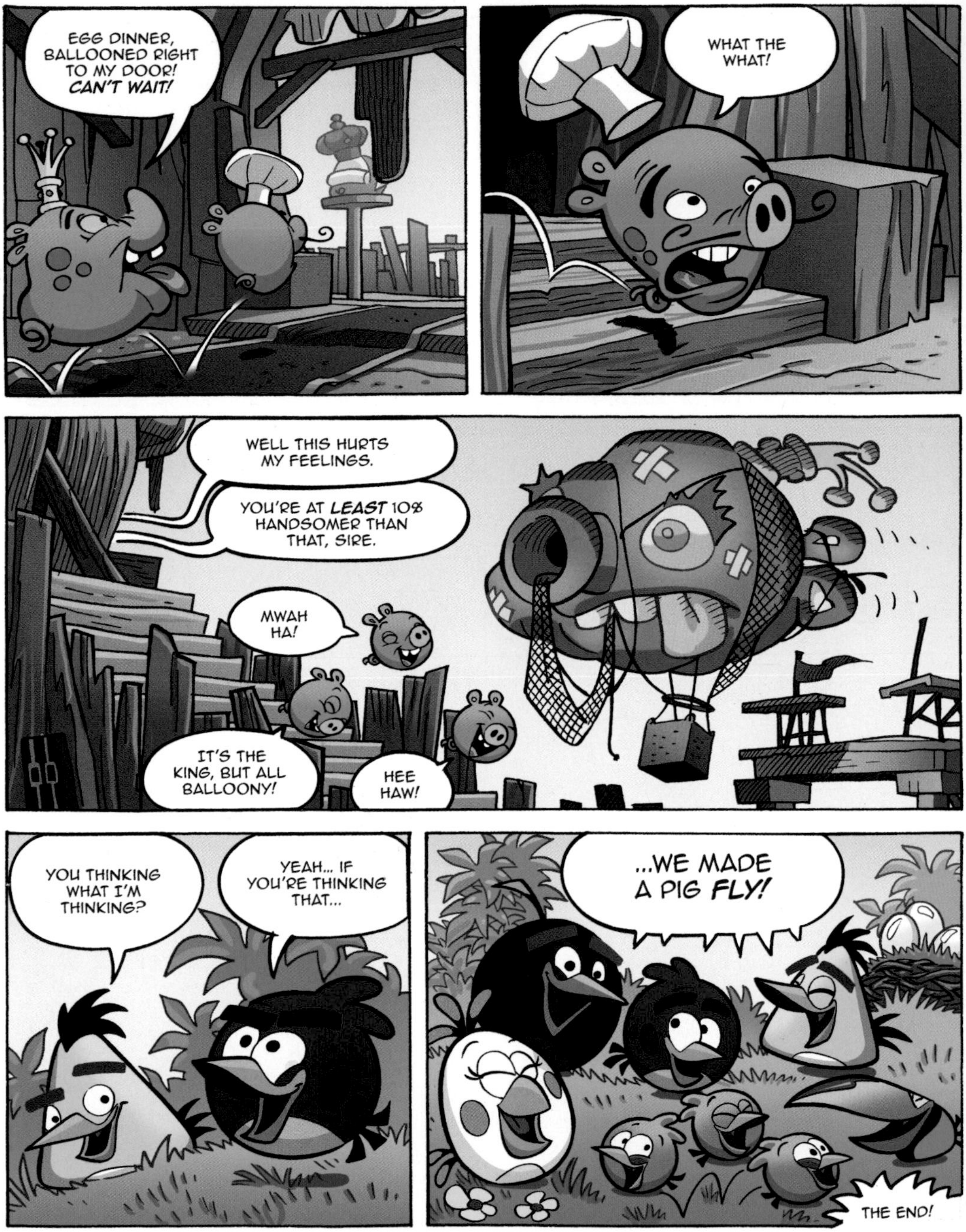
EGG DINNER, BALLOONED RIGHT TO MY DOOR! *CAN'T WAIT!*
WHAT THE WHAT!
WELL THIS HURTS MY FEELINGS.
YOU'RE AT *LEAST* 10% HANDSOMER THAN THAT, SIRE.
MWAH HA!
IT'S THE KING, BUT ALL BALLOONY!
HEE HAW!
YOU THINKING WHAT I'M THINKING?
YEAH... IF YOU'RE THINKING THAT...
...WE MADE A PIG *FLY!*
THE END!

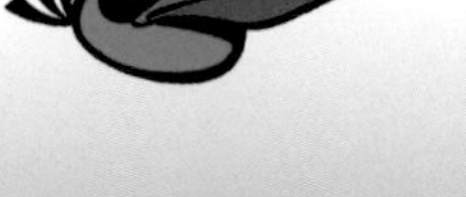

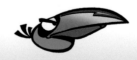

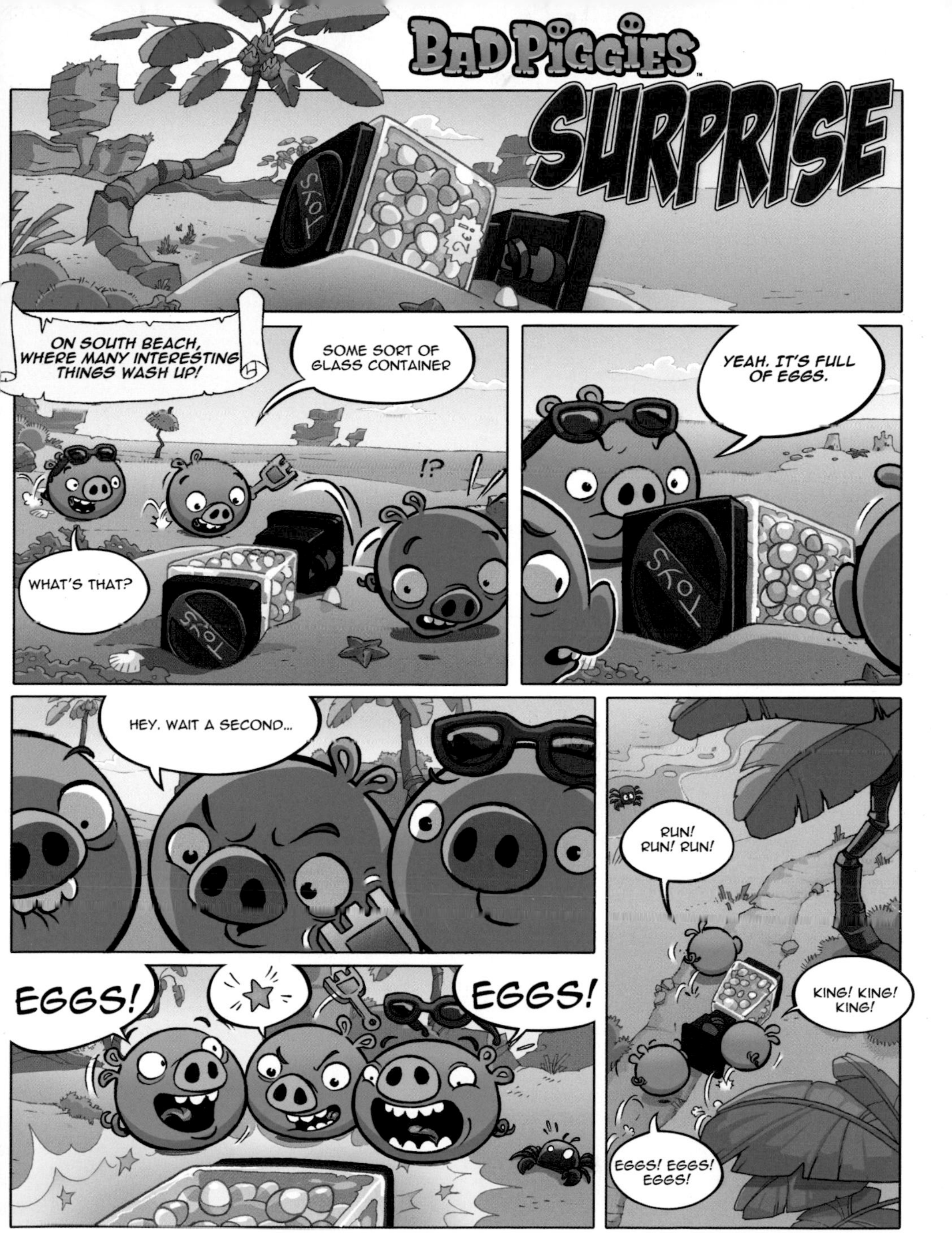
BAD PIGGIES
SURPRISE
TOYS
2¢!
ON SOUTH BEACH, WHERE MANY INTERESTING THINGS WASH UP!
SOME SORT OF GLASS CONTAINER
WHAT'S THAT?
!?
YEAH. IT'S FULL OF EGGS.
HEY. WAIT A SECOND...
EGGS!
EGGS!
RUN! RUN! RUN!
KING! KING! KING!
EGGS! EGGS! EGGS!

WRITTEN BY: PAUL TOBIN • ART BY: AUDREY BUSSI & ISA PYTHON • COLORS BY: DIGIKORE STUDIOS • LETTERS BY: ROVIO COMICS

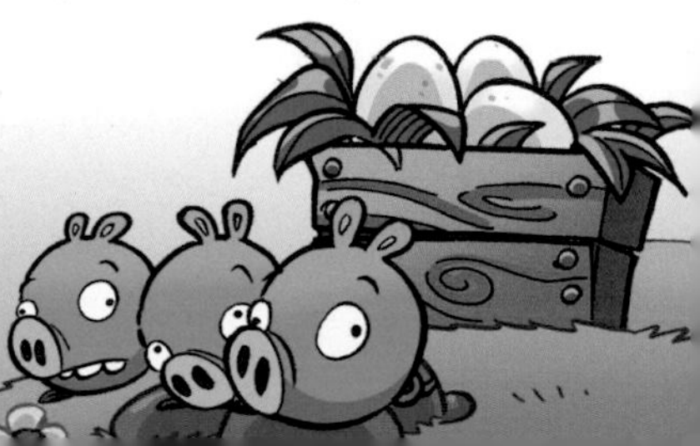

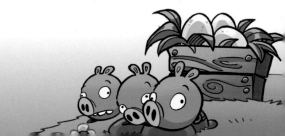

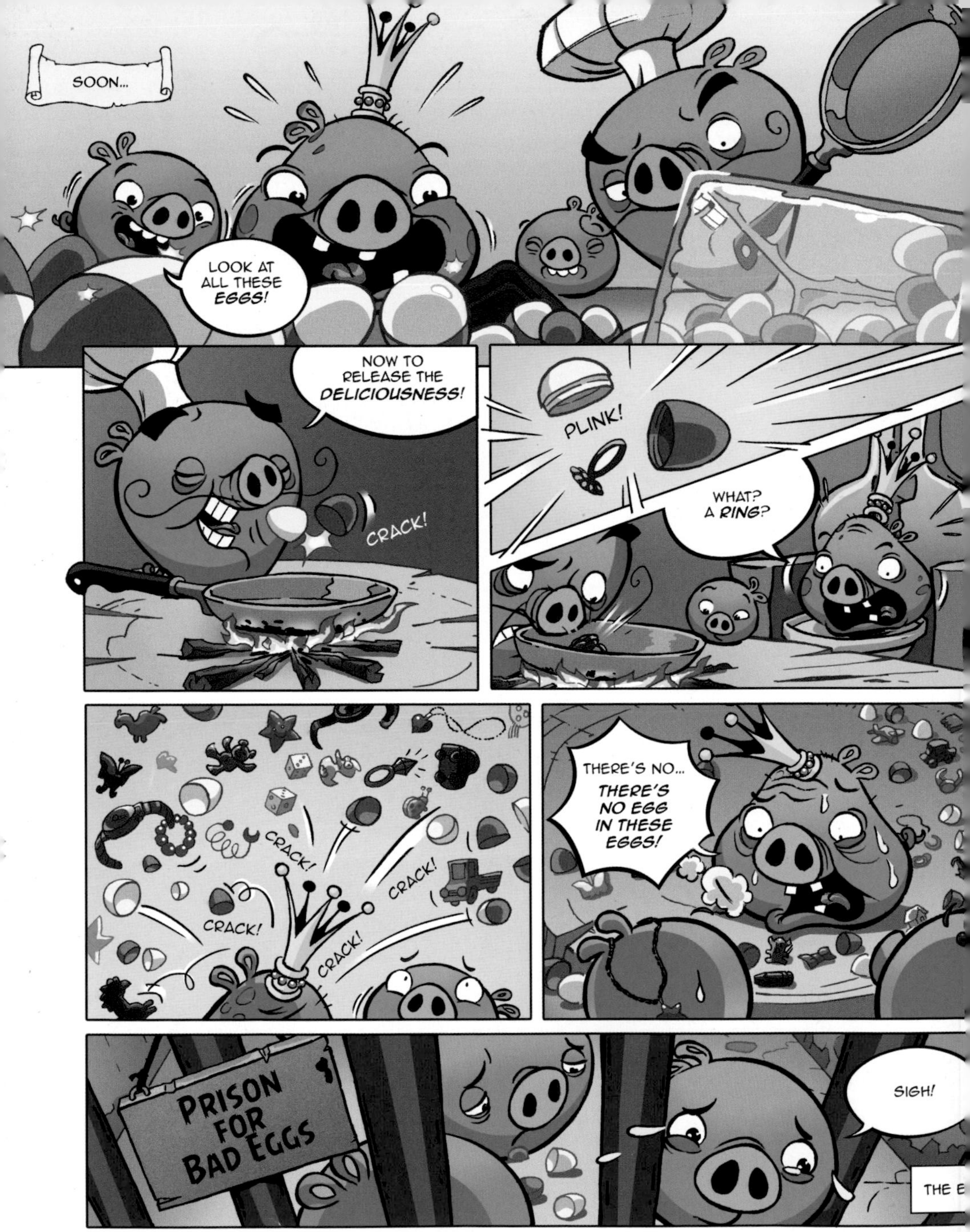
SOON...
LOOK AT ALL THESE EGGS!
NOW TO RELEASE THE DELICIOUSNESS!
CRACK!
PLINK!
WHAT? A RING?
CRACK!
CRACK!
CRACK!
CRACK!
THERE'S NO... THERE'S NO EGG IN THESE EGGS!
PRISON FOR BAD EGGS
SIGH!
THE E

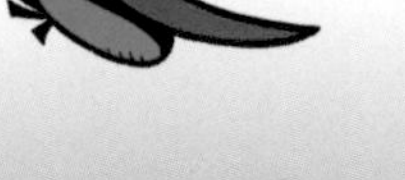

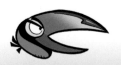

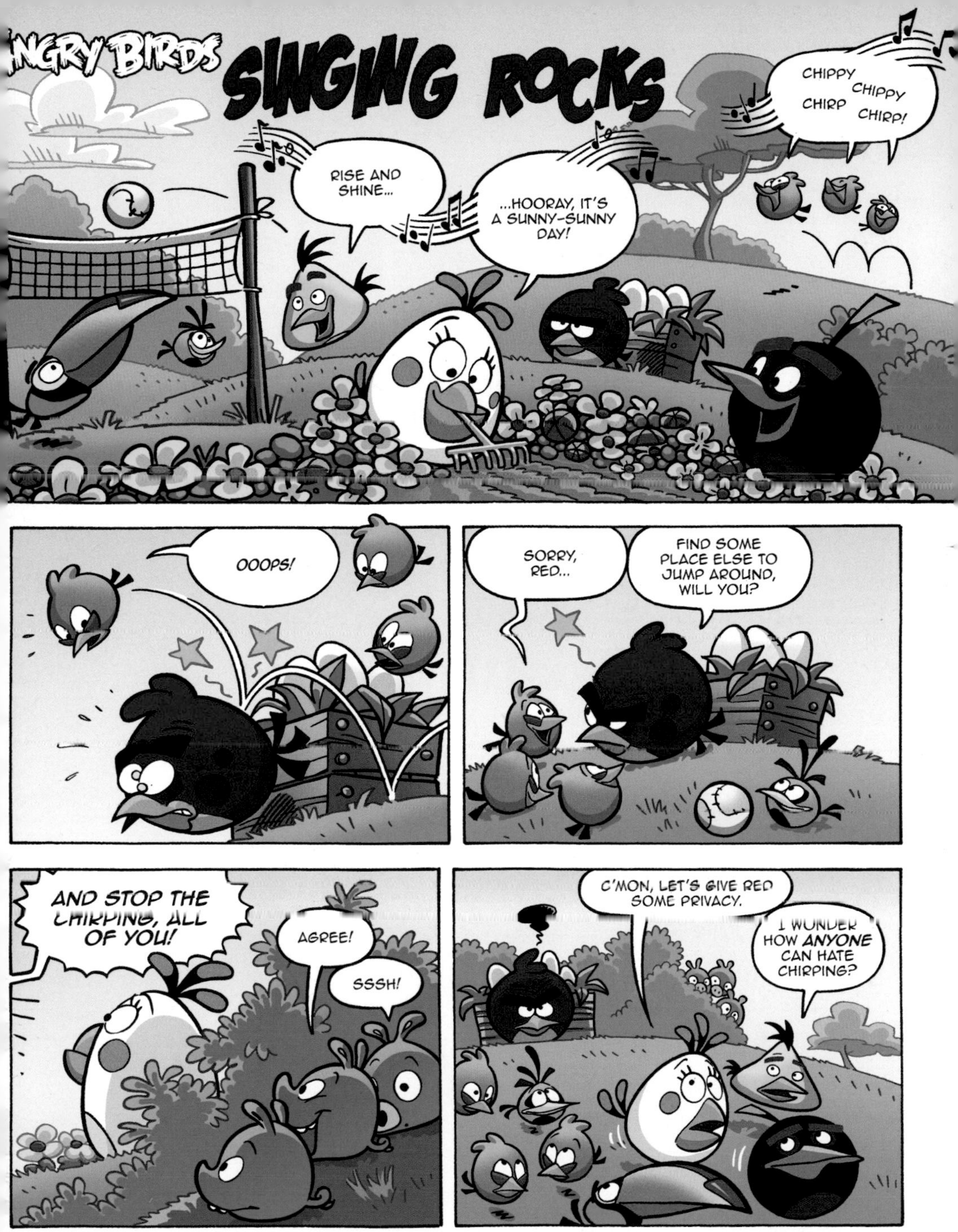
ANGRY BIRDS
SINGING ROCKS
RISE AND SHINE...
...HOORAY, IT'S A SUNNY-SUNNY DAY!
CHIPPY CHIPPY CHIRP CHIRP!
OOOPS!
SORRY, RED...
FIND SOME PLACE ELSE TO JUMP AROUND, WILL YOU?
AND STOP THE CHIRPING, ALL OF YOU!
AGREE!
SSSH!
C'MON, LET'S GIVE RED SOME PRIVACY.
I WONDER HOW *ANYONE* CAN HATE CHIRPING?

WRITTEN BY: JANNE TORISEVA • ART BY: GIORGIO CAVAZZANO • COLORS BY: DIGIKORE STUDIOS • LETTERS BY: ROVIO COMICS

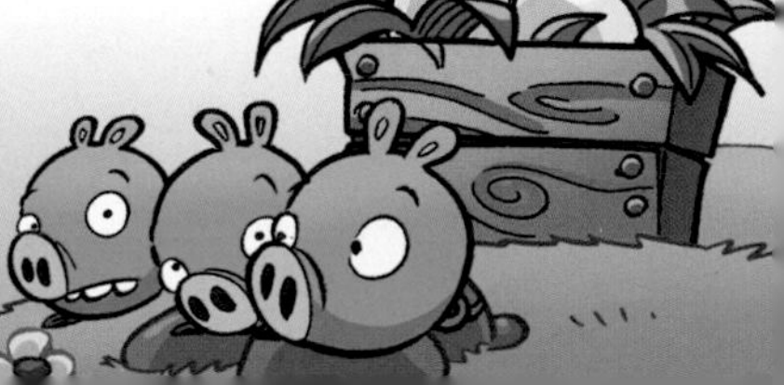

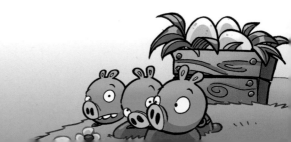

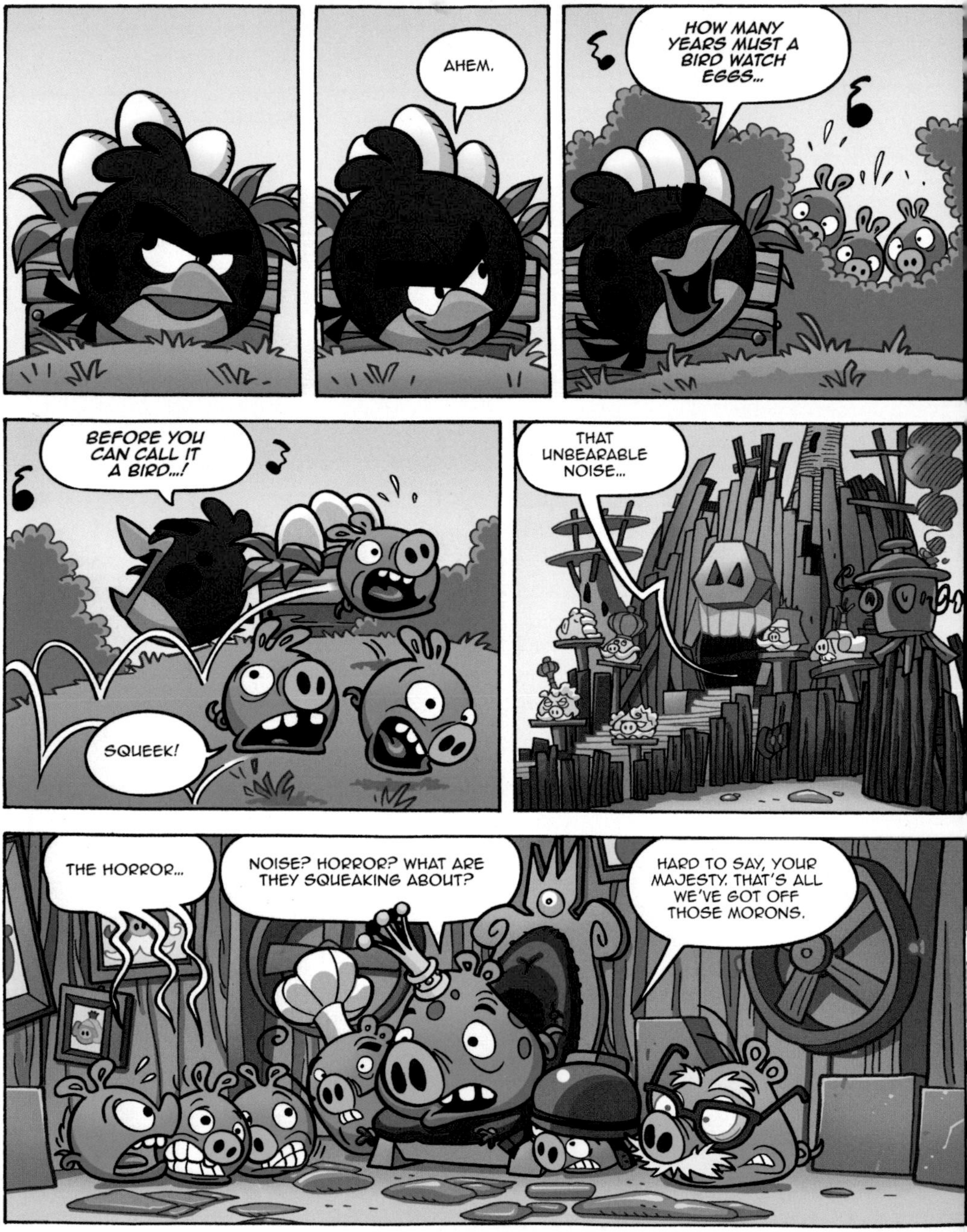
AHEM.
HOW MANY YEARS MUST A BIRD WATCH EGGS...
BEFORE YOU CAN CALL IT A BIRD...!
SQUEEK!
THAT UNBEARABLE NOISE...
THE HORROR...
NOISE? HORROR? WHAT ARE THEY SQUEAKING ABOUT?
HARD TO SAY, YOUR MAJESTY. THAT'S ALL WE'VE GOT OFF THOSE MORONS.

BRING ME THAT NOISE! I WANT TO KNOW WHAT'S GOING ON!

BUT SIR... IT'S *IMPOSSIBLE* TO CAPTURE A NOISE.

ACTUALLY... IT'S NOT.

"SOME TIME AGO I WAS WALKING ON THE BEACH AND THINKING, HOW WONDERFUL IT WOULD BE TO HEAR THE SOUND OF WAVES ANYWHERE..."

"AT THAT MOMENT I SAW A SHELL AND A FLAT ROCK AND I KNEW I HAD INVENTED A SOLUTION TO THE PROBLEM..."

STOP THE NONSENSE AND GET TO THE POINT!

CERTAINLY, YOUR HIGHNESS. MAY I INTRODUCE TO YOU THE...

ROCKORDER!

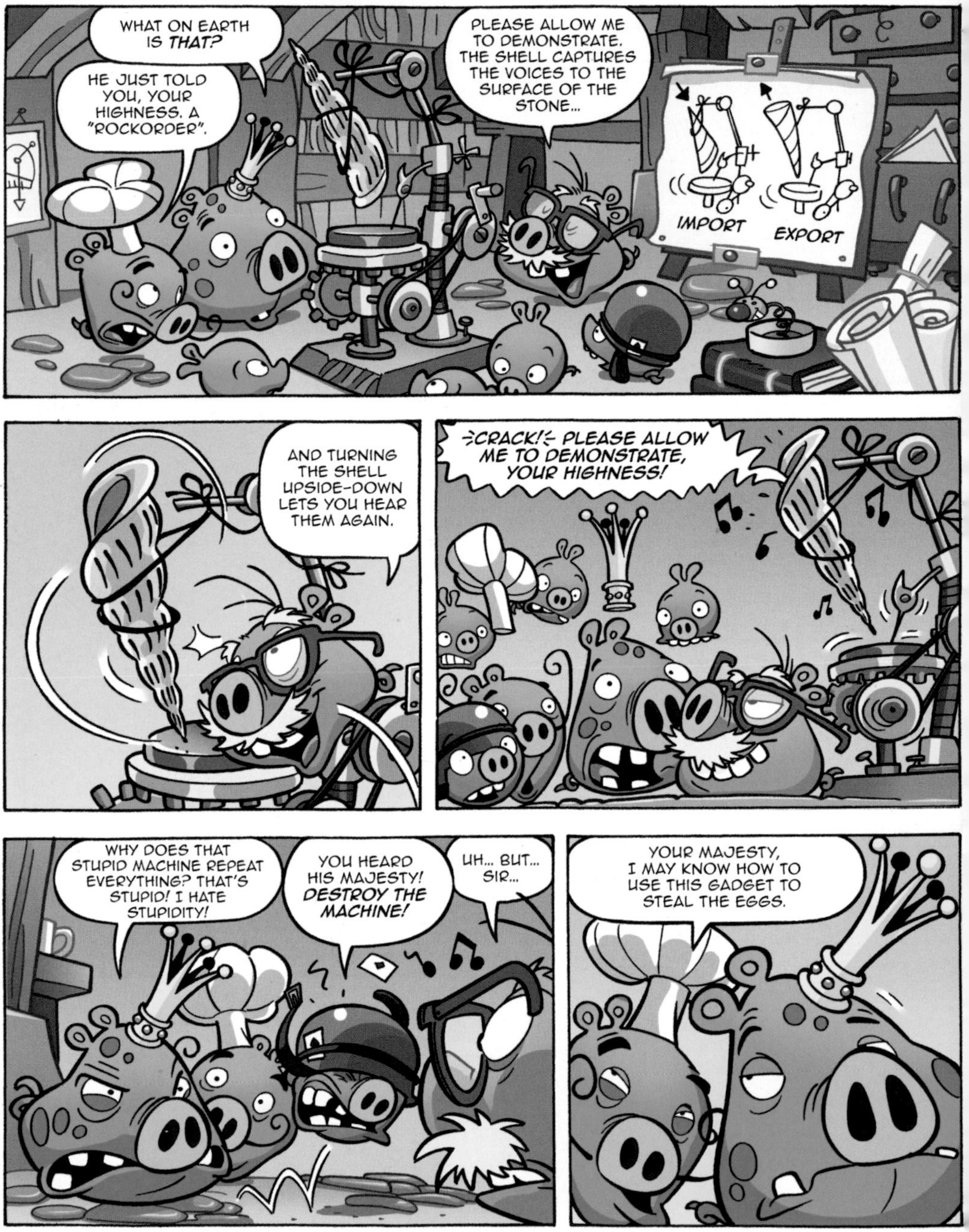
WHAT ON EARTH IS *THAT?*
HE JUST TOLD YOU, YOUR HIGHNESS. A "ROCKORDER".
PLEASE ALLOW ME TO DEMONSTRATE. THE SHELL CAPTURES THE VOICES TO THE SURFACE OF THE STONE...
IMPORT
EXPORT
AND TURNING THE SHELL UPSIDE-DOWN LETS YOU HEAR THEM AGAIN.
CRACK! PLEASE ALLOW ME TO DEMONSTRATE, YOUR HIGHNESS!
WHY DOES THAT STUPID MACHINE REPEAT EVERYTHING? THAT'S STUPID! I HATE STUPIDITY!
YOU HEARD HIS MAJESTY! *DESTROY THE MACHINE!*
UH... BUT... SIR...
YOUR MAJESTY, I MAY KNOW HOW TO USE THIS GADGET TO STEAL THE EGGS.

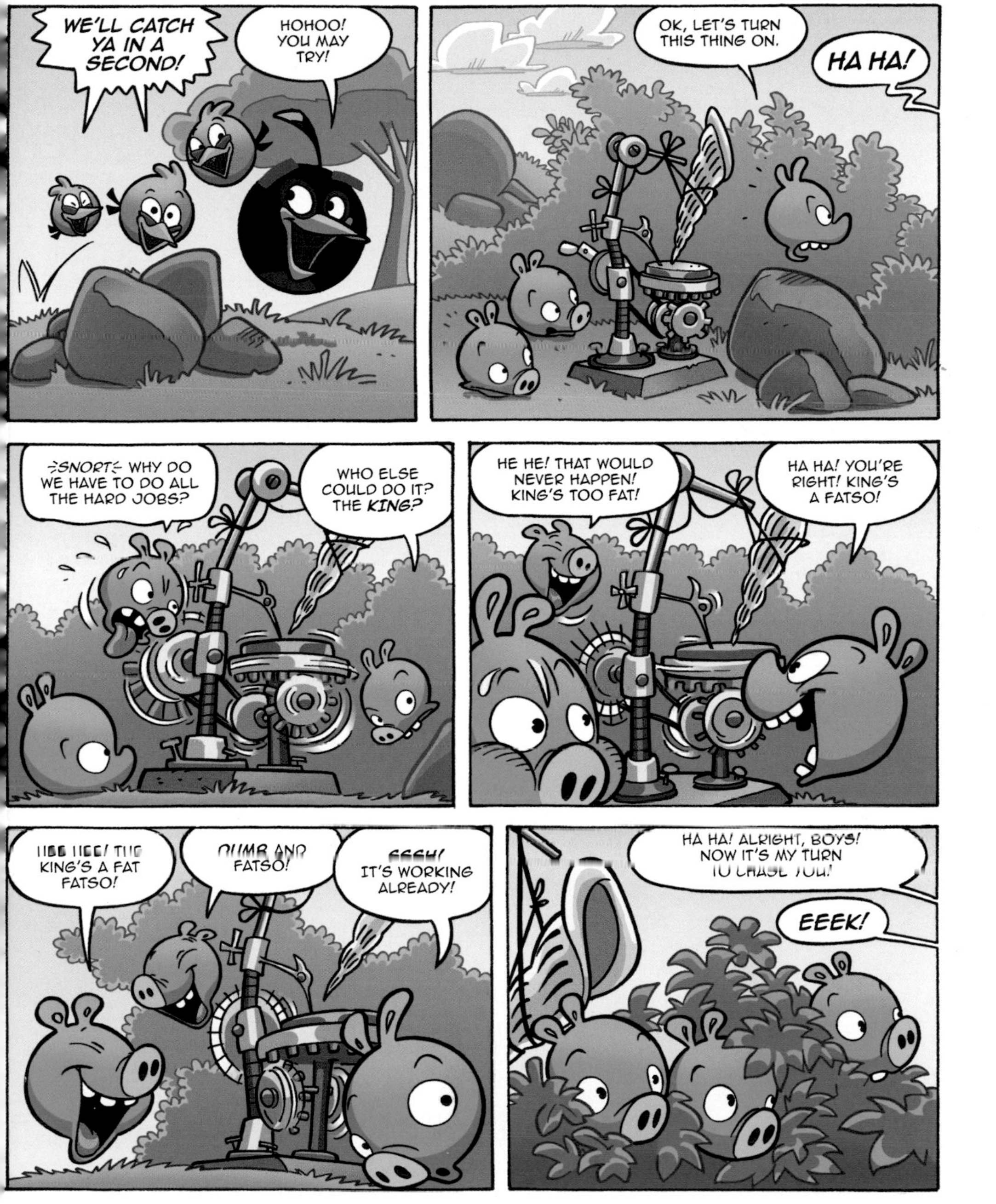
WE'LL CATCH YA IN A SECOND!
HOHOO! YOU MAY TRY!
OK, LET'S TURN THIS THING ON.
HA HA!
~SNORT~ WHY DO WE HAVE TO DO ALL THE HARD JOBS?
WHO ELSE COULD DO IT? THE KING?
HE HE! THAT WOULD NEVER HAPPEN! KING'S TOO FAT!
HA HA! YOU'RE RIGHT! KING'S A FATSO!
KING'S A FAT FATSO!
FATSO!
IT'S WORKING ALREADY!
HA HA! ALRIGHT, BOYS! NOW IT'S MY TURN
EEEK!

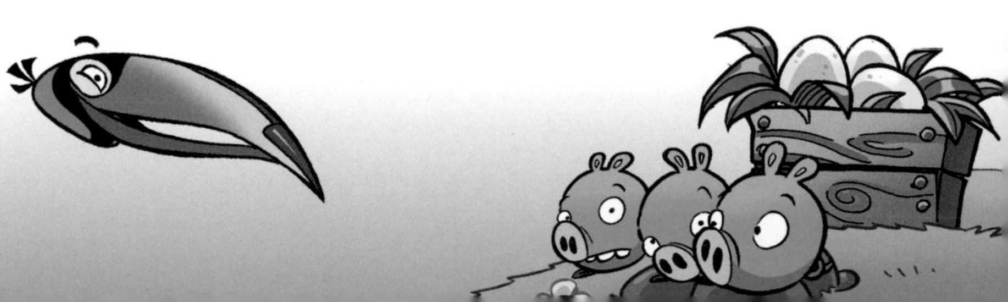

WE'RE GOING TO THE BEACH, RED!
WOULD YA JOIN US?
SOMEONE HAS TO GUARD THE EGGS, YOU KNOW.
WELL, *I* COULD GUARD THE EGGS FOR A CHANGE.
UH... THANKS, BUT I'M NOT IN A MOOD FOR THE BEACH TODAY.
SIGH. AS YOU SAY, RED.
C'MON, LET'S *GO!*

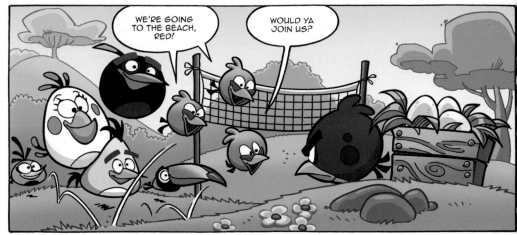

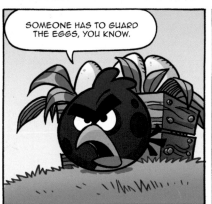

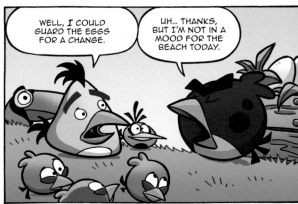

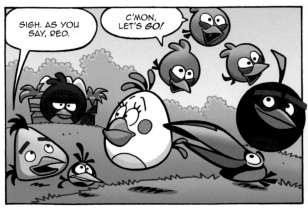

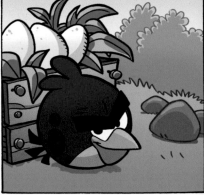

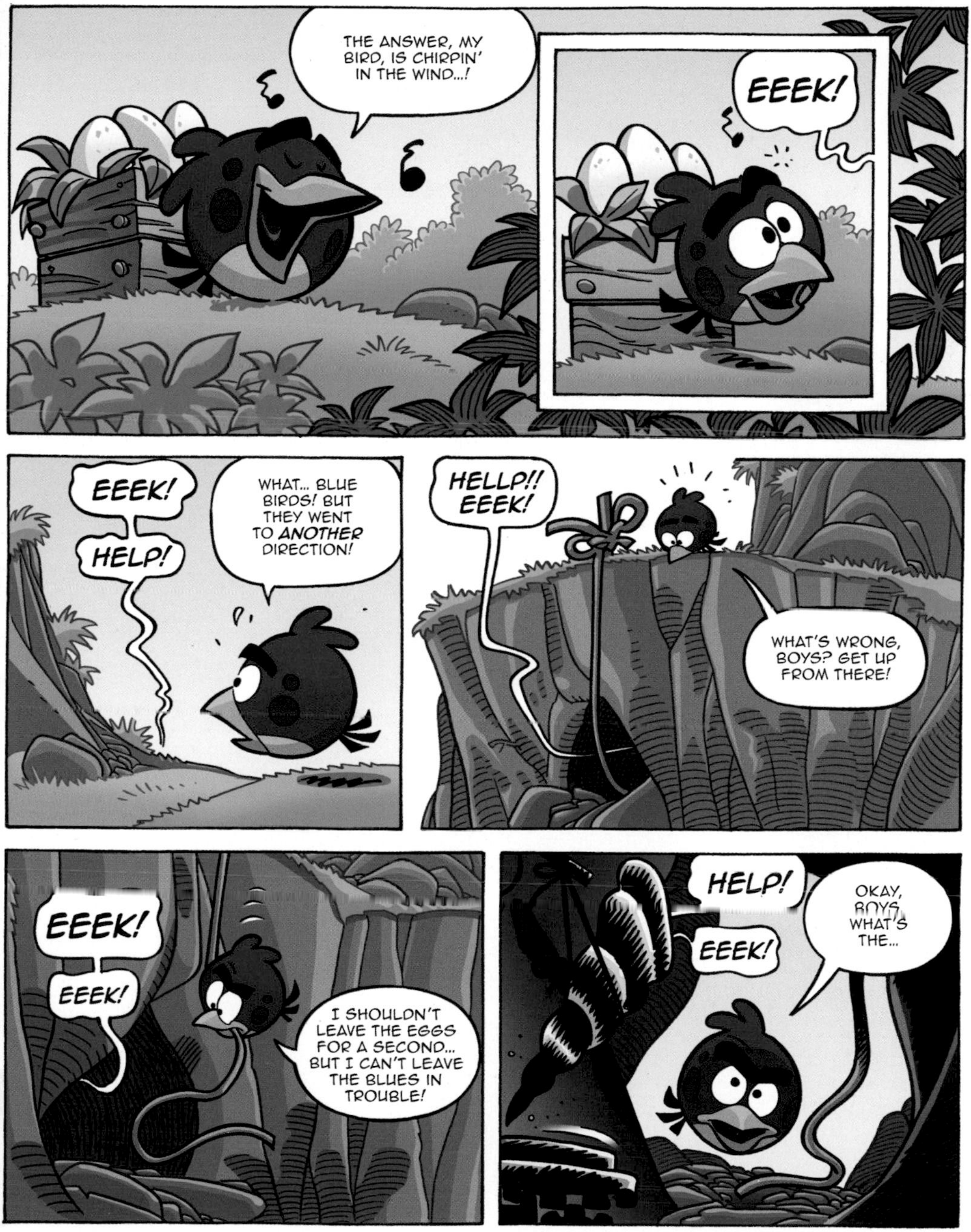
THE ANSWER, MY BIRD, IS CHIRPIN' IN THE WIND...!
EEEK!
EEEK!
HELP!
WHAT... BLUE BIRDS! BUT THEY WENT TO *ANOTHER* DIRECTION!
HELLP!! EEEK!
WHAT'S WRONG, BOYS? GET UP FROM THERE!
EEEK!
EEEK!
I SHOULDN'T LEAVE THE EGGS FOR A SECOND... BUT I CAN'T LEAVE THE BLUES IN TROUBLE!
HELP!
EEEK!
OKAY, BOYS, WHAT'S THE...

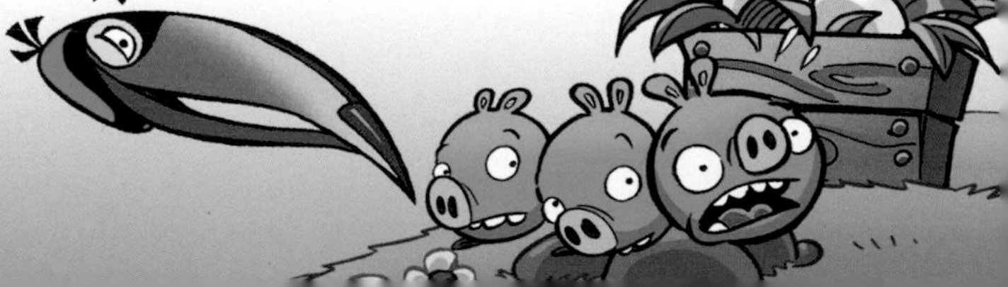

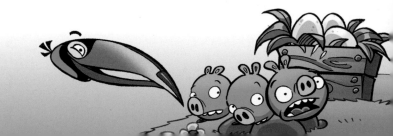

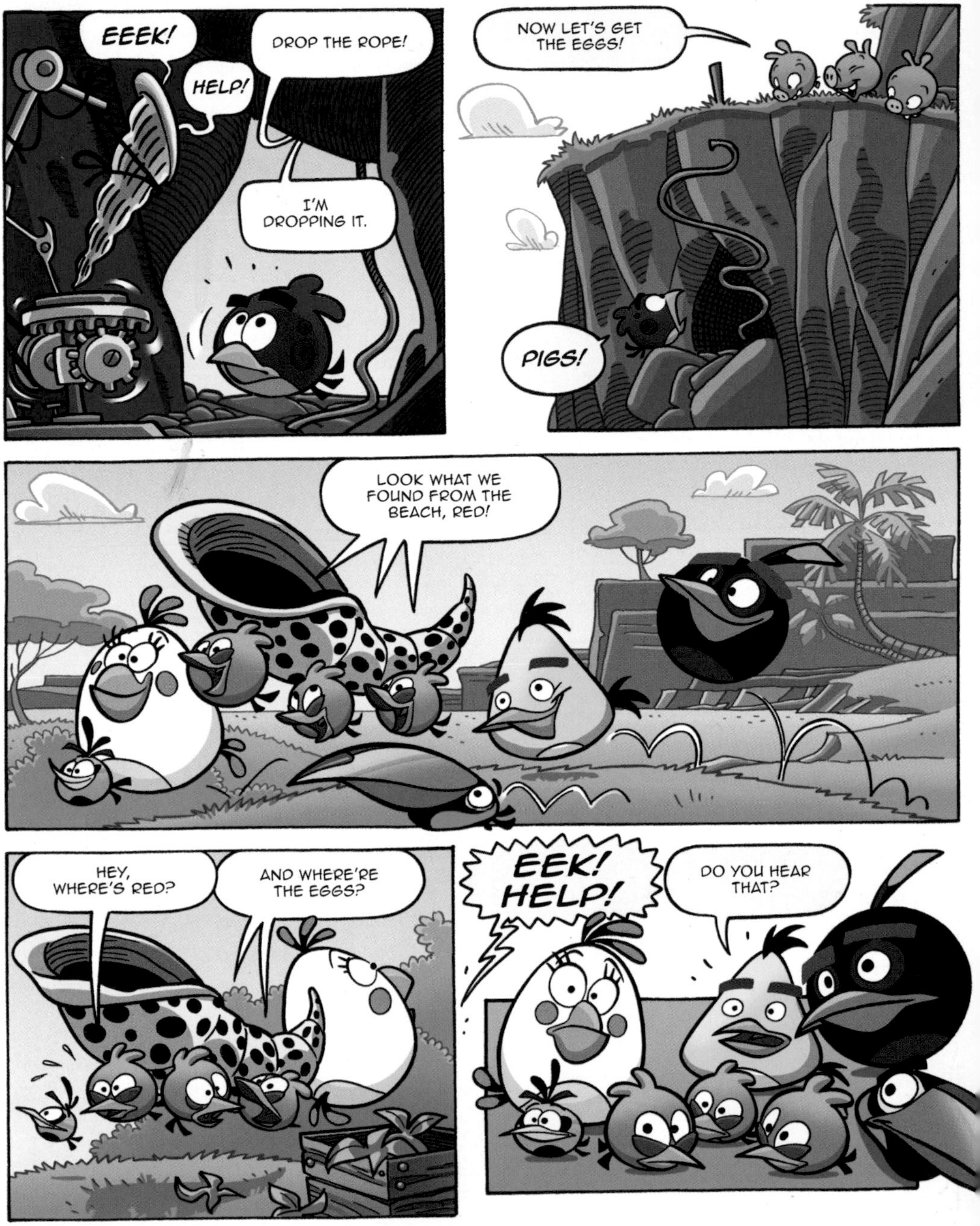
EEEK!
HELP!
DROP THE ROPE!
I'M DROPPING IT.
NOW LET'S GET THE EGGS!
PIGS!
LOOK WHAT WE FOUND FROM THE BEACH, RED!
HEY, WHERE'S RED?
AND WHERE'RE THE EGGS?
EEK! HELP!
DO YOU HEAR THAT?

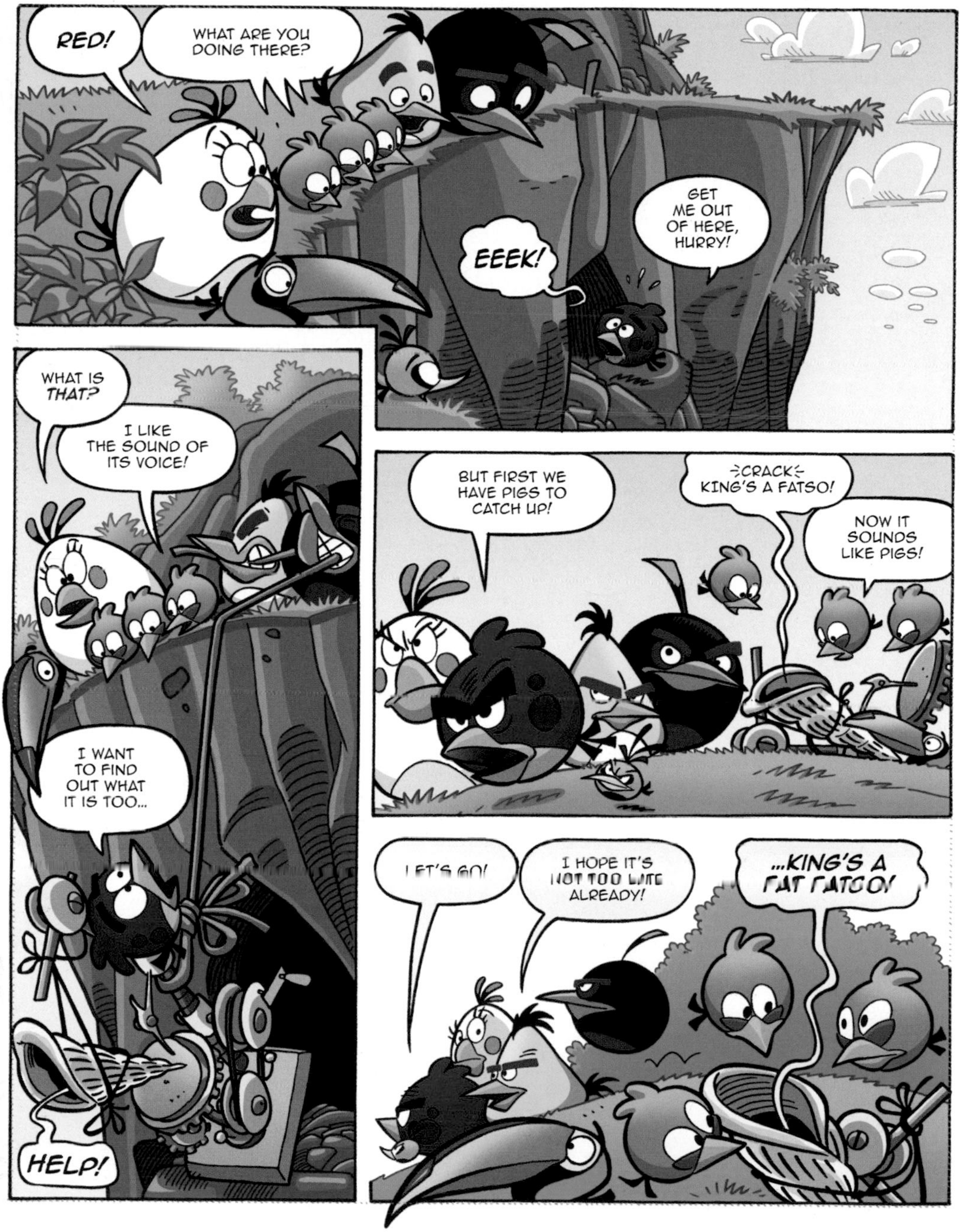
RED!
WHAT ARE YOU DOING THERE?
EEEK!
GET ME OUT OF HERE, HURRY!
WHAT IS THAT?
I LIKE THE SOUND OF ITS VOICE!
I WANT TO FIND OUT WHAT IT IS TOO...
HELP!
BUT FIRST WE HAVE PIGS TO CATCH UP!
CRACK KING'S A FATSO!
NOW IT SOUNDS LIKE PIGS!
LET'S GO!
I HOPE IT'S NOT TOO LATE ALREADY!
...KING'S A FAT FATSO!

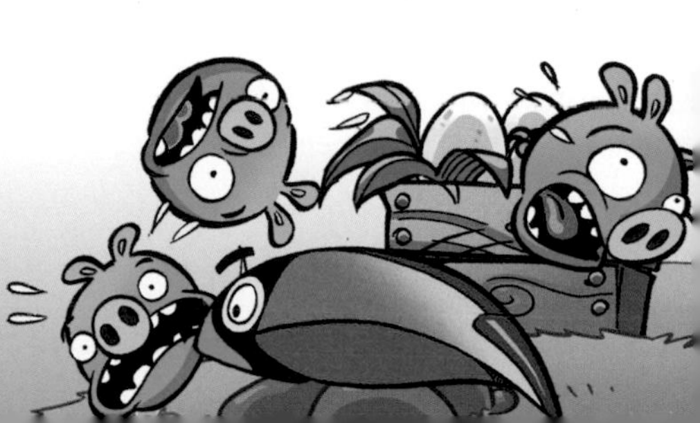

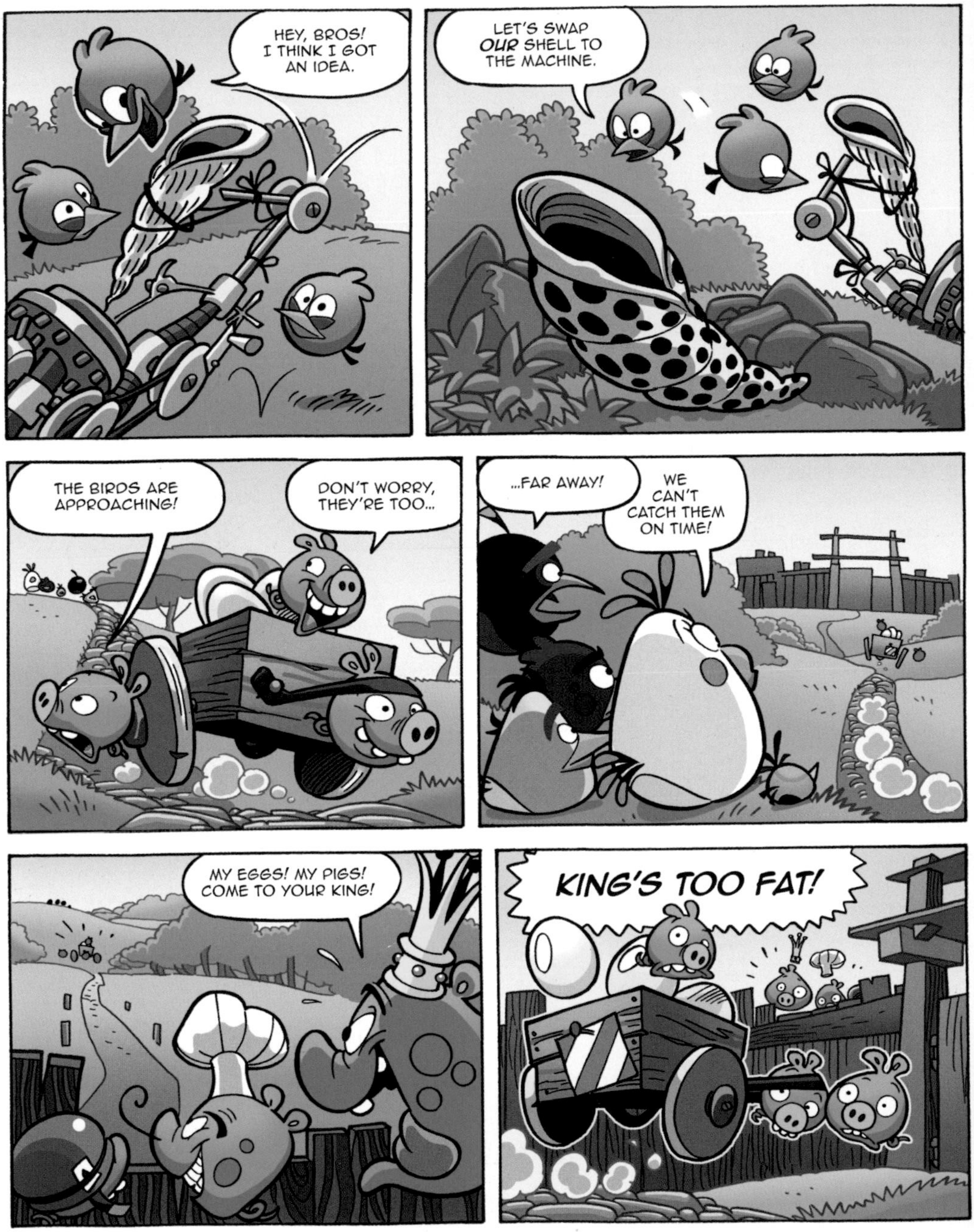
HEY, BROS! I THINK I GOT AN IDEA.
LET'S SWAP OUR SHELL TO THE MACHINE.
THE BIRDS ARE APPROACHING!
DON'T WORRY, THEY'RE TOO...
...FAR AWAY!
WE CAN'T CATCH THEM ON TIME!
MY EGGS! MY PIGS! COME TO YOUR KING!
KING'S TOO FAT!

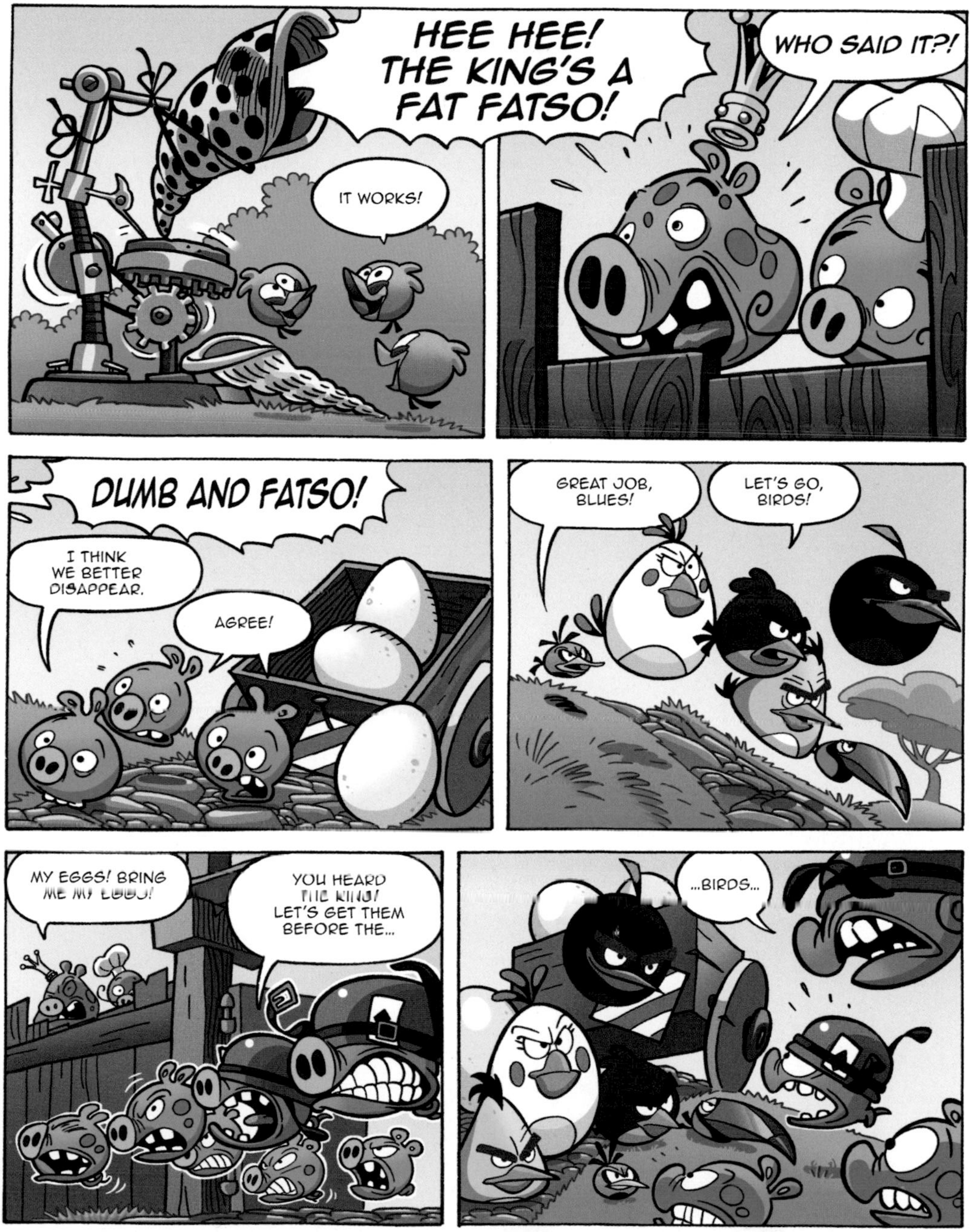
HEE HEE! THE KING'S A FAT FATSO!
IT WORKS!
WHO SAID IT?!
DUMB AND FATSO!
I THINK WE BETTER DISAPPEAR.
AGREE!
GREAT JOB, BLUES!
LET'S GO, BIRDS!
MY EGGS! BRING ME MY EGGS!
YOU HEARD THE KING! LET'S GET THEM BEFORE THE...
...BIRDS...

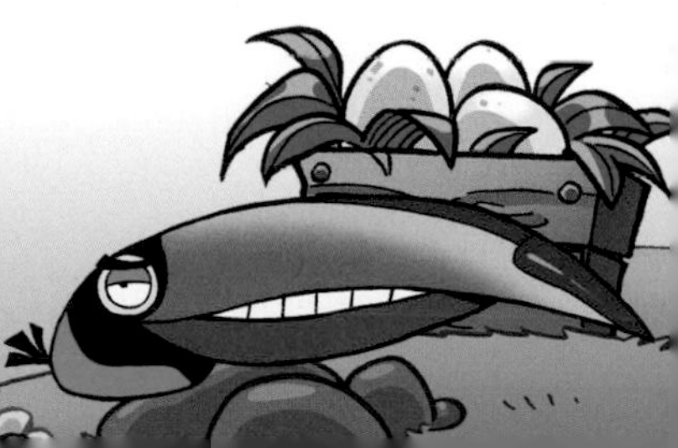

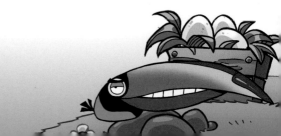

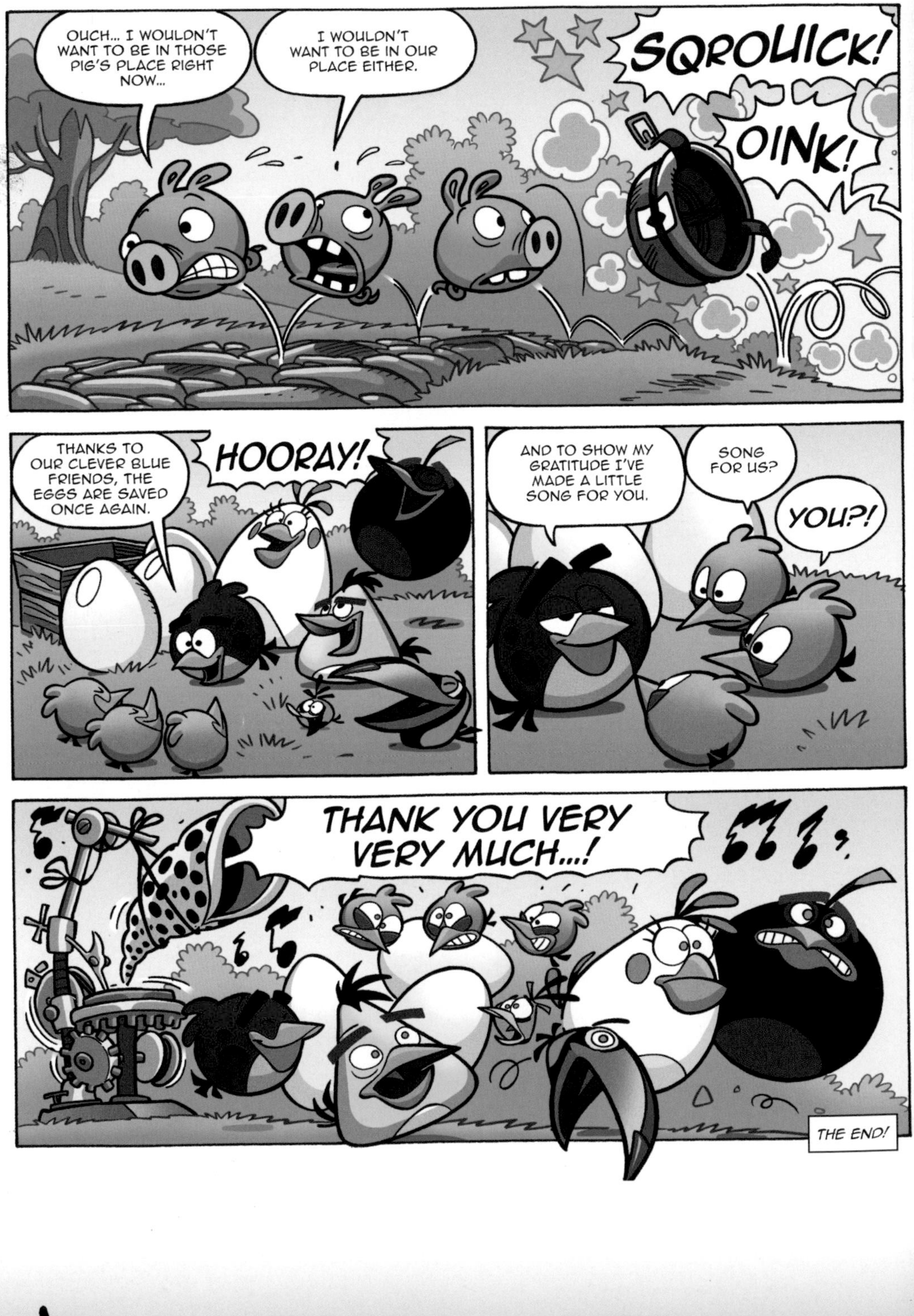
OUCH... I WOULDN'T WANT TO BE IN THOSE PIG'S PLACE RIGHT NOW...
I WOULDN'T WANT TO BE IN OUR PLACE EITHER.
SQROUICK!
OINK!
THANKS TO OUR CLEVER BLUE FRIENDS, THE EGGS ARE SAVED ONCE AGAIN.
HOORAY!
AND TO SHOW MY GRATITUDE I'VE MADE A LITTLE SONG FOR YOU.
SONG FOR US?
YOU?!
THANK YOU VERY VERY MUCH...!
THE END!

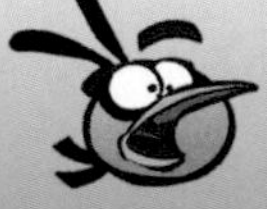

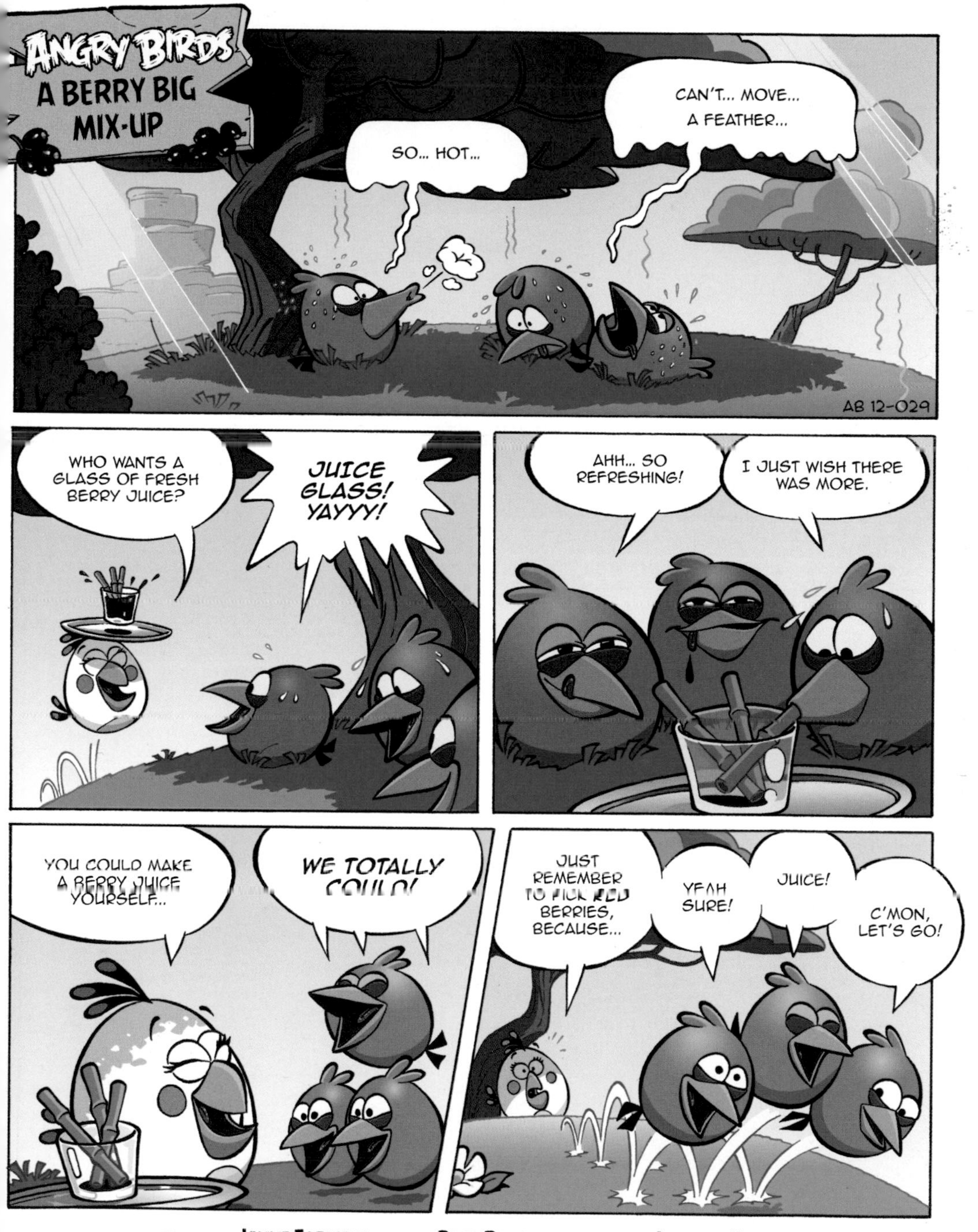
ANGRY BIRDS
A BERRY BIG MIX-UP
SO... HOT...
CAN'T... MOVE... A FEATHER...
AB 12-029
WHO WANTS A GLASS OF FRESH BERRY JUICE?
JUICE GLASS! YAYYY!
AHH... SO REFRESHING!
I JUST WISH THERE WAS MORE.
YOU COULD MAKE A BERRY JUICE YOURSELF...
WE TOTALLY COULD!
JUST REMEMBER TO PICK RED BERRIES, BECAUSE...
YEAH SURE!
JUICE!
C'MON, LET'S GO!

WRITTEN BY: JANNE TORISEVA • ART BY: PACO RODRIQUES • COLORS BY: JOSEP DE HARO

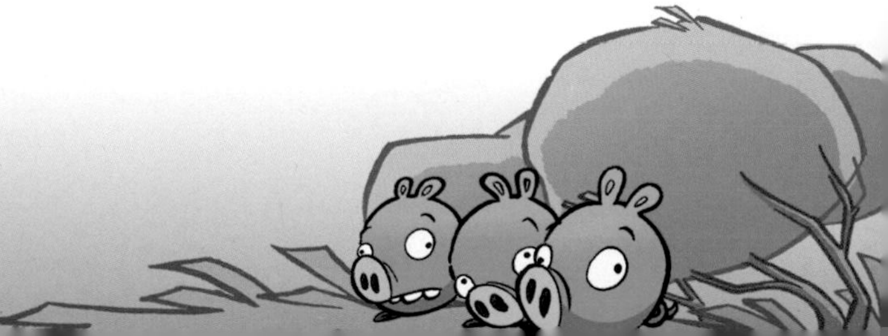

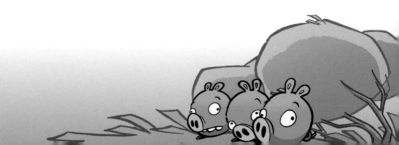

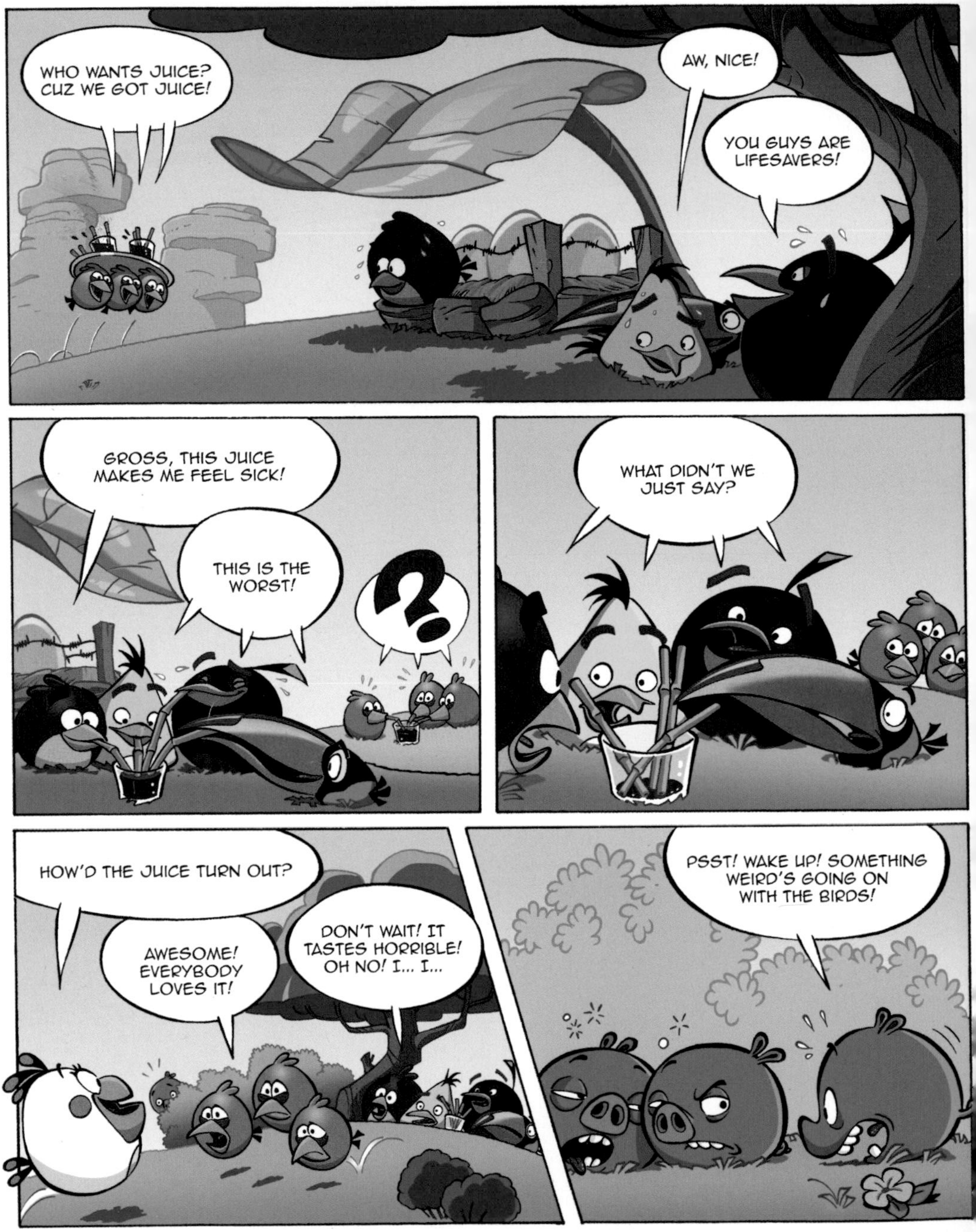
WHO WANTS JUICE? CUZ WE GOT JUICE!
AW, NICE!
YOU GUYS ARE LIFESAVERS!
GROSS, THIS JUICE MAKES ME FEEL SICK!
THIS IS THE WORST!
?
WHAT DIDN'T WE JUST SAY?
HOW'D THE JUICE TURN OUT?
AWESOME! EVERYBODY LOVES IT!
DON'T WAIT! IT TASTES HORRIBLE! OH NO! I... I...
PSST! WAKE UP! SOMETHING WEIRD'S GOING ON WITH THE BIRDS!

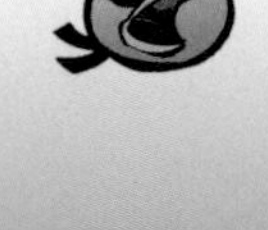

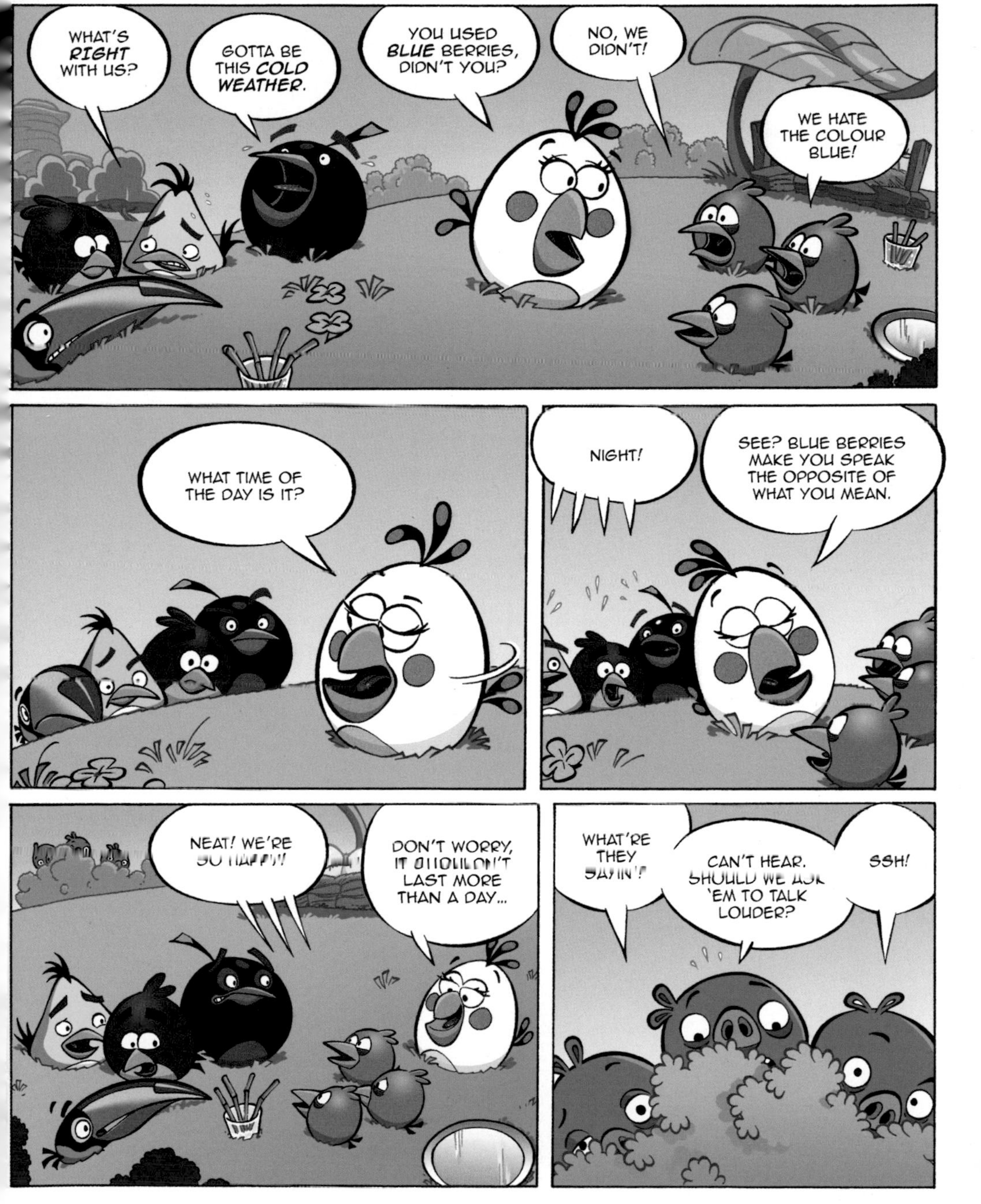

WHAT'S RIGHT WITH US?
GOTTA BE THIS COLD WEATHER.
YOU USED BLUE BERRIES, DIDN'T YOU?
NO, WE DIDN'T!
WE HATE THE COLOUR BLUE!
WHAT TIME OF THE DAY IS IT?
NIGHT!
SEE? BLUE BERRIES MAKE YOU SPEAK THE OPPOSITE OF WHAT YOU MEAN.
NEAT! WE'RE
DON'T WORRY,
LAST MORE THAN A DAY...
WHAT'RE THEY
CAN'T HEAR.
'EM TO TALK LOUDER?
SSH!

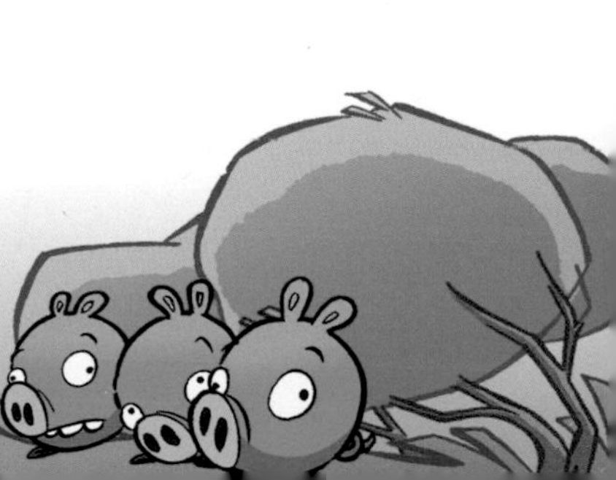

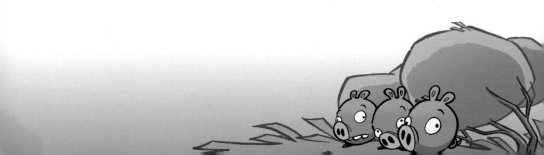

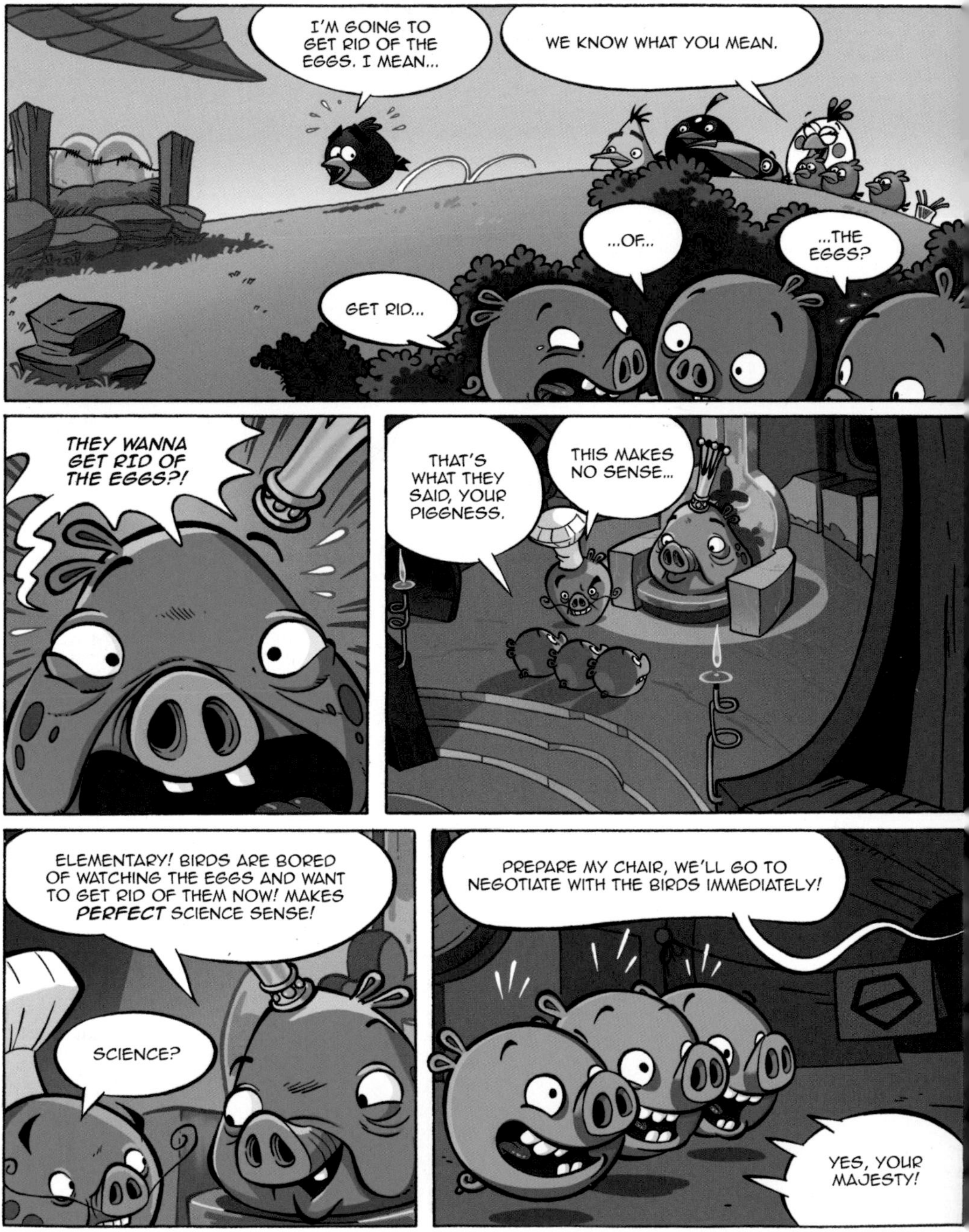
I'M GOING TO GET RID OF THE EGGS. I MEAN...
WE KNOW WHAT YOU MEAN.
GET RID...
...OF...
...THE EGGS?
THEY WANNA GET RID OF THE EGGS?!
THAT'S WHAT THEY SAID, YOUR PIGGNESS.
THIS MAKES NO SENSE...
ELEMENTARY! BIRDS ARE BORED OF WATCHING THE EGGS AND WANT TO GET RID OF THEM NOW! MAKES PERFECT SCIENCE SENSE!
SCIENCE?
PREPARE MY CHAIR, WE'LL GO TO NEGOTIATE WITH THE BIRDS IMMEDIATELY!
YES, YOUR MAJESTY!

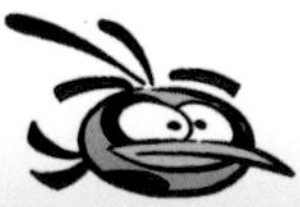

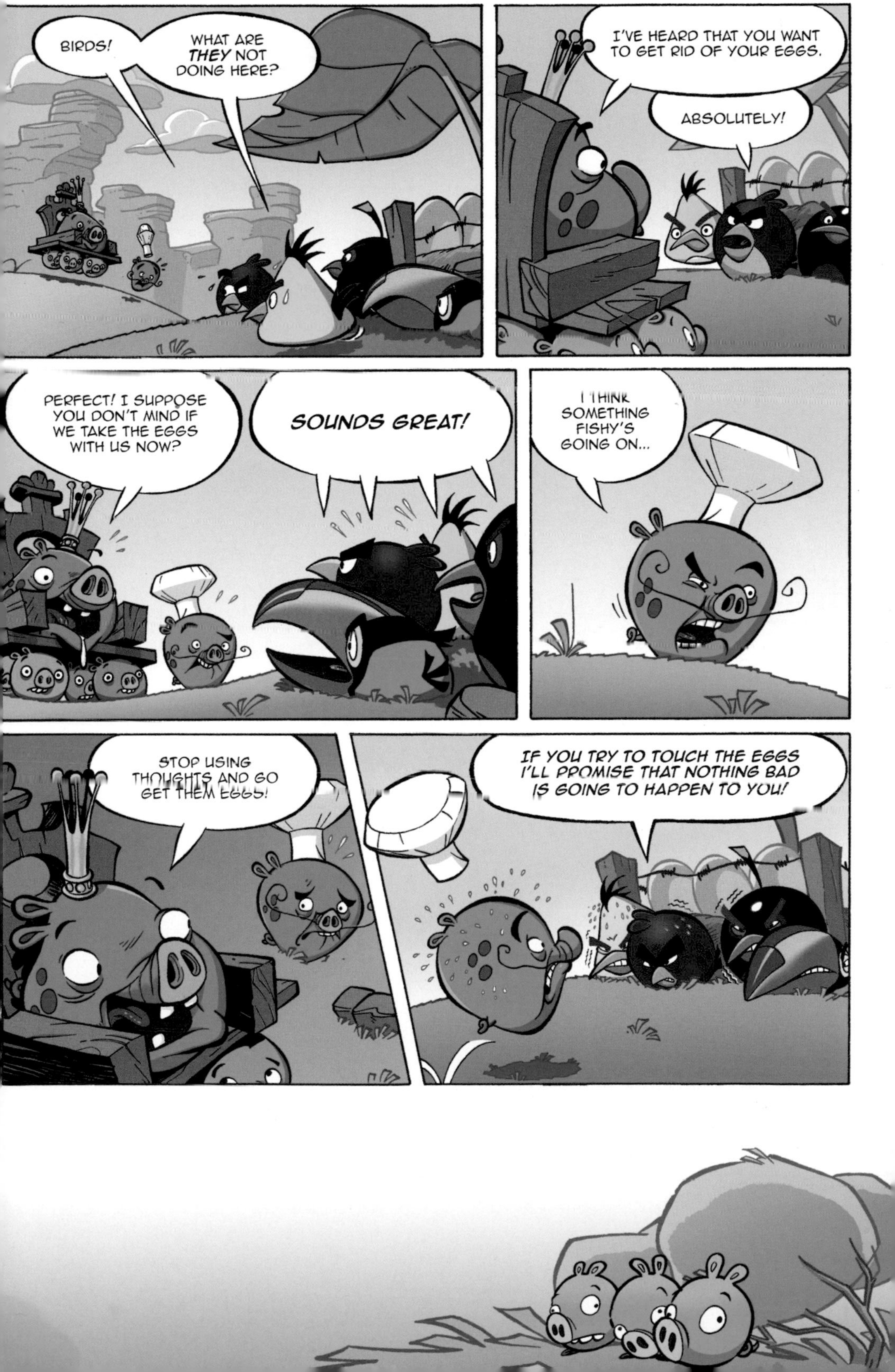

BIRDS!
WHAT ARE *THEY* NOT DOING HERE?
I'VE HEARD THAT YOU WANT TO GET RID OF YOUR EGGS.
ABSOLUTELY!
PERFECT! I SUPPOSE YOU DON'T MIND IF WE TAKE THE EGGS WITH US NOW?
SOUNDS GREAT!
I THINK SOMETHING FISHY'S GOING ON...
STOP USING THOUGHTS AND GO GET THEM EGGS!
IF YOU TRY TO TOUCH THE EGGS I'LL PROMISE THAT NOTHING BAD IS GOING TO HAPPEN TO YOU!

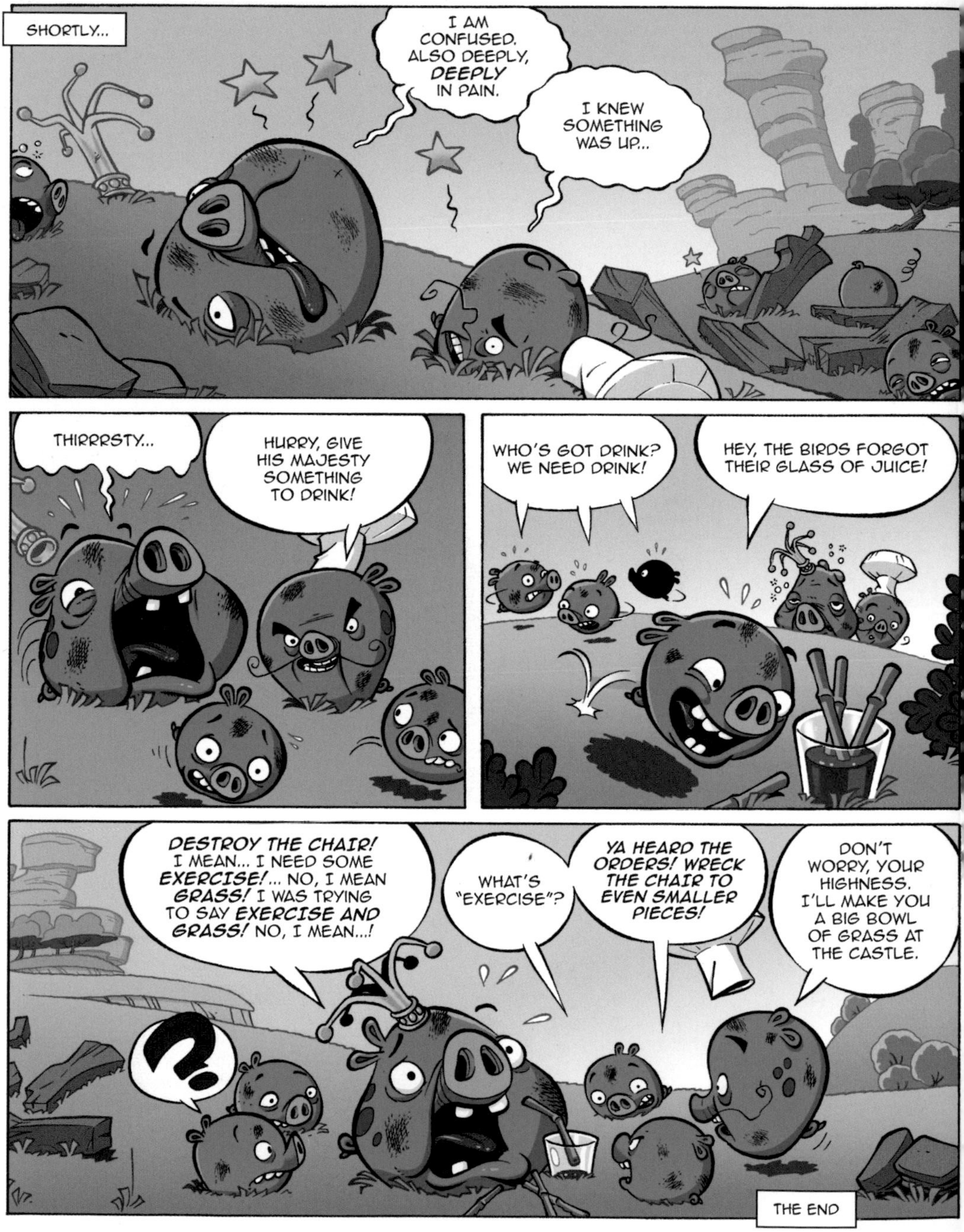
SHORTLY...
I AM CONFUSED. ALSO DEEPLY, DEEPLY IN PAIN.
I KNEW SOMETHING WAS UP...
THIRRRSTY...
HURRY, GIVE HIS MAJESTY SOMETHING TO DRINK!
WHO'S GOT DRINK? WE NEED DRINK!
HEY, THE BIRDS FORGOT THEIR GLASS OF JUICE!
DESTROY THE CHAIR! I MEAN... I NEED SOME EXERCISE!... NO, I MEAN GRASS! I WAS TRYING TO SAY EXERCISE AND GRASS! NO, I MEAN...!
?
WHAT'S "EXERCISE"?
YA HEARD THE ORDERS! WRECK THE CHAIR TO EVEN SMALLER PIECES!
DON'T WORRY, YOUR HIGHNESS. I'LL MAKE YOU A BIG BOWL OF GRASS AT THE CASTLE.
THE END

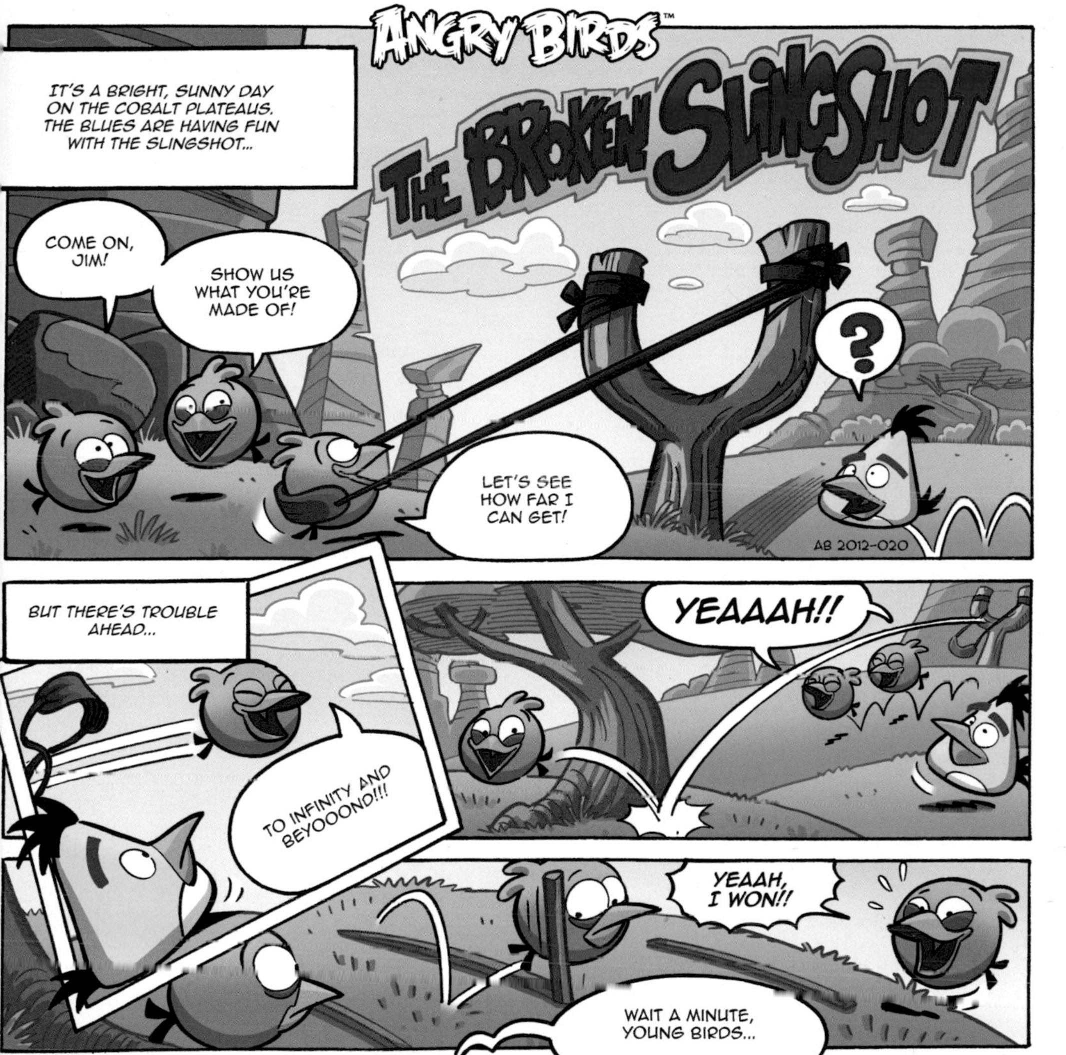
ANGRY BIRDS™
THE BROKEN SLINGSHOT
IT'S A BRIGHT, SUNNY DAY ON THE COBALT PLATEAUS. THE BLUES ARE HAVING FUN WITH THE SLINGSHOT...
COME ON, JIM!
SHOW US WHAT YOU'RE MADE OF!
LET'S SEE HOW FAR I CAN GET!
?
AB 2012-020
BUT THERE'S TROUBLE AHEAD...
TO INFINITY AND BEYOOOND!!!
YEAAAH!!
YEAAH, I WON!!
WAIT A MINUTE, YOUNG BIRDS...
YOU THINK THAT WAS FAR? PFFT!
YOU DON'T KNOW THE MEANING OF FAR!
WHATEVER YOU SAY, CHUCK...

WRITTEN BY: ANASTASIA HEINZL • ART BY: MARCO GERVASIO • COLORS BY: DIGIKORE STUDIOS

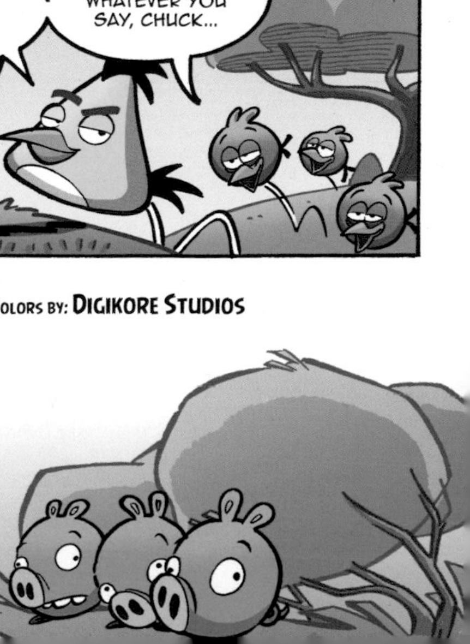

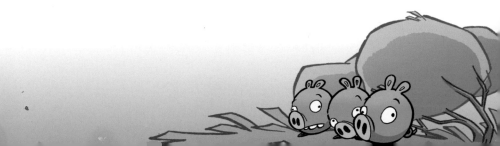

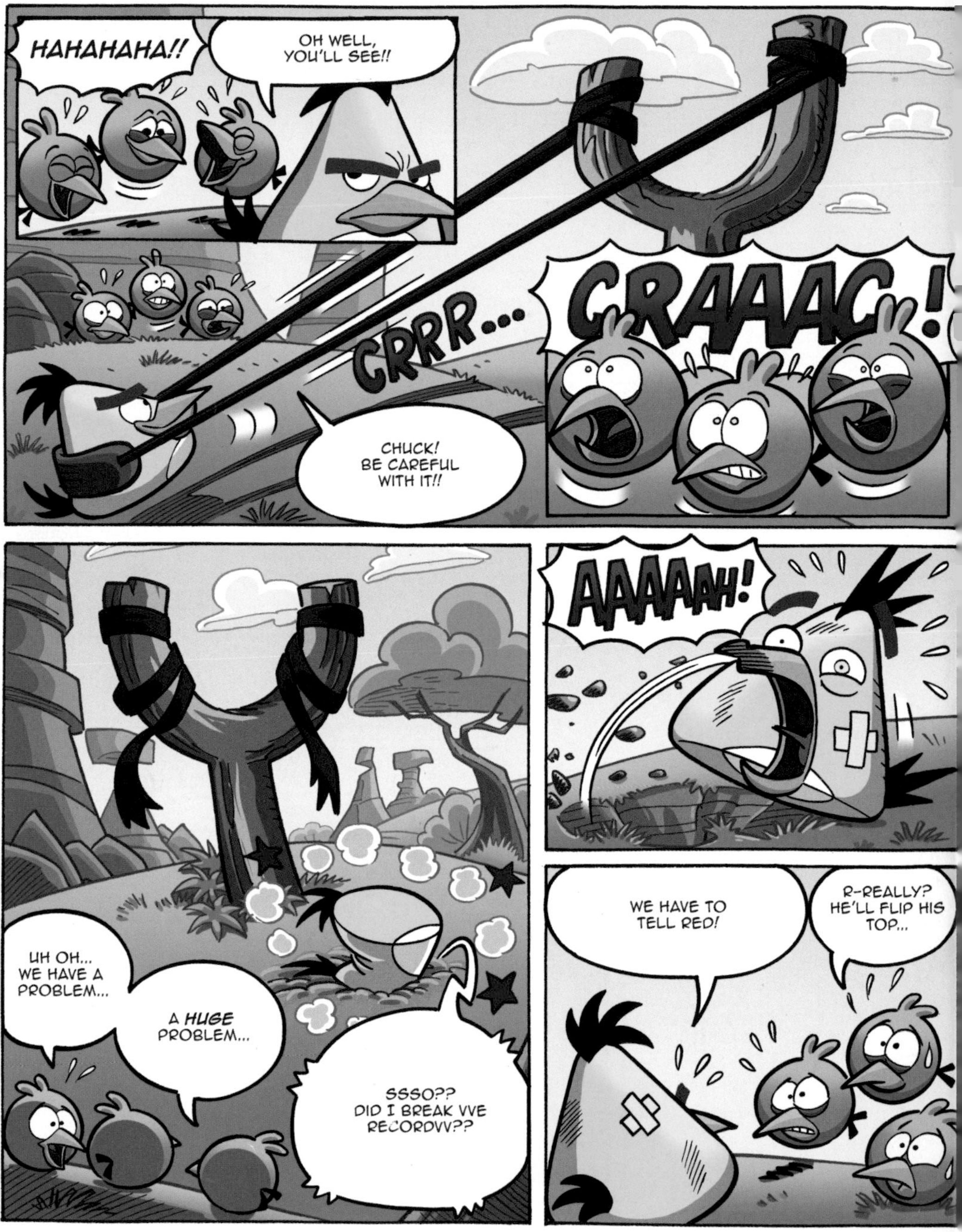
HAHAHAHA!!
OH WELL, YOU'LL SEE!!
CRRR...
CHUCK! BE CAREFUL WITH IT!!
CRAAAC!
AAAAAH!
UH OH... WE HAVE A PROBLEM...
A HUGE PROBLEM...
SSSO?? DID I BREAK VVE RECORDVV??
WE HAVE TO TELL RED!
R-REALLY? HE'LL FLIP HIS TOP...

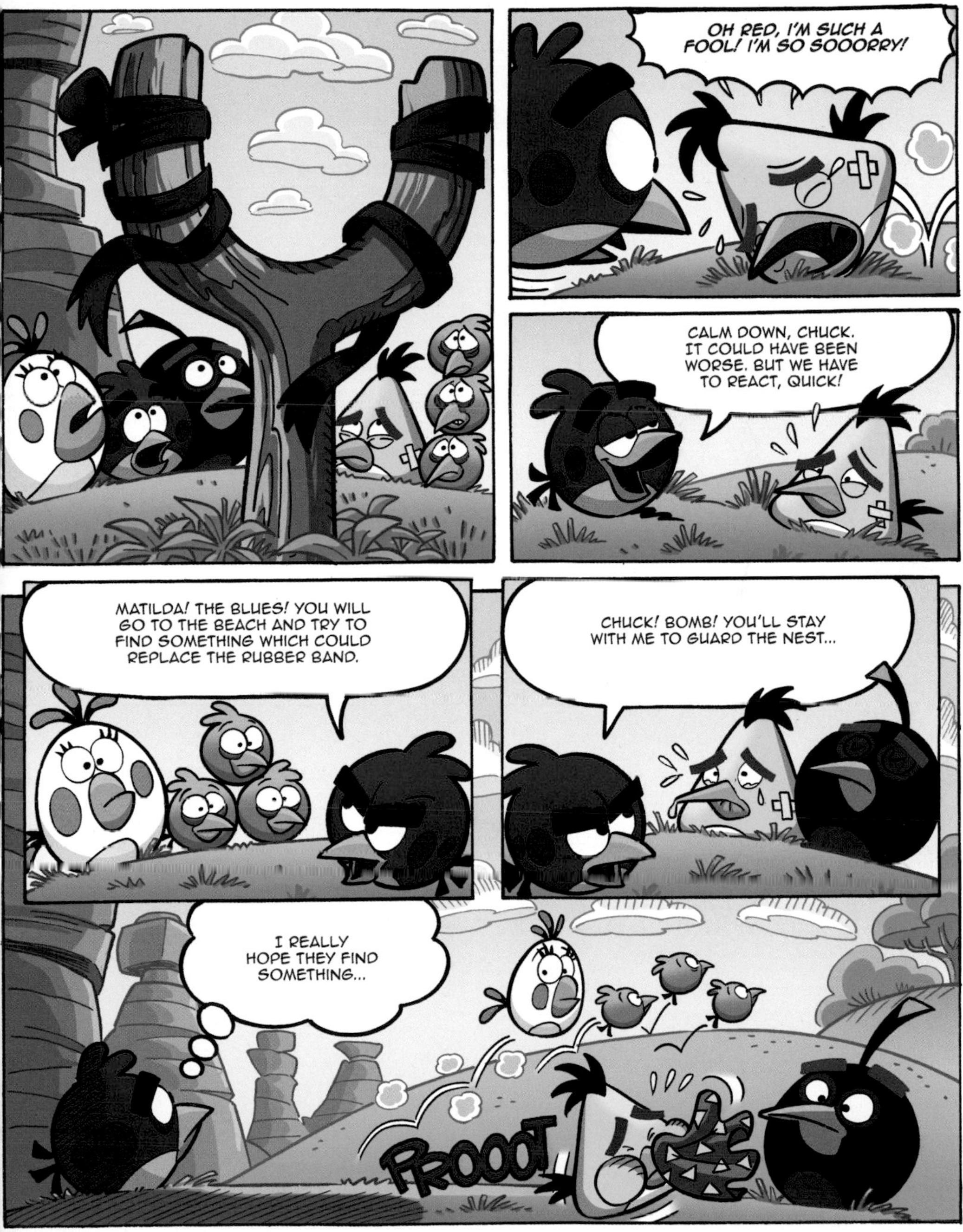
OH RED, I'M SUCH A FOOL! I'M SO SOOORRY!
CALM DOWN, CHUCK. IT COULD HAVE BEEN WORSE. BUT WE HAVE TO REACT, QUICK!
MATILDA! THE BLUES! YOU WILL GO TO THE BEACH AND TRY TO FIND SOMETHING WHICH COULD REPLACE THE RUBBER BAND.
CHUCK! BOMB! YOU'LL STAY WITH ME TO GUARD THE NEST...
I REALLY HOPE THEY FIND SOMETHING...
PROOOT

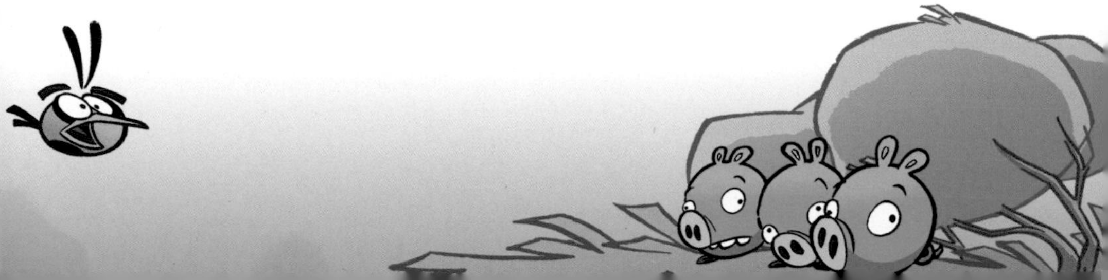

LATER...
I CAN'T FIND ANYTHING ELASTIC!
ME NEITHER!
UH? WHAT'S THIS?
IT'S WARM! A SURVIVAL BLANKET?
NO! A TUNNEL TO OUTER SPACE!
?
!
TCHOING!
IT'S PERFECT! WELL DONE, MATILDA!

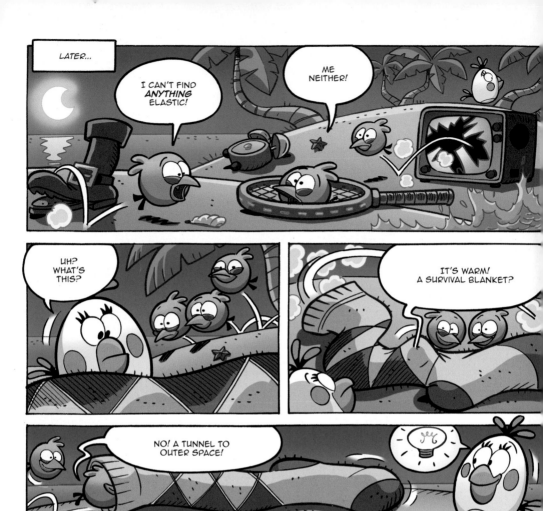

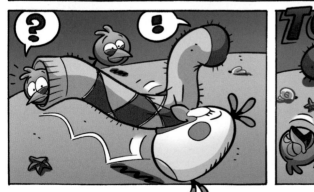

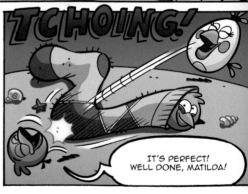

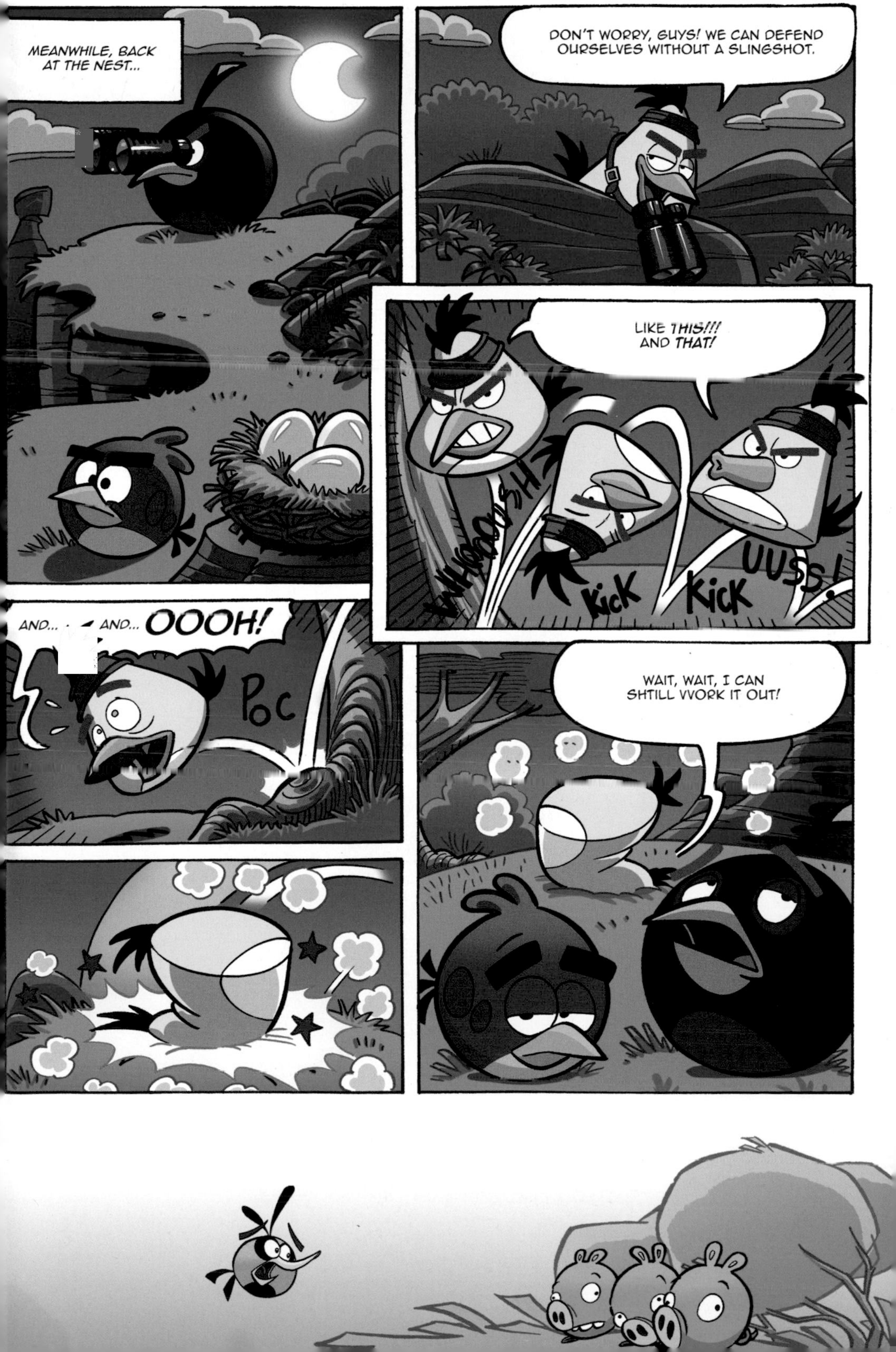
MEANWHILE, BACK AT THE NEST...
DON'T WORRY, GUYS! WE CAN DEFEND OURSELVES WITHOUT A SLINGSHOT.
LIKE THIS!!! AND THAT!
KICK
KICK
UUSS!
AND... AND... OOOH!
POC
WAIT, WAIT, I CAN SHTILL VVORK IT OUT!

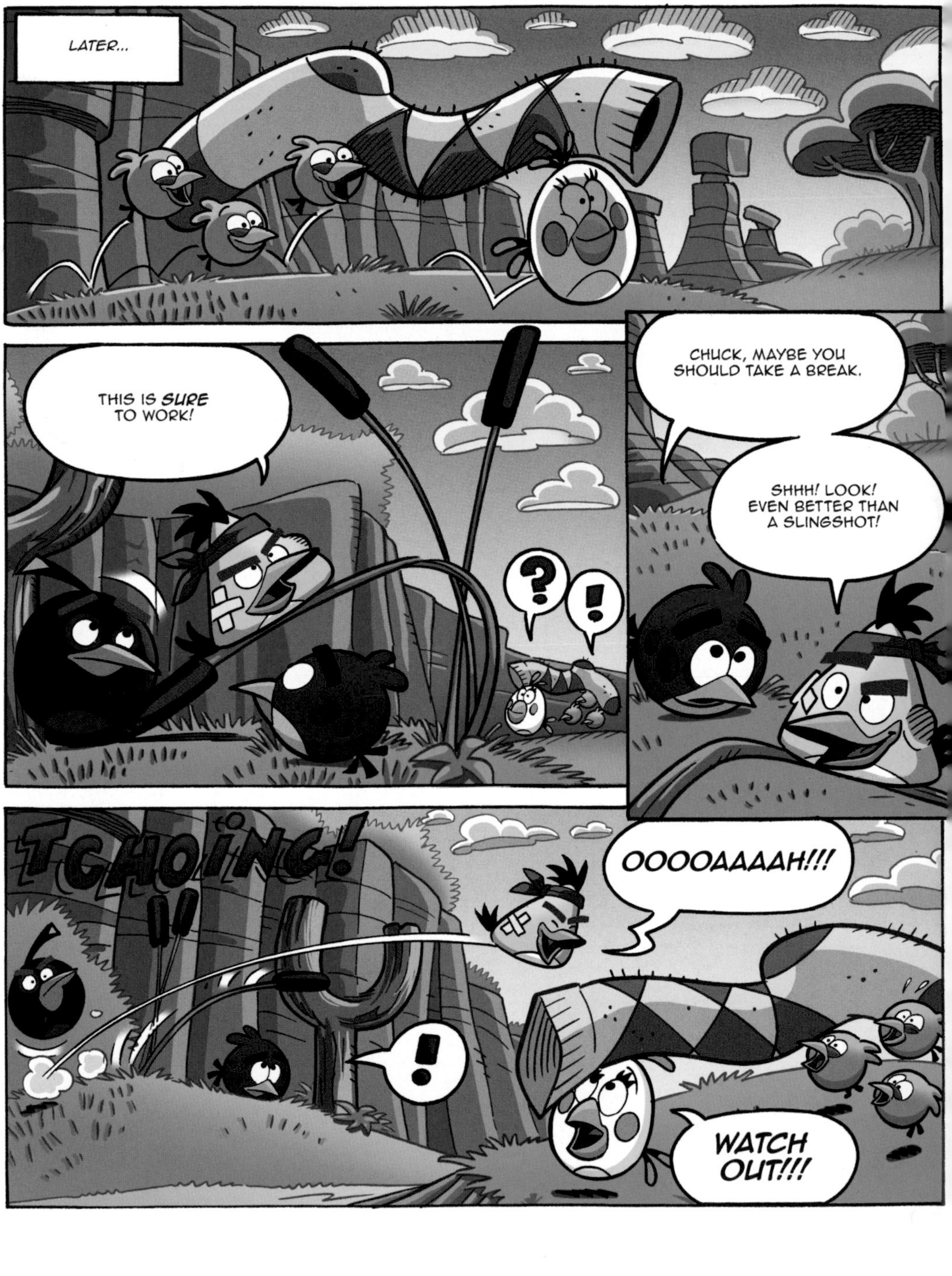
LATER...
THIS IS SURE TO WORK!
?
!
CHUCK, MAYBE YOU SHOULD TAKE A BREAK.
SHHH! LOOK! EVEN BETTER THAN A SLINGSHOT!
TCHOING!
OOOOAAAAH!!!
!
WATCH OUT!!!

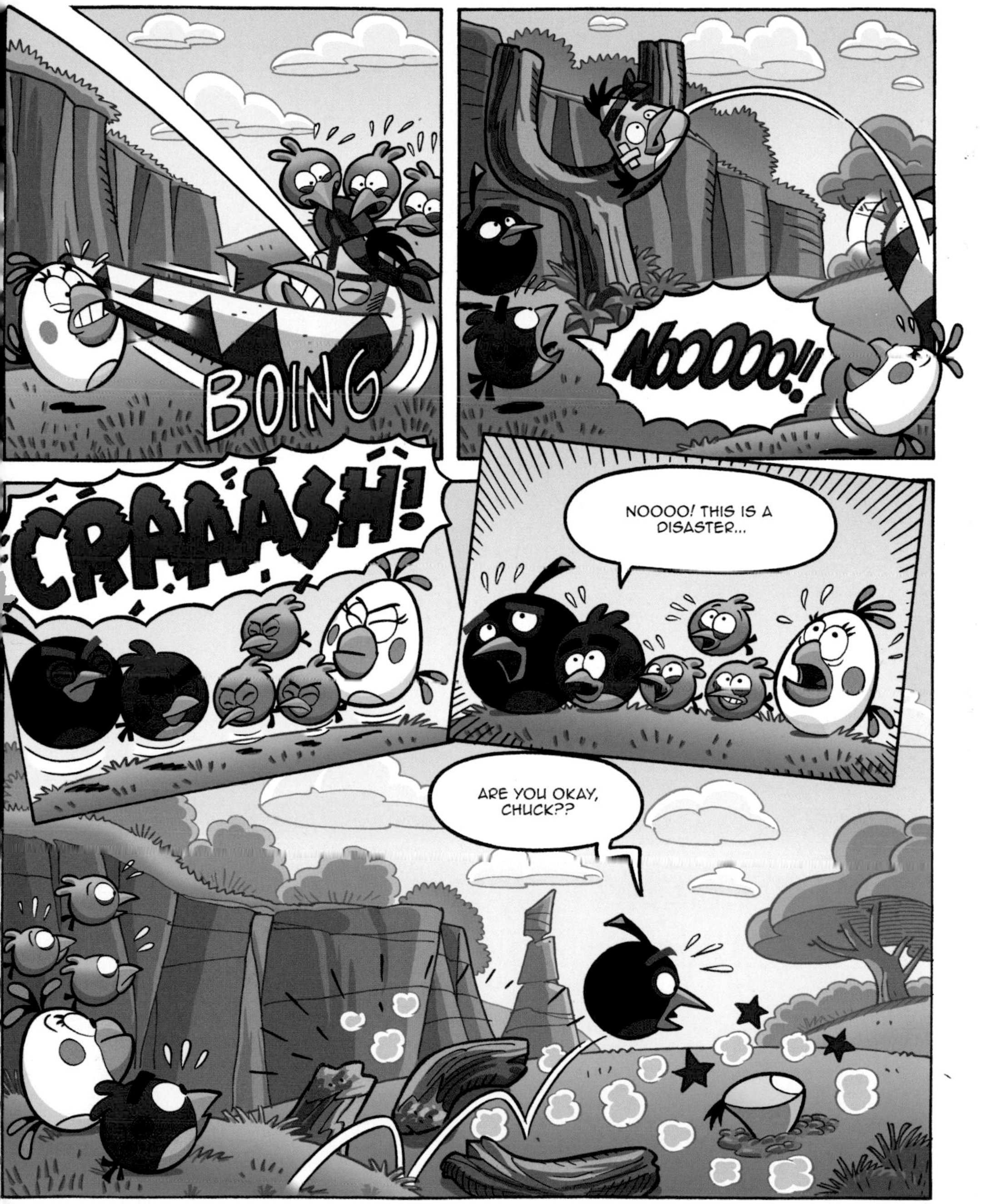
BOING
NOOOOO!!
CRAAASH!
NOOOO! THIS IS A DISASTER...
ARE YOU OKAY, CHUCK??

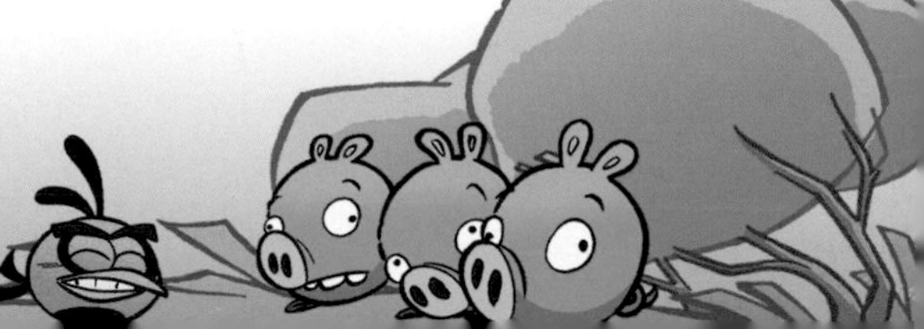

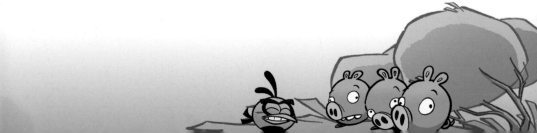

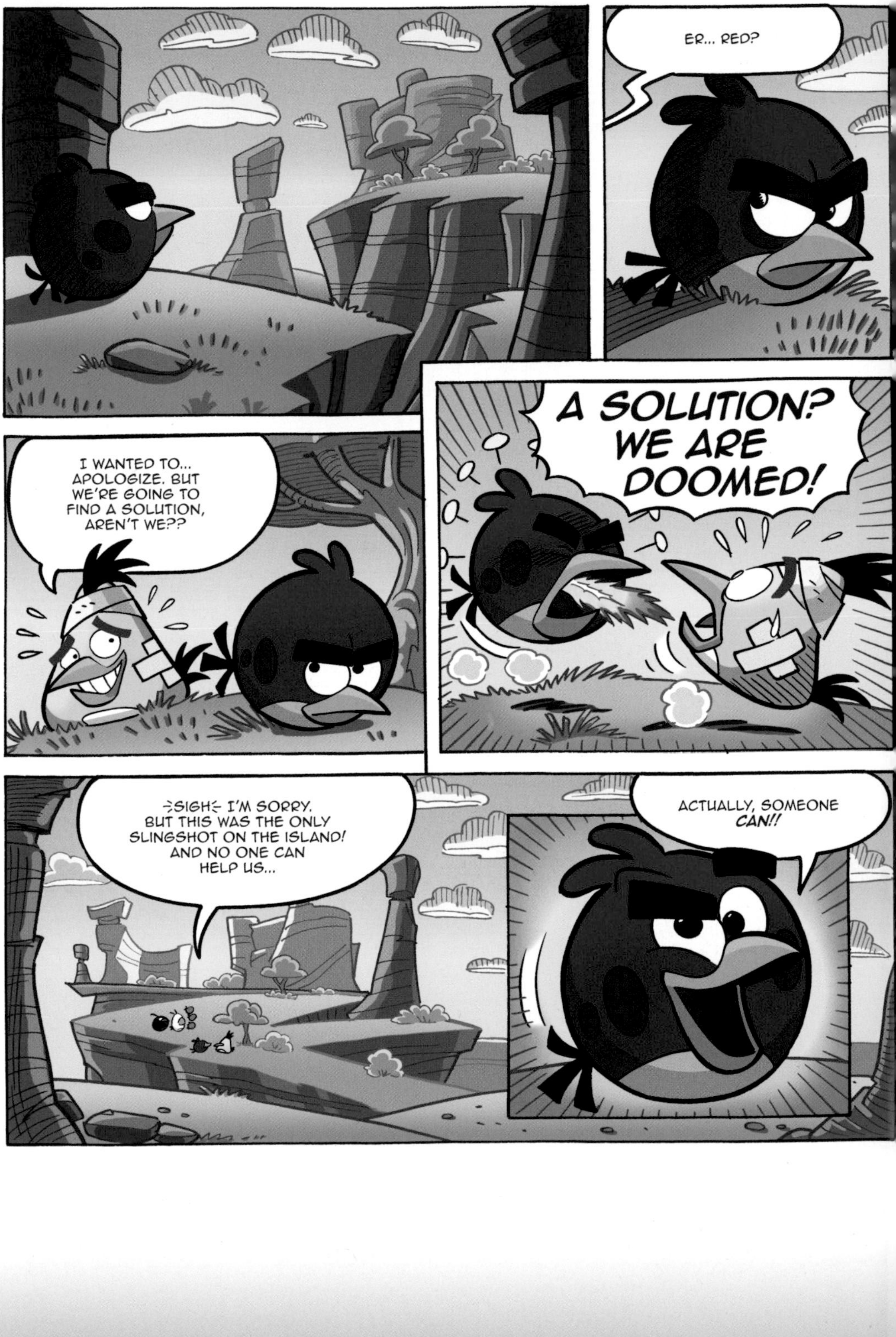
ER... RED?
I WANTED TO... APOLOGIZE. BUT WE'RE GOING TO FIND A SOLUTION, AREN'T WE??
A SOLUTION? WE ARE DOOMED!
SIGH I'M SORRY. BUT THIS WAS THE ONLY SLINGSHOT ON THE ISLAND! AND NO ONE CAN HELP US...
ACTUALLY, SOMEONE *CAN!!*

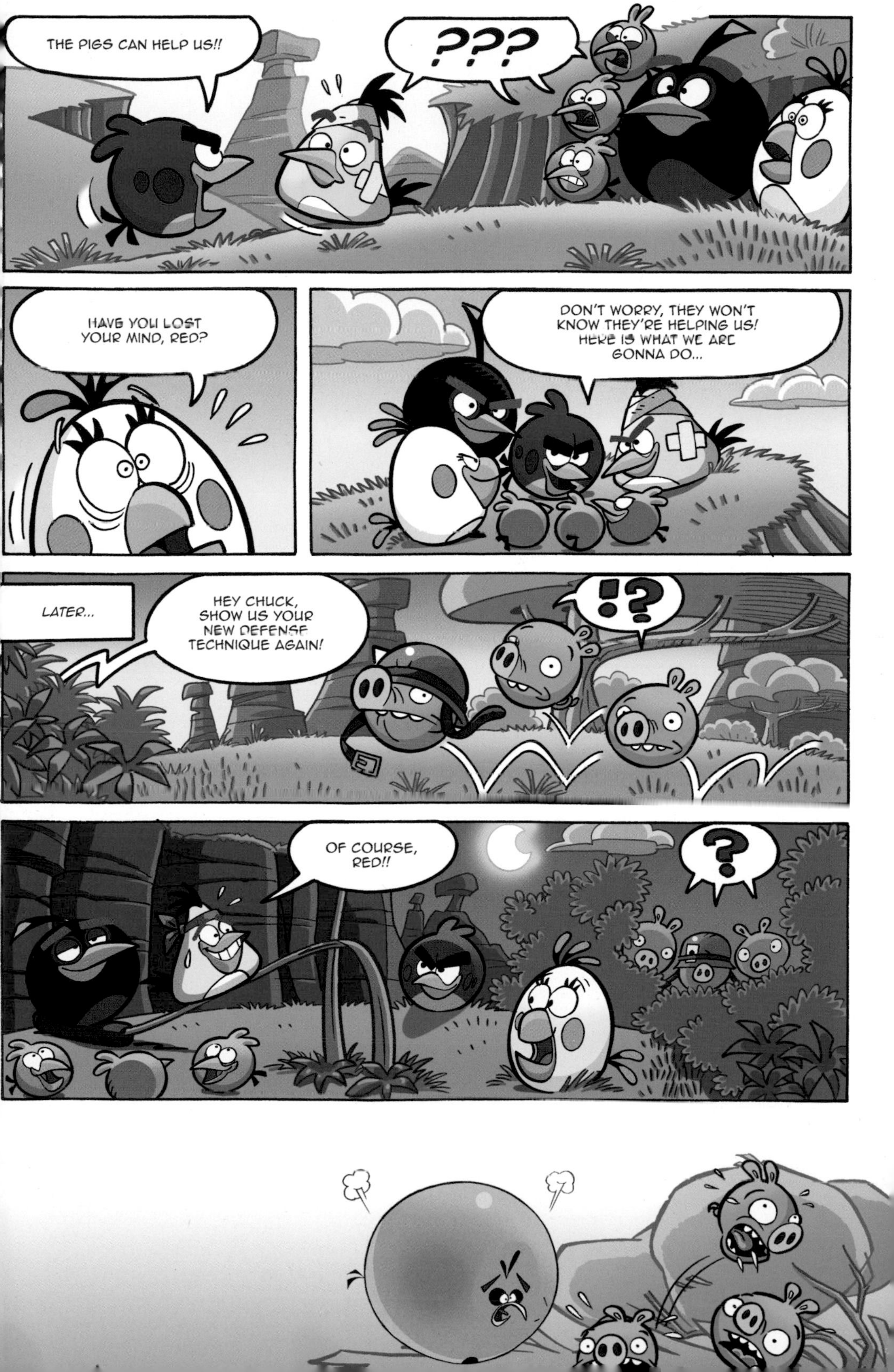

THE PIGS CAN HELP US!!
???
HAVE YOU LOST YOUR MIND, RED?
DON'T WORRY, THEY WON'T KNOW THEY'RE HELPING US! HERE IS WHAT WE ARE GONNA DO...
LATER...
HEY CHUCK, SHOW US YOUR NEW DEFENSE TECHNIQUE AGAIN!
!?
OF COURSE, RED!!
?

AAAAAAHH!
TOOOING
EXCELLENT! MUCH BETTER THAN THE SLINGSHOT. BOMB?
FAREWELL, SLINGSHOT!
TOK
HOLY BACON! IF WE REPAIR THIS SLINGSHOT, WE WILL BE ABLE TO USE IT AGAINST THOSE STUPID BIRDS!!
I HOPE YOU KNOW WHAT YOU ARE DOING, RED...

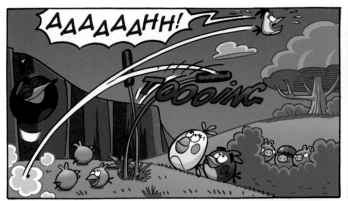

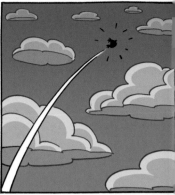

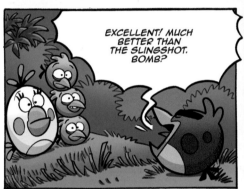

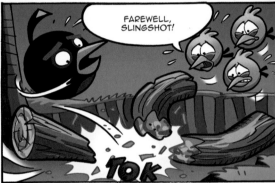

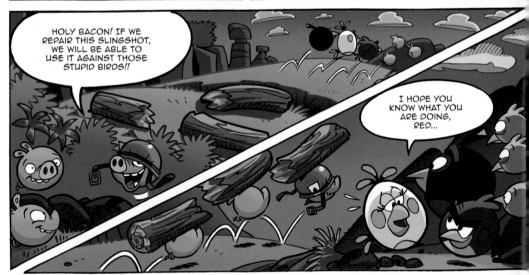

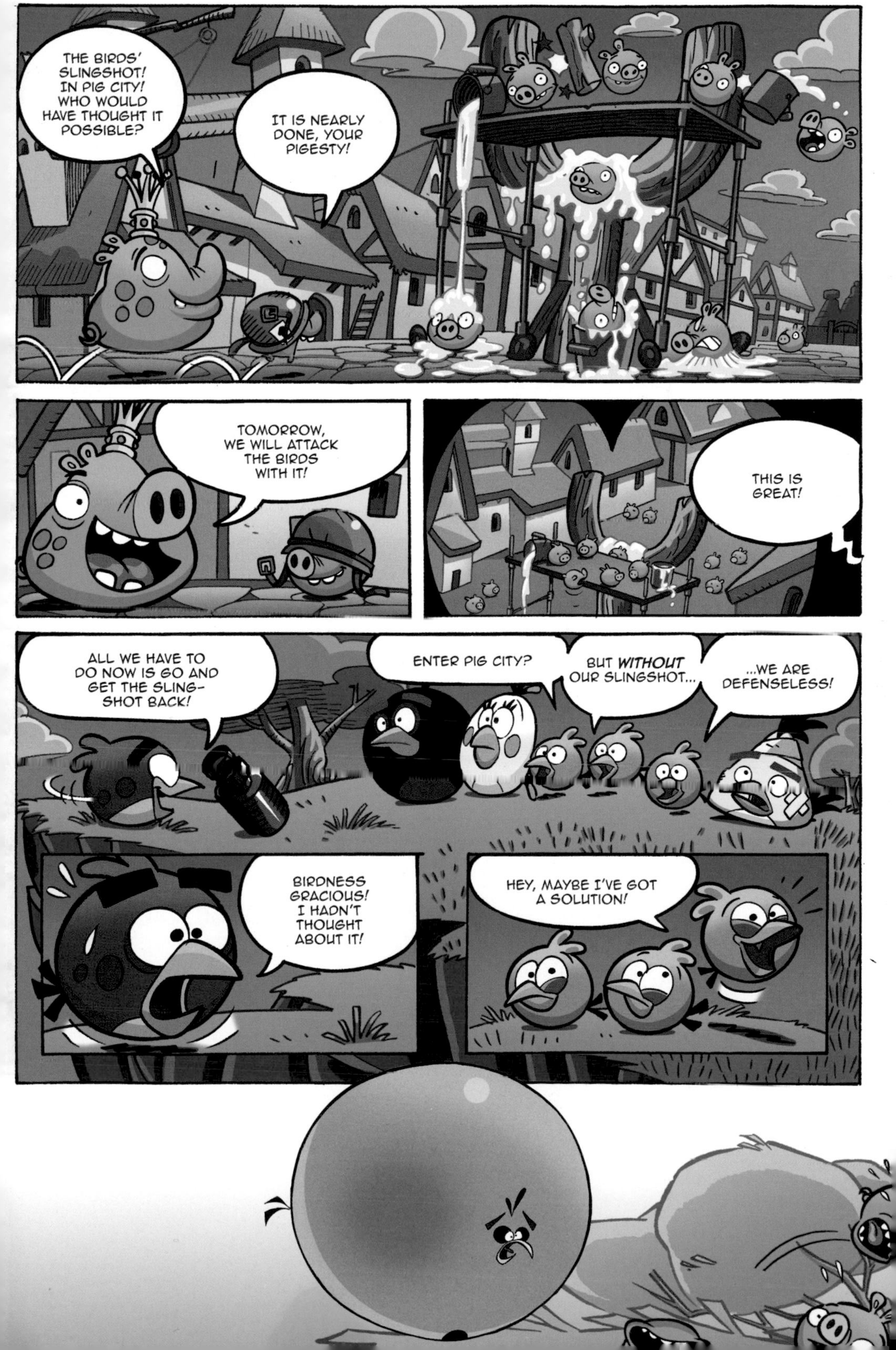
THE BIRDS' SLINGSHOT! IN PIG CITY! WHO WOULD HAVE THOUGHT IT POSSIBLE?
IT IS NEARLY DONE, YOUR PIGESTY!
TOMORROW, WE WILL ATTACK THE BIRDS WITH IT!
THIS IS GREAT!
ALL WE HAVE TO DO NOW IS GO AND GET THE SLING-SHOT BACK!
ENTER PIG CITY?
BUT *WITHOUT* OUR SLINGSHOT...
...WE ARE DEFENSELESS!
BIRDNESS GRACIOUS! I HADN'T THOUGHT ABOUT IT!
HEY, MAYBE I'VE GOT A SOLUTION!

NIGHT FELL ON PIG CITY...

OUCH! WATCH OUT!

SSSSSHHH!! WE'RE NEARLY THERE!

SSSSSSS!!!

AAAAAH!!! A SNAKE!

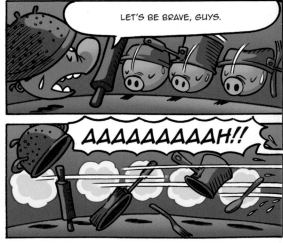

LET'S BE BRAVE, GUYS.

AAAAAAAAAAH!!

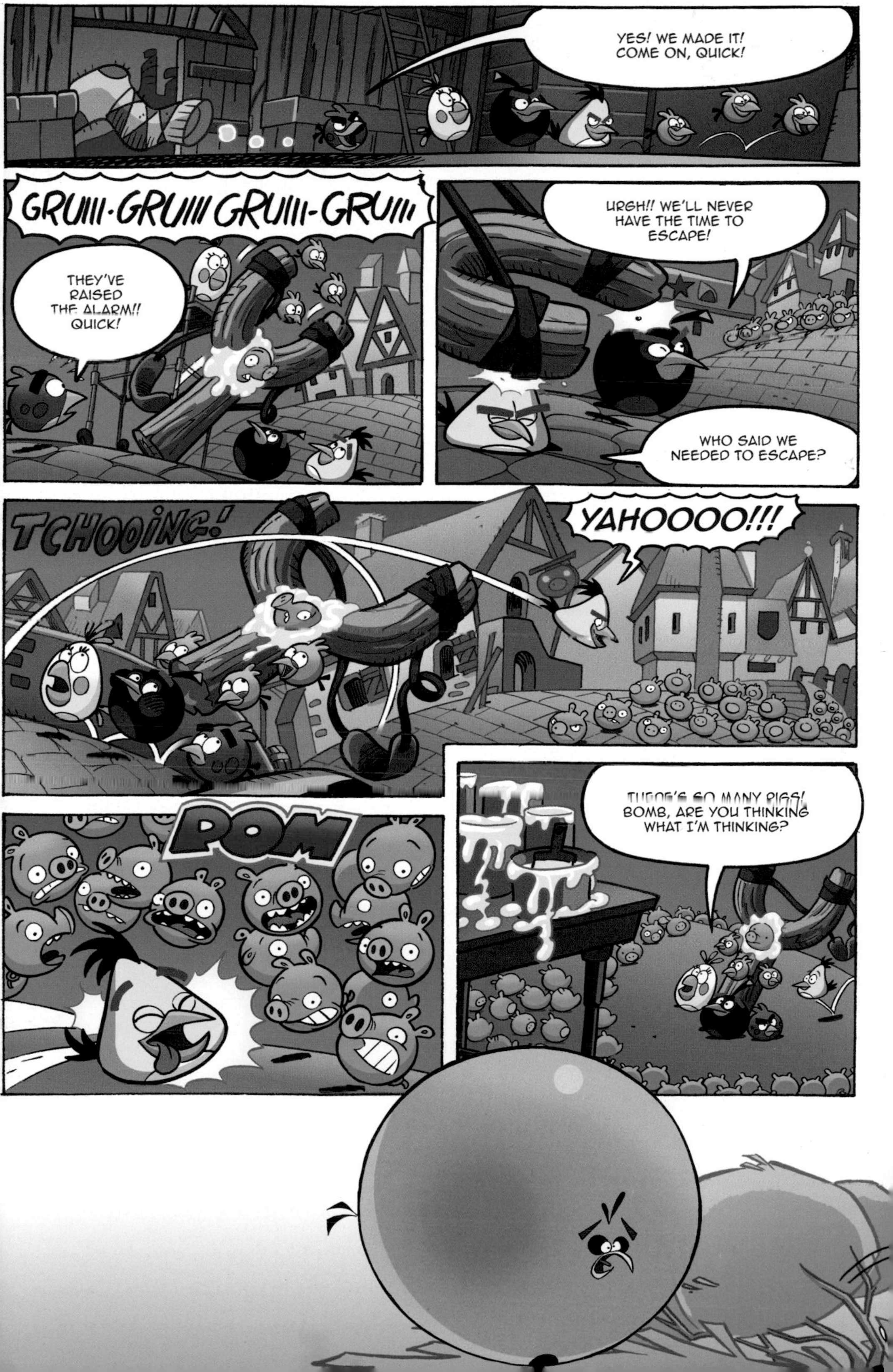
YES! WE MADE IT! COME ON, QUICK!
GRUIII-GRUIII GRUIII-GRUIII
THEY'VE RAISED THE ALARM!! QUICK!
URGH!! WE'LL NEVER HAVE THE TIME TO ESCAPE!
WHO SAID WE NEEDED TO ESCAPE?
TCHOOING!
YAHOOOO!!!
POM
BOMB, ARE YOU THINKING WHAT I'M THINKING?

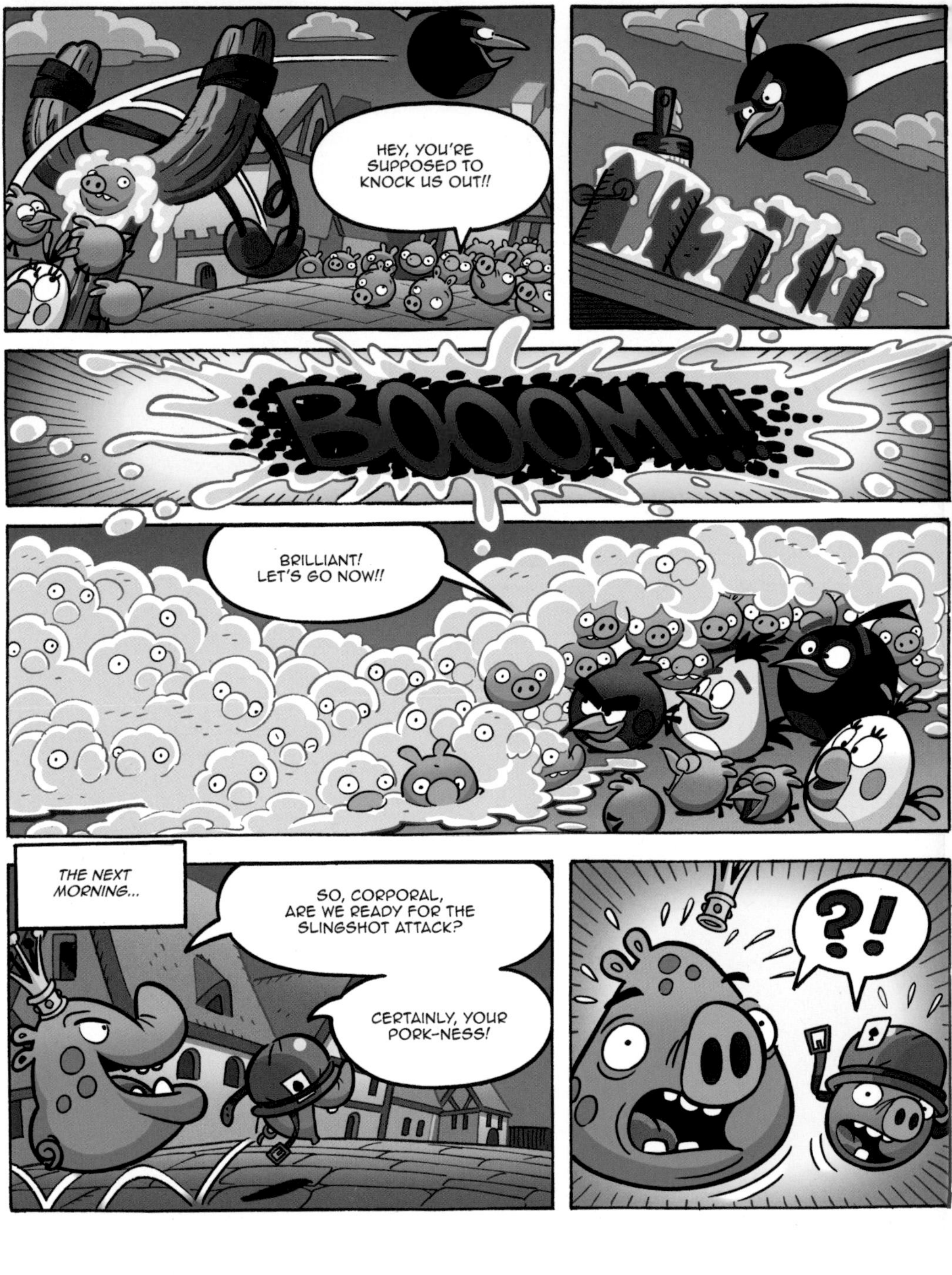
HEY, YOU'RE SUPPOSED TO KNOCK US OUT!!
BOOOM!!!
BRILLIANT! LET'S GO NOW!!
THE NEXT MORNING...
SO, CORPORAL, ARE WE READY FOR THE SLINGSHOT ATTACK?
CERTAINLY, YOUR PORK-NESS!
?!

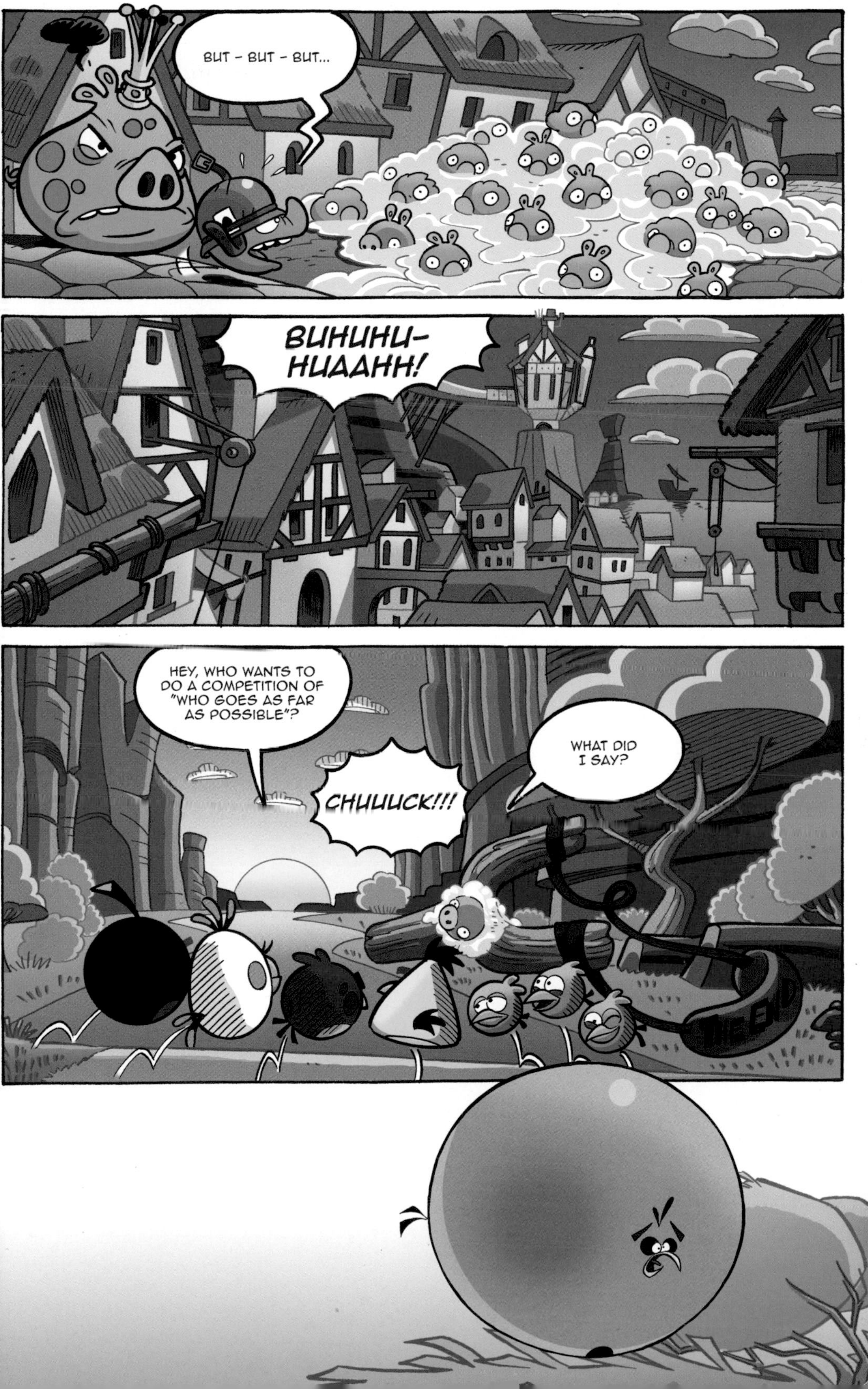
BUT - BUT - BUT...
BUHUHU-HUAAHH!
HEY, WHO WANTS TO DO A COMPETITION OF "WHO GOES AS FAR AS POSSIBLE"?
CHUUUCK!!!
WHAT DID I SAY?

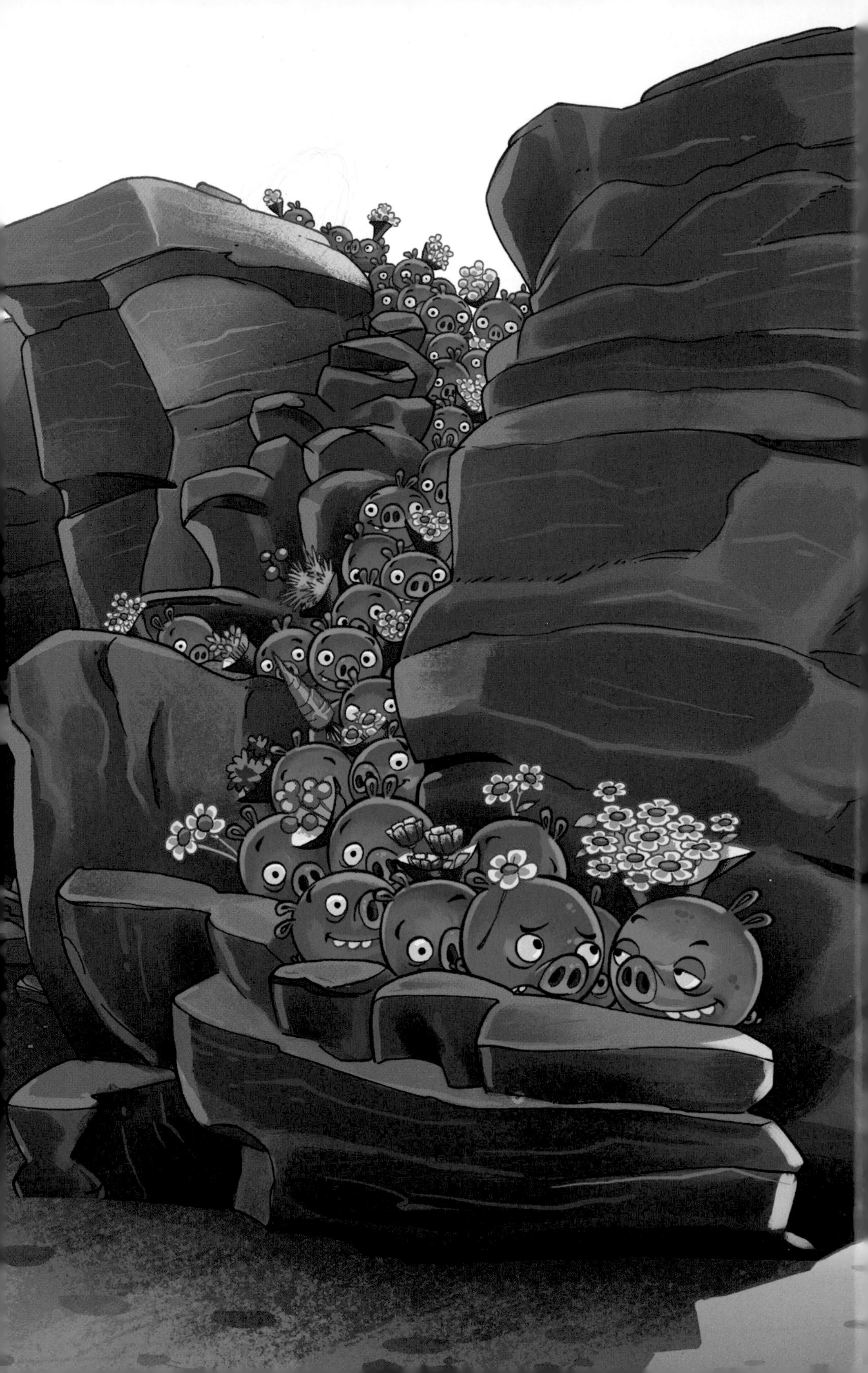

Artwork by Paco Rodriques
Colors by Digikore Studios

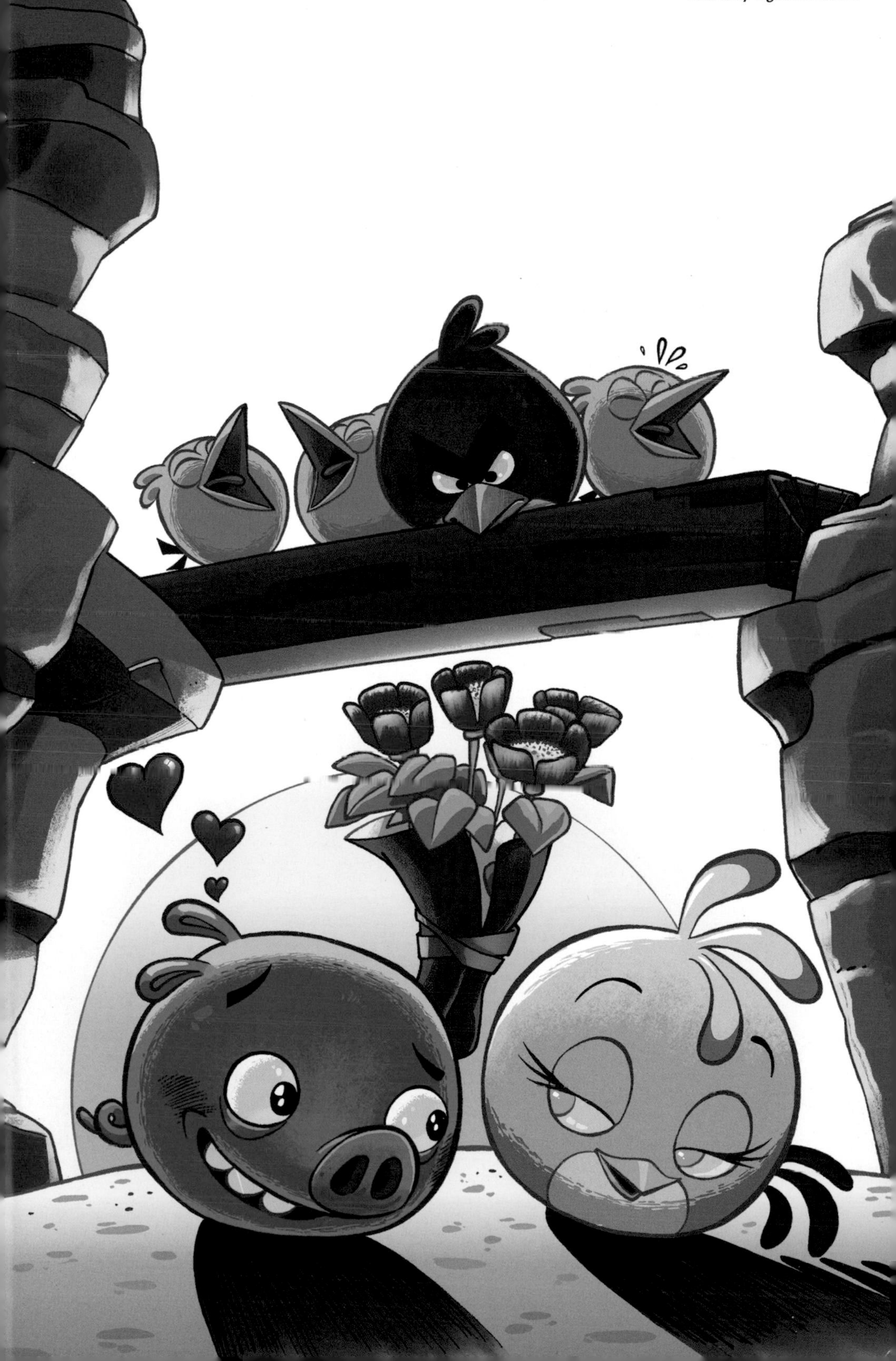

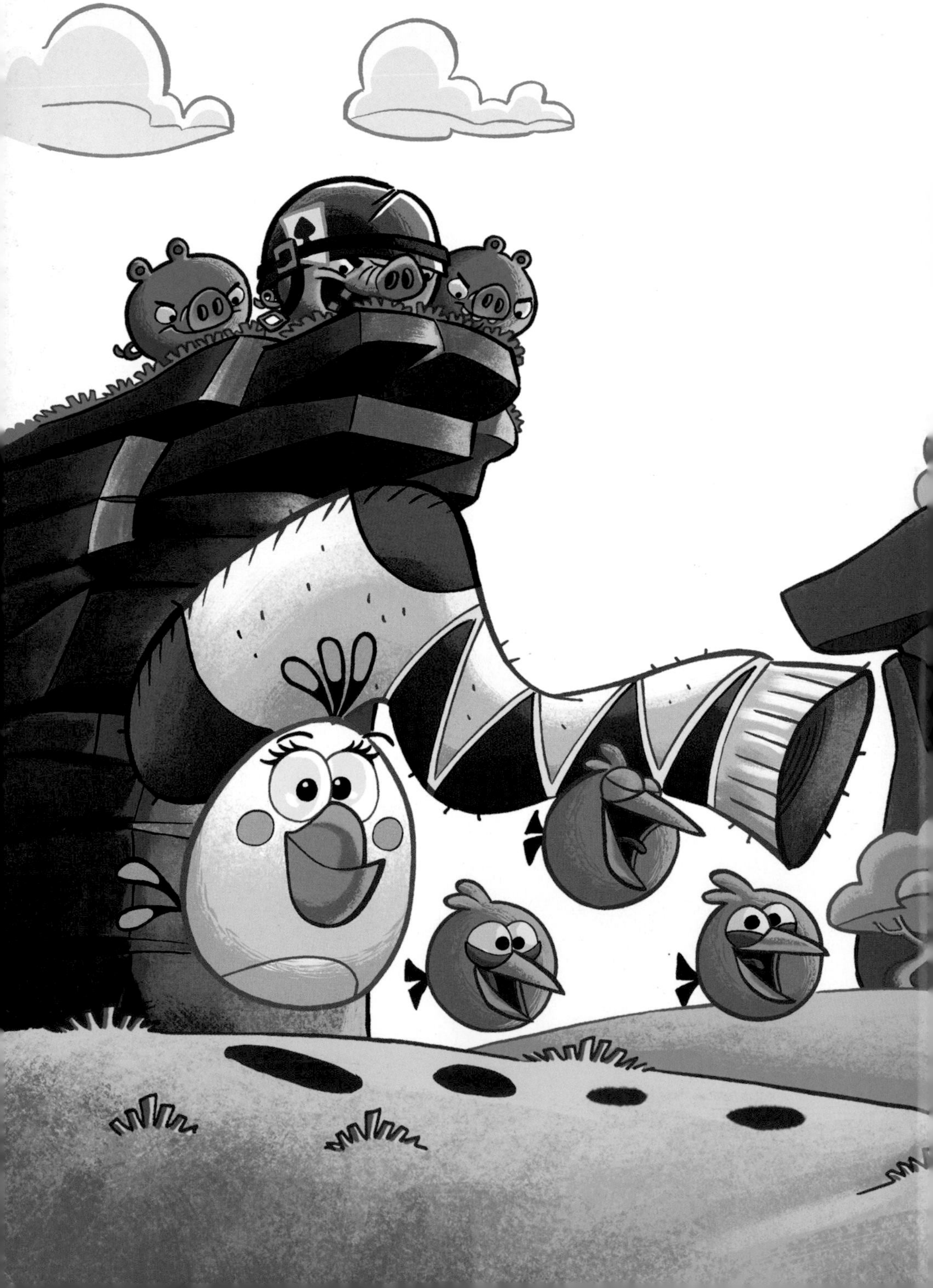

Artwork by Marco Gervasio

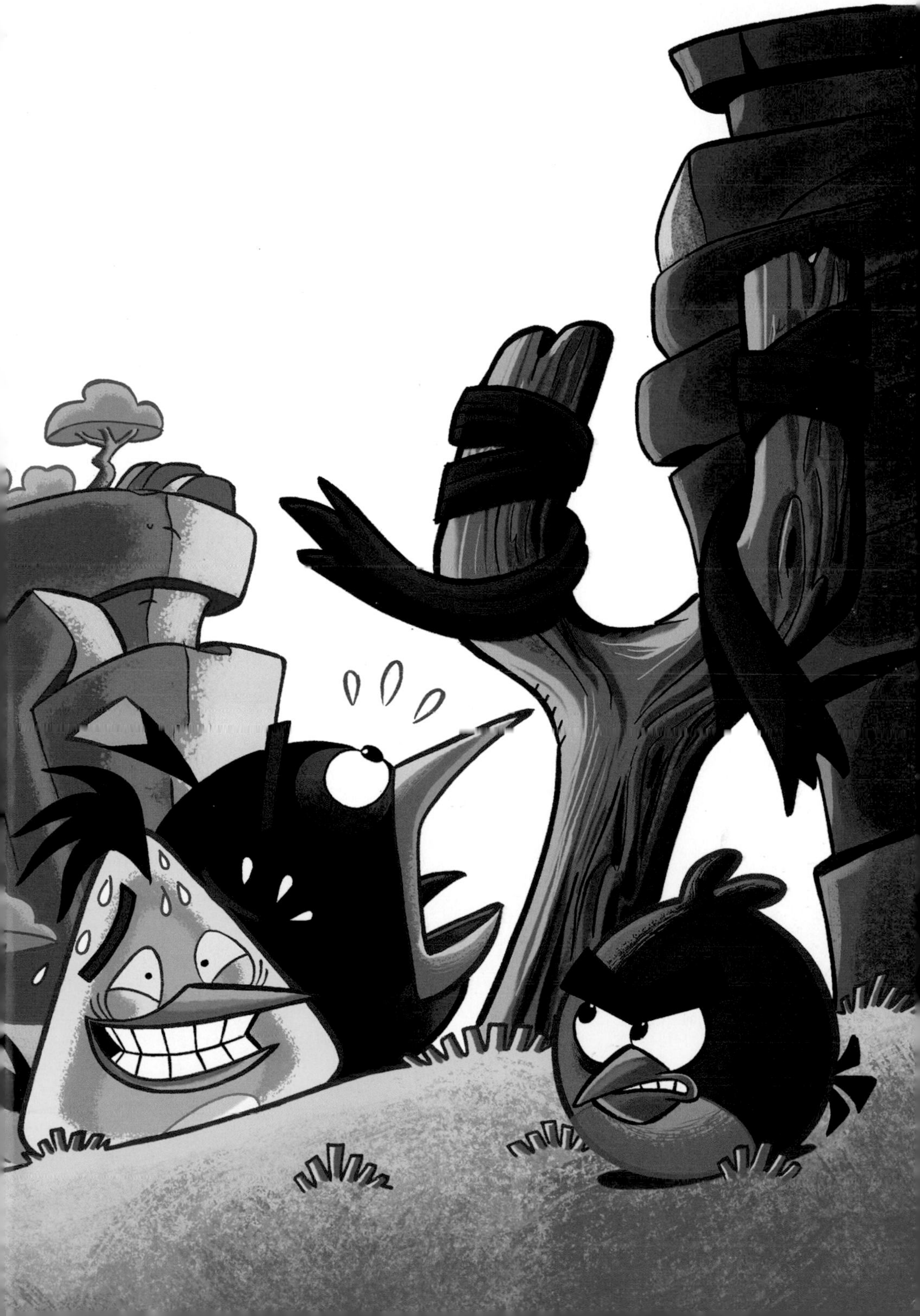

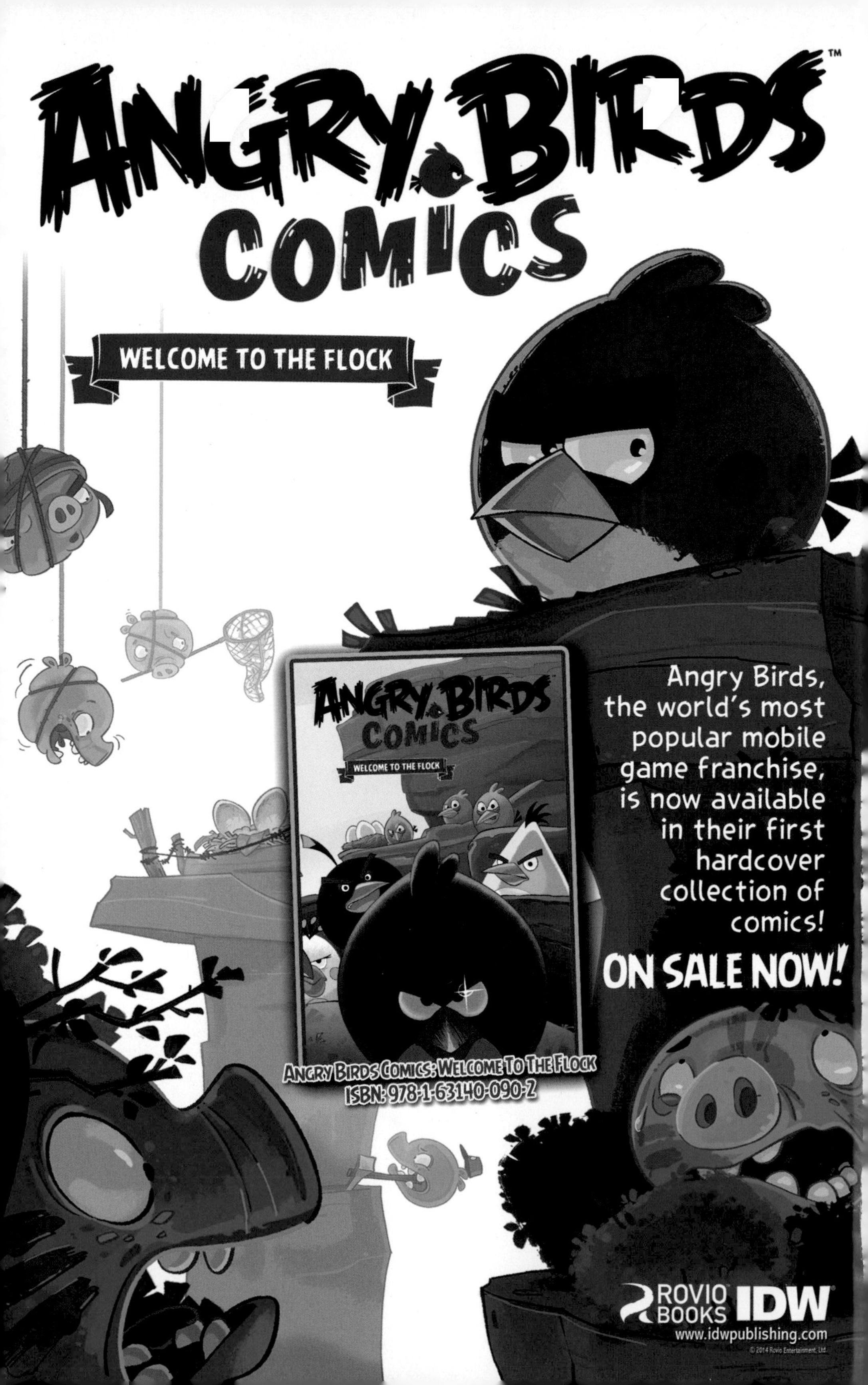
ANGRY BIRDS™
COMICS
WELCOME TO THE FLOCK
ANGRY BIRDS
COMICS
WELCOME TO THE FLOCK
ANGRY BIRDS COMICS: WELCOME TO THE FLOCK
ISBN: 978-1-63140-090-2
Angry Birds, the world's most popular mobile game franchise, is now available in their first hardcover collection of comics!
ON SALE NOW!
ROVIO BOOKS
IDW
www.idwpublishing.com
© 2014 Rovio Entertainment, Ltd.